CAXTON TEMPEST
AT THE END OF THE WORLD

KEN PRESTON

The Council
of 7 are
watching you!
Best Wishes
Ken Preston
18th Oct. '07

CAXTON TEMPEST
AT THE END OF THE WORLD

British Library Cataloguing In Publication Data
A Record of this Publication is available
from the British Library

ISBN 978-1-84685-883-3

First Published 2007 by
Exposure Publishing,
an imprint of
Diggory Press Ltd
Three Rivers, Minions, Liskeard, Cornwall, PL14 5LE, UK
and of Diggory Press, Inc.,
Goodyear, Arizona, 85338, USA
WWW.DIGGORYPRESS.COM

For Matthew and Jack

Chapter One
The Mutilated Corpse

Dark, viscous pools of blood glistened in the yellow light of the sputtering gas lamps mounted on the walls. In the middle of the room lay the mutilated corpse of a fat, middle-aged man. The blood had finished gushing from his ripped flesh hours ago, leaving his skin pale and waxy. He now looked like a hideous mutilated doll. Spatters of dark red decorated the walls where his arteries had sprayed blood, soaking into the flock wallpaper and dripping from the expensive paintings, ruining them forever. Large, bloody handprints marked the glass of the shop door where the man had tried to escape, or maybe just seek help, but it had been too late. His blood was already spouting from his lacerated throat, filling his lungs, drowning him in his own bodily fluids.

Jim Kerrigan, standing in an open doorway at the back of the shop, stared involuntarily at the grisly scene before him. Hypnotised by the carnage, he jumped when his younger brother bumped into him from behind.

"Jim!" the ten-year-old boy said, coughing, and wiping the soot from his eyes. "Why've you stopped?"

"Keep your voice down!" Jim said. "He might still be here."

"Who might still be here?"

"I dunno," Jim said, his voice dropping low now. "I dunno."

George wiped the last of the soot from his eyes and stretched to look over Jim's shoulder. He drew in his breath at the sight of the slaughtered body on the shop floor, and gripped his brother's arm.

"Do you think he's dead?"

"Course he's dead!" Jim hissed.

"Somethin' got him bad. Look at him."

"I know," Jim said. He turned to look at his brother. "Stay here, I'm going to have a look around."

"Don't go in there, we should go back. The coppers'll be here soon," George replied, tugging at Jim's filthy shirtsleeve.

"Just stay here and keep your mouth shut. I'm just going to have a look, that's all."

Jim pushed his brother down into a sitting position on the flagstone floor and turned back to face the shop. He pushed the door open a little wider so he could see the whole room from where he stood.

More blood, splattered on the walls, the shelves of *objets d'art*, the antique books, the glass vials and coloured vessels, the wall hangings of bright colours and intricate patterns, blood *everywhere*.

Jim took a few cautious steps into the shop, carefully avoiding the deep red pools of congealing gore. He looked back at George, framed by the doorway of dark oak, his eyes wide and riveted upon his brother. Jim put his finger to his lips, silently imploring him to keep quiet, and turned back to face the shop. Quietly, slowly, he gingerly stepped round and over the dark expanses of blood, making his way to the body by the front door.

Jim looked down at the man's fleshy, waxen face, his eyes wide open in terror, and his red, pudgy lips parted in a grimace of fear exposing his yellowing, chipped teeth. Jim knew him, recognised him from a couple of days ago when Mulready had brought him down here. They had not gone into the shop straight away; Mulready had taken him round the back first, pointed to the chimney stack, crumbling away at the top, allowing him to climb down and get inside. Then he took Jim back out onto the street and they went inside and admired the expensive, unusual antique items on display. Mulready pointed at certain pieces, giving him a little nudge in the small of his back, *that one, nick that one!*

Jim and Mulready had dressed up for their trip into town but none of their worn, tattered clothing could disguise their poverty row origins in the Dials. The shop owner had watched them carefully from the moment they entered. After a few minutes it became obvious they were buying nothing, and the fat, middle-aged man bustled them out of his shop, threatening them with the police.

"Fat old shit!" Mulready hissed back out on the street. "Yer'll show 'im tonight. What yer can't nick, smash up, smash the place to smithereens. That'll teach 'im."

Jim looked around. Nothing to nick now, everything covered in blood and gore like that.

"Jim!" George hissed from the doorway.

"What, what is it?" Jim said, looking back down at the murdered shop proprietor.

"I want to go. Please, let's go!"

Jim waved his hand absently towards his little brother. "In a minute."

Something about the dead man's posture unsettled the young boy. His arms were outstretched beside him as if he had been crucified, and his legs stretched wide apart. Jim doubted that he could have fallen down into that position. Had his killer arranged his victim like that?

Something had torn at the man's throat, leaving a gaping, ragged wound. How the shopkeeper had managed to live long enough to attempt an escape from his attacker as the blood had gushed from his neck was a mystery. The splashes and pools of blood indicated that he had put up a strong fight.

Jim looked at the man's face again. He had seen dead bodies before, drunks passed out in the street, worn out by a life of hardship, their frail bodies killed by the cold of the night. Once he had seen a man who had starved to death. He had been lying in a back alley, his body so wasted and thin Jim could have encircled one of the man's legs with his hand. His eyes bulged from his yellowing skin stretched tight over his skull, the cheeks sunken and hollow, the lips drawn back from his teeth.

But he had never seen anyone who had died so violently. The expression of fear etched so vividly on the man's face unnerved Jim more than the blood. The way his eyes stared in terror straight at him.

No, not straight at him, but past him. Jim turned and looked behind him. A large painting hung on the wall, sprayed with blood like the others. In it a winged, demonic figure hurtled towards the earth shrouded in cloud. Jim wasn't sure if the demon was flying or simply falling to earth. All around stars penetrated the inky blackness of the night.

"Jim!"

"What?"

"Somebody's comin'!"

Jim could hear the voices now, the footsteps on the street coming closer. He looked around the room, panic gripping him instantly. If he were to be found here, with the dead body . . .

He scuttled to the back of the shop, quickly and silently running around the pools of blood. A quick glance behind told him how close he was to being discovered; the light steadily growing outside the dirty shop front windows, no doubt policemen approaching with their lamps.

Jim darted through the doorway into the back of the shop, quietly pulling the door to behind him. George stood in front of him hopping from one filthy, bare foot to the other, casting agitated glances at the door behind him.

"Can we go now?" he said.

"Sshh!" Jim hissed, his finger to his mouth. "Be quiet will you!"

He turned back to the door and knelt down on the cold flagstones, and put his eye to the keyhole. The two shadowy figures stood at the door, one of them fumbling with the lock, cursing as he struggled to release it. Finally he managed to open the door, and the two men entered the shop.

"There," said the one, "just like I said."

The other man let out an exclamation of surprise at the grisly scene before him.

"Who is it? Who's there?" George whispered, still silently bouncing from foot to foot behind Jim as though he desperately needed to pee.

"It's a couple o' peelers," Jim whispered. He turned to look at his agitated little brother and said, "Keep still, before they hear you, and come and throw both of us in stir."

George stopped his jigging and stood stock still, a look of terror on his grimy face. Satisfied he would have no more trouble from his little brother, Jim turned his attention back to the policemen in the shop.

The two constables now circled the mutilated corpse, stepping over and around the congealing pools of deep crimson, drawing ever closer to the object of their morbid fascination. Neither of them spoke; the clip of their shoes on the cold hard floor and the rustle of their uniforms as they moved were the only sounds they made. Their movements had a careful, awesome reverence about them, as though they were in a cathedral, and they were approaching the altar.

Suddenly one of the constables stopped and turned to look at his companion.

"D'you reckon 'e's still 'ere?" he said. He was tall, and thin, and towered over his colleague, whose face was forever to be insulted by his large, protruding nose.

Jim nicknamed them Lanky and Beaky.

"Who?" Beaky replied.

"Why, the blighter who did this, who do you think?"

Beaky drew himself up to his full height, which wasn't much, and puffed out his chest and said, "No, he scarpered pretty sharpish like, when he saw me."

"You saw 'im? Did you get a good look at 'im? I hear they've been after 'im a long time now, he's been halfway across the world murdering innocent people in their beds at night, and you got a look at 'im . . ."

"Well maybe not a good look," said Beaky, his shoulders drooping slightly now.

"And maybe you didn't see 'im at all, because maybe he'd long gone by the time you got here," Lanky said, laughing. "Don't go telling Inspector Behrends you've been seeing something when you ain't, or else he'll have you back looking for toshers in the sewers underneath Mayfair again."

"Not bloody likely," he said, and shuddered at the thought.

They both looked at the butchered corpse again.

"They say he's killed people everywhere, all across the world. Always antique collectors, and people selling curios and artefacts, like. And they say the victims' bodies are always drained of blood."

"What's 'e doin', you reckon? What's brought 'im over 'ere? Ain't it bad enough we got Jack the Ripper? We don't need another one."

"No, this one's different, they say."

10

"Why, because he ain't interested in dolly-mops? He might have an 'igher class of victim but he still kills 'em."

"No, because he drinks their blood, that's why. I've heard that most of 'em have not a drop of blood left in their body, an' not a drop spilt on the floor either."

Beaky shuddered. "Didn't get much of a drink this time, did he?"

Lanky played the light of his lamp across the blood-bespattered walls of the shop and over the congealing pools of blood.

"Looks like Mr Antrobus put up a fight, an' didn't give him a chance to have a drink like," he said.

The bell on the shop door jingled as another figure entered, his sharp intake of breath when he saw the carnage audible to Jim in the rear. He shifted position slightly, trying to get a better view of the newcomer. He pressed his face against the door, his eye against the keyhole, straining to see.

The man was dressed up for an evening out, at the theatre perhaps. He was portly and his face held the dour expression of one who is harassed and overworked. His bald head shone a little under the yellow glare of the sputtering gas lamps.

"Figgis, Cotton," he said, "I hope the two of you have left the scene of the crime undisturbed, as I instructed."

"Yes sir," said Lanky. "Left exactly as we found it sir, just as you said."

Inspector Behrends, as Jim assumed the newcomer to be, stepped carefully around the puddles of blood until he reached the corpse. He looked for a long time at the man's face, seemingly studying it.

"Do you think it's 'im sir?" Beaky said.

"And who might you be talking about, Constable Figgis?"

"Why, 'im what's been murderin' poor folks in their bed at night all over the world an' drinking their blood."

"Really Figgis, if you spent more time concentrating on police work and less reading those penny dreadfuls then I might not be so inclined to send you down the sewers looking for missing valuables so often."

"Hmmph!" Beaky spluttered, taking a step back.

"Be careful, you blundering buffoon!" Behrends shouted, but it was too late.

Beaky stepped back into a large, dark expanse of blood and slipped. Arms and legs flailing wildly, he fell on his back and slithered across the slippery floor. Shouting in disgust and horror, he began thrashing about frantically in an attempt to get back on his feet, but only managed to cover more of himself in the dead man's blood.

Jim clapped a hand over his mouth, stifling a giggle. He hated the police, and enjoyed seeing Beaky's mortification.

"Constable Figgis, pull yourself together," Inspector Behrends shouted.

Beaky finally stopped his frantic writhing and looked up, large, round white eyes peering out from his blood red face.

Behrends squatted over the corpse now saying, almost absently, "Figgis, I'll have you disciplined for compromising the crime scene. You're a disgrace to the force."

Again he examined the dead man for several moments while Beaky made a few unsuccessful attempts to get back onto his feet.

Lanky walked over to the Inspector and stood by him. "Any ideas sir?" he said.

"Only one, Cotton," the Inspector replied. "I hate to say this, but if this is indeed the same killer who has been on a murder spree in New York and Paris, then I begin to feel that we are a little out of our depth. Perhaps it is time I paid Caxton Tempest a visit and sought his counsel."

As Behrends spoke, Beaky had kept up a continual litany of grunts and exclamations as he tried to stand up. Every time he seemed to be about to gain his feet once more he slipped again, until he looked like a blood-soaked corpse himself.

"Cotton, help your colleague up will you?" Behrends said.

Jim watched as Behrends continued examining the corpse, his mind racing at the thought of the great Caxton Tempest becoming involved in this murder case. He had heard of Tempest and his adventures many times, of his explorations in Africa and his exploits in the army. It was said he could speak every language in the world, that he was as skilled with a sword as a man with a gun, and that he could outfight an army of thugs and murderers all by himself. Slum Lassie Sal claimed to have seen him once, striding through Regent's Park. She said he was tall and handsome, and everything a girl could wish for in a man, that she felt fair faint as he had walked past her. Beside him had walked Johnny Chen, the only Chinaman in London to be allowed service in the private rooms of the Café Royal in Regent Street. Sal had said Johnny Chen was handsome too, in an Oriental way if that was your preference.

Finishing his examination of the corpse, Behrends stood up and watched Lanky carefully help Beaky struggle to his feet, with much spluttering and uttering of curses.

"Careful, careful," he said.

With a colourful oath Beaky once more fell onto the blood-smeared floor, this time taking Lanky with him. The two constables wrestled each other for a while, cursing and swearing, until Lanky was just as covered in blood as his colleague.

Jim looked away, sticking his fist in his mouth, his whole body shaking with silent laughter, sure that at any moment a great guffaw would escape him and reveal their presence behind the door. After a few moments he managed to compose himself and pressed his face against the door once more, staring through the keyhole.

And saw Behrends pointing directly at him.

"We may have the murderer yet," he was saying. "Look, the footprints lead that way."

Jim looked down at his shoes. There was blood on the soles, bloody footprints on the floor where he had walked.

He leapt to his feet and ran to George, still standing motionless behind him.

"C'mon," he said, bundling George ahead of him to the open fireplace they had made their illegal entry through. "Quick, start climbing, they're coming."

"Are they gonna throw us in stir, Jim?" he said, fat tears rolling down his face, cutting a clean path through the soot on his cheeks.

"Not if you get up that chimney," Jim said, pushing his brother up the filthy, dark flue. He pushed at George's bottom as he began climbing, soot getting into his eyes and mouth, making him cough and splutter. George's feet flailed around Jim's head, threatening to give him a good kicking. Jim grabbed his feet and gave him a firm push up. The young boy managed to gain a foothold and began climbing unaided.

Jim started climbing next, feeling his way up the rough, jagged stone. Another few feet and he would be in complete darkness. He heard the door below opening, heard them coming in to the room and exclaiming at the mess they found, the clouds of soot spewing from the fireplace.

Just another few feet and then they would be on the rooftops, able to make their escape into the night. Just another few feet . . .

And then Jim lost a foothold. He scrabbled for a handhold as he began his fall, the jagged edges of the chimney ripping the skin off his hands and tearing at his fingernails, until he finally landed with a sickening thump in the fireplace.

"Come here, we've got you now," said Lanky, grabbing him with bloodstained hands and dragging him into the middle of the room.

Disoriented, blind and retching from the clouds of soot swirling around him, Jim lay on the flagged floor. He rubbed at his eyes and saw the feet of his captors surrounding him. Slowly he looked up.

Inspector Behrends looked down at him.

Chapter Two
Down in the Cellar

Lying on his back on the cold, hard floor, Jim looked up through the swirling clouds of soot at Inspector Behrends. Behrends stood over Jim, his fists on his hips, staring back at the teenage boy.

Jim coughed and a small cloud of soot billowed from his mouth. Behind him he could hear Lanky and Beaky laughing and clapping their hands, singing, "We got him, we got him!"

"Who are you, boy?" Behrends said.

"Jim Kerrigan, sir," he replied.

"And what were you doing in the chimney, Jim Kerrigan?"

"Nothing, sir."

"You were creating an awful lot of disturbance doing nothing. Are those your footprints on the shop floor?"

Jim opened his mouth to say no, but the look in Behrends' eyes made him think again.

"Yes, sir," he said.

"And what were you up to in the shop then, my young lad?"

"Nothing, sir."

"Nothing, sir," Behrends repeated. His chubby, dour face twitched a little, as though it might be about to break into a smile, and he said, "Go on, be off with you."

The Inspector turned and walked back to the corpse. As Jim struggled to his feet, Lanky and Beaky ceased their celebrations and turned as one, a look of indignation on both their faces.

"What?" said Lanky. "You're letting him go?"

"You can't do that," said Beaky. "We've caught him dead to rights, he's the murderer. Caught him dead to rights, we have."

"Figgis, Cotton, if you two believe this young lad capable of scouring the world for victims to kill and drain of blood then you are even more imbecilic than I first thought," said Inspector Behrends, casting a vicious glance at the two bloody, dirt encrusted policemen hovering by the fireplace. "You will both report to me in the morning for your new duties. I'm taking you off the beat as you both seem incapable of a sensible thought or action between you."

After taking a moment to enjoy the two constables' embarrassment, Jim made to leave through the shop entrance.

"Where do you think you're going?" Behrends said, blocking his path to the front door.

"You said I could go, sir."

"Yes I did, but not by the front door. That mode of entrance and exit is reserved for honest people. You can leave the way you came."

Jim hesitated for a moment, and then turned and ran past Lanky and Beaky, and began climbing the inside of the chimney once more.

Soon he was clambering out of the crumbling open top of the chimney, and into the cool night breeze. The young boy collapsed on his back on the roof, gasping for air after the confines of the chimney. Gulping down great lungfuls of the night air, his field of vision filled with stars shimmering against the velvet blackness of the night sky, he began laughing at his lucky escape. The memory of Lanky and Beaky struggling to extricate themselves from each other, slipping and sliding on the blood wet floor, made him laugh even harder.

A sound behind him cut short his laughter, and he jumped to his feet, ready to fight whoever was sneaking up on him.

"Jim!" George said, his grimy face split wide open by a smile of delight, though his eyes still looked red and puffy from the tears he had been crying. "I thought for sure they'd got you, thought I ain't never gonna see you again."

Jim relaxed, laughing again.

"Ain't I told you before, George, there ain't nobody can hurt a Kerrigan, especially a couple o' peelers. You knew I weren't gonna leave you up here by yourself, didn't you?"

"I . . . I suppose," said George, sniffing.

Jim reached out a dirty hand and ruffled his brother's equally dirty hair.

"C'mon," he said. "Let's get back."

The two boys ran across the rooftop, shinned their way down to street level and began running through the late-night, deserted London streets. As they ran, Jim told his younger brother of his encounter with Inspector Behrends, and mention of the mysterious Caxton Tempest. He embellished the story in the telling so that soon he was fighting off the peelers with his bare hands, and only narrowly escaping arrest and a spell in jail. George listened to it all with the unquestioning trust of a little brother, knowing that every word Jim told him was the absolute truth.

They ran and ran, Jim slowing down occasionally when he saw his young brother flagging, unable to keep up the pace. Sometimes they would walk for a spell, and then begin running again when their breathlessness had eased. Jim told George about Lanky and Beaky, and he threw himself on the ground imitating their thrashing about, and George fell down too, helpless with laughter.

And then they ran again.

Soon the affluence of inner-city London disappeared, and the streets closed in on them, becoming darker and dirtier. Here all manner of life still carried on, even at such a late hour. The dirty windows of illegal drinking dens blazed with yellow light and raucous noise, drunkards wandered the streets looking for their next cheap drink and the dolly-mops stood on the street corners, waiting for their next pick-up.

The two boys slowed their pace now, not wanting to attract too much attention. They walked past a young woman sitting on the dirty, wet ground, clasping a baby to her chest. She glanced at Jim and George, and then looked away again, knowing it would be a waste of time to beg money from the likes of them.

They walked on, past the open slaughterhouses discharging their stinking effluent out onto the streets to mingle with the dirty river of sludge flowing down the main thoroughfares. A filthy, decrepit old drunk staggered towards them, his ragged clothes hanging from his wasted body.

"Spare a ha'penny for a drink?" he said, his voice a hoarse whisper.

Jim took hold of George's hand and they ran around the old man, and on deeper into the rabbit warren of narrow alleyways and courtyards that was their home. Finally, down an alleyway that was so narrow a full grown man had to turn sideways to walk down it, the two boys entered a courtyard of dark, decrepit, wooden houses, two storeys high and leaning inwards at a precipitous angle. In the middle of the courtyard stood a single, rusty standpipe, dripping water. This standpipe was the only source of water for all the residents of the courtyard.

The brothers entered a doorway and started down a flight of rickety steps into the cellar. They were brought to a halt by a shout from above them.

"Kerrigan! C'mere you useless little toe-rag."

Jim turned and began a slow, reluctant ascent of the stairs, George following him.

Marchek Mulready shuffled out of his room, a battered cigarette dangling from his lips and a tin mug of cheap gin in his hand. He looked at the two boys through eyes narrowed down to tight slits, and smiled a greedy, toothless smile.

"Where is it, then?" he said. "Where's the loot?"

"I ain't got nothing," Jim said.

"What?" Mulready said, the toothless smile disappearing as if he had been slapped across the face. "You ain't got nothin'! What do yer mean, you ain't got nothin'?"

George moved closer to Jim, searched out his hand with his, and held on tight.

17

"The shopkeeper, he were already dead when we got there, he'd been done in something nasty, like."

Mulready shuffled a bit closer and took a gulp of his gin.

"That should have made it easier for yer to nick stuff then, shouldn't it?"

"But the coppers came before I had chance."

"Coppers, eh?"

"And there was blood everywhere, all over everything, there weren't no use nicking nothing."

"Blood, eh? Blood everywhere?"

"Yeah, and then another copper turned up, and he almost caught me an' all."

Mulready finished the last of his drink and then hurled the tin mug at Jim's head, shouting, "You lying little toe-rag! You got scared, didn't yer? There weren't no coppers, there weren't no dead bodies, you just got scared!"

The old man lashed out and grabbed Jim by the arm, pulling him to the ground. He gave him a couple of vicious punches to the head, cracking his skull against the hard, earthen floor. Jim curled himself up into a ball, protecting his head with his arms.

"Stop it, stop it!" George shouted.

"You stay where you are, less'n you want more of the same," Mulready snarled at the young boy. He leant down over Jim, prying his arms from his head with tobacco-stained hands, and pushed his face up against the boy's, his foul, sickly sweet breath making Jim gag.

"Yer can't fool old Mulready, can yer boy? There weren't no dead body, were there? There weren't no coppers. There were just you, wettin' yer pants, 'cos yer were too scared to go thieving. I've got plenty o' lads to go thieving for me, Kerrigan, just 'cos yer used to be the best, don't mean I won't replace yer in a flash."

He looked over at George, crying now, and said, "Maybe I should send yer little brother out on a job. 'Bout time he cut his teeth on his own, ain't it?"

"Leave them alone."

Mulready turned around slowly, still holding Jim's arms in a vice-like grip. A plain, thin-looking woman stood in Mulready's doorway, holding a tattered, worn shawl about her shoulders. She looked tired and hungry, beaten down by years of hardship, yet she still carried about her a certain presence, as though once she had been beautiful, and had known that, and lived in simple enjoyment of it.

"Stay out of this, Slum Lassie Sal, it ain't none of your business," growled the old man.

"Of course it's my business," she said. "You choose to run this den of little thieves and ragamuffins and mudlarks. You give them shelter and food, not enough, mind, and that's the Lord's truth. But they're yours, Lord pity them, and that makes you their father, of a sorts. And if you're their father, then that makes me their mother, seen as how you count me as your wife. And so, as their mother, I'm saying, leave them alone."

Mulready took a long moment looking at the woman he called his wife, and then he hauled Jim to his feet and gave him a kick, sending him tumbling down the cellar steps.

"G'warn with yer," he snarled, and stalked back into his room. Sal gave George a last pitying look, and then followed the old man.

George, crying softly, turned and ran down the cellar steps, and helped Jim get to his feet.

"I'm okay," he said, wiping a sliver of blood from his lips. They walked together into the damp, dark cellar, which they shared with several other children, and over to a corner where they had a sheet that they slept on. The only light came from a single sputtering oil lamp, which threw flickering shadows across the room, barely lighting it.

The two boys huddled down together, wrapping the sheet around them for warmth.

"Did 'e 'it yer hard, Jim?" said a voice from the gloom.

"No, not too hard."

"He's been drinkin'," said another. "It's always worse when he drinks."

"Him and Slum Lassie Sal were arguin' earlier," said the first boy. "Shoutin' and screamin' at each other."

"I dunno why she stays here, it's not like she has to. She's tapped, s'got to be."

George snuffled and sniffed underneath the sheet, still crying. Jim put a protective arm around him.

"Don't worry," he whispered. "We'll be out of here one day soon. Just you wait and see."

"I want to go now," George said, gulping back more tears. "Why can't we go now, tonight?"

"You know why, we ain't got enough money yet. Just a little while longer, just 'til we got a bit more."

"But he'll find out, I know he will. He'll find out you been stealing from him, an' holdin' stuff back for yourself, an' he'll kill you."

"No he won't, he's too stupid, too drunk all the time."

"But what if he finds it? What if he finds the money?"

"Sshh," Jim whispered. "We don't want nobody to know about that, do we? It's our secret, remember? We don't even tell the others, okay?"

"But what if—?"

"He ain't gonna find it, nobody ain't. I've hidden it good and proper. Okay?"

"Okay," said George.

"An' what are we gonna do with the money, George? What are we gonna do when we've got enough?"

"We're gonna buy a barrow," George said.

"Yeah, that's right. An' what are we gonna do with the barrow?"

"We're gonna sell fruit and veg to all the fine ladies and gents."

"That's right, an' fresh fish, too. 'Come an' get your fresh fish, freshly caught this mornin', cheapest fish in all London', that's what you'll be saying. Calling it out across the streets first thing in the mornin'. An' all the pretty ladies will be coming up and buying the fish an' what have you, an' they'll be lookin' at you an' sayin' how handsome you are, like, an' 'would you care to come back for a cup of tea in my living room?' they'll say."

George giggled.

"An' we'll be the finest pair of costermongers London's ever seen," Jim said.

"An' what are we gonna do then?" George said, although he already knew the answer.

"We're gonna get ourselves a little shop, so we won't be costermongers no more, we'll be proper shopkeepers."

"I'd like that," George said, snuggling up closer to his brother, trying to keep warm.

"So would I," Jim said. "So would I."

Chapter Three
Murmur

Eliza pulled her bright red shawl tighter around her shoulders to ward off the coolness of the evening. She had made up her mind to pull one more trick and then she would finish for the night and go back to her doss. Tonight was too cold to be standing around outside, shivering in the damp air coming off the Thames. She'd had enough of watching the dockers and bargemen stagger past in their groups, singing their bawdy songs set to salvation music and occasionally shouting drunken obscenities at her. She ignored the groups; it was the solitary traveller she was after: the jolly Jack tar on shore leave, eager for some drink and some fun, after too many months spent at sea. Or, better still, the gentleman slummer, prowling the East End in search of cheap booze and cheaper sex.

The sailors were easy to spot, some of them wobbling down the street, not yet having found their land legs, and looking for all the world as though they were already drunk. The gentleman slummer stood out too, his well-dressed figure marking him out as a stranger. Eliza would hang around outside one of the local drinking dens, where they sold cheap booze and asked no questions, until she found a likely dupe. As her unsuspecting prey approached the pub, intent on satisfying his craving for alcohol, Eliza would step up to him, entwining her arm through his, asking her poor, gullible victim if he would buy a girl a drink.

Distracted by her gaudy clothes and seductive manner, he would not notice the figure behind him, the cosh raised high, until it was too late. Eliza and Bill would then quickly divest their unconscious victim of all his valuables, and leave him lying in the street as they went and looked for their next dupe.

Seventeen-year-old Eliza had been playing this dangerous game for eight months now, ever since she had arrived in London after running away from her home in Salford. She had run away from home before, but not far enough. Her father always found her after a few weeks, and took her back and beat her with a rope. The last time he had locked her in her room for a week, feeding her nothing but bread and water, and sitting with her every night, reading to her from the Bible. She promised herself that the next time she ran away she would go far enough that she would never be found.

So she came down to London, and for a while she tried to make an honest living selling flowers. But the hardship of life on the streets ground her down, and soon she was immersed in a life of petty crime, and living in doss-houses and padding-kens.

And then she met Bill. He was a professional beggar; knew more ways of parting a person from their money than she would have imagined possible. When she met him it was midwinter, and he was using the 'shivering dodge'. She accompanied him once, watching from the sidelines as he went through his performance. And what a performance it was; wearing the thinnest of clothes he shook and shivered and silently implored the well-dressed passers-by for their assistance. He did well by it, too. But he decided to give up on that particular dodge; knew one beggar who used it too much, and now he couldn't stop trembling, even on the hottest of summer days.

So Bill and Eliza decided to team up. No more begging, Bill decided. He'd heard of easier ways of getting money, quicker too. All it needed was for Eliza to tart herself up a little, and for Bill to use a bit of muscle. Couldn't be safer. Easy money.

Eliza rubbed her hands together and blew on them. It was getting colder now; she was definitely calling it a night.

But then she felt something snaking around her ankles. She looked down and there was a cat, jet-black, twisting and turning between her feet, rubbing its sleek body up against her legs.

"Hello," she said, bending down to stroke it. The cat responded to her attention by rubbing its head against her hands, purring deeply now, still twisting and turning, and flicking its tail from side to side.

There were many cats in the neighbourhood, but none like this one. It looked groomed and well fed, and . . . what was that around its neck? She fingered the leather collar with its strange symbols and signs printed on it. Eliza had never seen a cat wearing a collar before.

"Ah, I see you've met my friend, Lucifer."

Eliza jumped at the sound of the voice, a gasp of surprise escaping from her lips, and looked up. A tall, thin stranger stood in front of her. He wore a long, black overcoat and a black chimneystack hat. The hat cast a shroud of darkness across his face, apart from his eyes, which flashed green at her from under the brim. His voice sounded strange to the young girl, as though he were speaking from a bottomless chasm, his voice echoing from unfathomable depths.

"You scared me," she said. She stood up, but still the stranger towered over her.

"Don't be scared, such a pretty young thing, don't be scared," he whispered, stepping closer, and reaching out a gloved hand to caress her face.

She could see Bill now, appearing spirit-like from the darkness behind the stranger, raising his arm with the cosh, bringing it down.

In one swift movement the stranger turned and fastened his long, gloved fingers around Bill's arm, and pulled him to the floor. As Eliza watched, suddenly frozen with fear, the stranger stooped over her companion, enveloping him in his black overcoat. The cat shrieked and hissed, arching its back, its fur sticking from its body in sharp little spikes. Bill's hand reached out to Eliza from underneath the stranger, the fingers stiffening claw-like in a desperate, silent plea for help. As she watched, paralysed with fear, the skin on Bill's hand began to dry and shrivel up, tightening across the bones until every last ridge and knuckle was plain to see, finally cracking and turning to dust.

The stranger stood once more, turning to look at Eliza. Behind him lay Bill's emaciated, desiccated corpse.

"What . . . what do you want? I ain't got no money."

"I'm not after your money, young girl. I've had more than enough of the riches of this world to satisfy me several lifetimes over. Oh no, it's not your money I want."

Eliza took a step back, and another, until she backed into a wall. The dark figure moved closer, his gloved hand caressing her face once more. She flinched at each soft touch of his fingers upon her cheek.

"I'll scream," she said, breathless with fear, and knowing that she had lost the power to scream, that somehow he had already taken this from her.

"But why?" he whispered. "There's no need to scream, no need at all." He stooped over her now, like a bird of prey, his fetid, freezing breath already sucking the life from her.

"Please . . . please, don't."

Eliza felt herself slipping, fading away, succumbing beneath his power. She felt herself falling to the ground, only to be caught in the stranger's arms. He gathered her up, his touch as tender as a lover's embrace, and kissed her gently on the mouth. She lifted up her hands, trying to ward off the freezing winter invading her body, and knocked away the stranger's hat, revealing his cadaverous face and greedy, sunken eyes.

"Who . . . who are you?" she said, breathless with fear, and . . . excitement.

"I'm a warrior, in charge of thirty legions and more. I'm a duke. I'm a philosopher. Stop trembling child, soon your trial will be over, and you will live forever."

With the tenderness of a father comforting his sick child, the stranger stroked Eliza's hair, pushing it back from her face.

"What . . . what's your name?" she said.

"My name?" the stranger said. "My name is Murmur."

And he kissed her again, sucking the life from her body, her flesh drying up and cracking, and falling from her bones like dust.

"Read all about it!"

The newsvendor held the large sheet newspaper in front of him, various headlines emblazoned in bold on it.

"Ghastly murder in city antique shop!"

Jim and George ran across the street to the newsvendor, who looked down at the two dirty, scruffy boys with undisguised suspicion.

"What do you want?" he asked them.

"Was this the murder that happened last night?" Jim said.

"Yeah. What's it to you?"

"Does it mention anything in the paper about Caxton Tempest?"

"It might do. Like I said, what's it to you?"

"Oh, nothing," Jim said.

"If you're that interested why don't you buy yourself a paper, 'stead of wasting my time asking me lots of foolish questions. Oh, but then I guess," he said, bending down to the two boys, "you ain't got the money to buy a paper, and even if you had, you wouldn't be able to read it anyway."

"Jim doesn't need to read your stupid paper," George shouted, "'cos he was there when it happened."

"Go on, scarper!" the newsvendor shouted, aiming a kick at the boys' bottoms as they turned and ran, giggling.

"Read all about it! Mutilated corpse found in city antique shop!"

Jim and George ran down the West End streets, dodging round the ladies and gentlemen out for a walk in all their finery, giggling and laughing, shouting insults at each other and pulling faces at the passers-by. A policeman blew his whistle at them, but they simply stuck their tongues out at him and carried on running. The policeman decided they were not worth his time bothering with and carried on his beat. Soon they came to a halt and found a side street to sit down in, still laughing and playfully punching each other.

And then Jim said they needed a plan.

"We ain't got no money from last night, so we need to make some today, if we're ever gonna buy that barrow."

"What are we gonna do?" said George.

"I dunno," said Jim, thinking. "We could do a spot of pickpocketing, I suppose, but it's a risky business, and the chances are we won't get much."

Jim pulled from his pocket the small, sharp knife he kept for pickpocketing. He would pretend to stumble against someone, as though he were about to faint, and quickly slice open the man's pocket with his knife, and remove the contents. It was quite often some time later that his

24

victim would realise what had happened, and Jim would be long gone by then. The big disadvantage with pickpocketing was that you had to get up close to your victim, and they would get a very good look at you.

Jim turned the knife over and over in his hands, watching the blade flash in the sunlight. Then he put it away again.

"Nah, pickpocketing's no good, too dangerous. Everybody's getting wise to it."

He sat in thought for a moment, furrowing his brow as he concentrated. Then he clicked his fingers and a wide smile crept across his face.

"I got it," he said. "C'mon, let's go."

He hauled his brother to his feet and they started running again, up and down the streets, Jim turning his head this way and that, always on the lookout.

Until he found what he wanted.

"Matches! Matches for sale! Come and get yer matches!"

The young lad, about Jim's age, his cap set at a jaunty angle on his head, strode up and down the pavement, holding a box of matches in the air as he shouted. A wooden tray containing more boxes hung from his neck and lay against his chest. Draped around his neck also was a sign advertising his goods – Bryant and May's Alpine Vesuvians.

As Jim watched, a man stopped to buy a box from the young match seller.

"Brimstone matches these are sir," said the young boy. "Not even a bloody good gust of wind'll blow one of these things out."

After the man had gone Jim and George approached the young lad. They sized each other up for a few moments in silence.

The match seller said, "What do you want?"

"How'd you like to earn some extra money today?" Jim said.

"Yeah, course I would," the boy replied, still suspicious though.

Jim explained his plan, cajoling the initially reluctant boy until he was persuaded of Jim's moneymaking scheme.

They found another street where the young match seller had not been seen that day and gave George a couple of boxes of matches. Jim and the match seller found somewhere to hide while they watched George.

He walked out into the street and started shouting, "Matches for sale, come and get your matches!" all the while holding the two boxes in the air. He made sure to walk near dirty, muddy pools of water, and then artfully bumped into an old lady, dropping the matches into the puddles. Immediately he sat down on the pavement and began howling.

"Look at him go," said Jim. "Ain't he a good 'un?"

Flustered, the old lady began apologising, but George just howled even more, tears now rolling down his face. Soon a crowd had gathered around the pitiable-looking young boy and his ruined matches. So heart wrenching was the sight that the onlookers were compelled to give the poor little mite money to recompense him for his ruined goods, far more than he would have made by simply selling them. Then George began picking up the sodden matches, saying, "p'raps I can dry 'em out," and helped of course by one or two of the crowd, before carrying on his way.

A minute or two later he met with his two conspirators. They counted out their ill-gotten gains, and then moved on to other streets and repeated the trick again and again, using the same two boxes of now ruined matches. By the end of the morning they had made close to eighteen shillings.

"Blimey!" the match seller said, his eyes popping out of his head. "Me dad don't make that much in a week!"

They began to split the money between them, but as none of them were very good with maths they managed to disagree about how it should be done. A furious argument developed into a full-blown fight between the two young lads, George pitching in with a few well-aimed kicks at the match seller's shins. The coins had now scattered across the pavement, so George took the opportunity to collect as much as he could, and then run. Jim pushed his opponent over, who landed heavily on his tray of matches. The young boy ran as fast as he could, leaving the match seller shouting curses after his departing former companions in crime, but with enough coins scattered around him to give him a small profit on the morning's work.

The two brothers ran deeper into the heart of the West End, past hansom cabs and horse-drawn trams, off the busy Holborn thoroughfare and down onto Great Russell Street. George stopped running to watch an organ grinder and his monkeys, all wearing waistcoats, and surrounded by a group of children.

Jim turned and was about to tell his brother to come on, when he saw Inspector Behrends, and walking beside him Caxton Tempest. Jim stood with his mouth open, forgetting that he had been about to speak, and watched Tempest as he approached.

He was leaving the British Museum with Inspector Behrends. They were so deep in conversation they did not see Jim, despite walking close enough that he could have reached out and touched the two men. Jim had never seen Tempest before, but he had no doubt that this was the great man. He was as handsome as Slum Lassie Sal had said he was, tall and powerful enough to dwarf the Inspector walking beside him.

George was still watching the monkeys. Jim punched him on the arm.

"That's him!" said Jim. "I know it is, it's got to be him!"

"Huh?" said George.

"Tempest, Caxton Tempest, I've just seen him. C'mon!"

He pulled at George's arm, dragging him away from the entertainment. Despite his brother's protestations, they began following Behrends and his companion.

They left Great Russell Street and began walking down Drury Lane. The two men walked quickly and the brothers occasionally had to break into a trot to keep up with them. Tempest led them into the quieter London streets, where he stopped and talked to the Inspector.

Jim drew as close as he dared to the two men, straining to hear the words passing between them.

"Of course, Mr Tempest," Behrends said, "I'll come right by to let you know anything I find out."

"You can find me in the lecture hall of the African Association later this afternoon," Tempest replied. "I'm delivering an address there, but we can talk afterwards and in some privacy. This sounds very serious indeed."

The two men said their goodbyes and parted company. Jim shrank back into the shadows, pushing George behind him. Behrends pulled his heavy overcoat closer around himself as he walked, in an attempt to cut out the chill wind sweeping through the tiny street.

Jim decided to continue following Behrends. He had no interest in a lecture that Tempest might give and would not be allowed in such a prestigious establishment as the African Association anyway. But the Inspector was still investigating the murders, and Jim wanted to be there when he found his next clue.

Jim held George's hand tightly as they ran, afraid he might stray too far ahead and give them away. Every now and then George asked his older brother what they were doing, but Jim just shushed him and gave no answer.

Behrends finally halted in front of a dark, dismal-looking shop in a deserted, narrow alleyway. The shop appeared to be closed, but the Inspector tried the door anyway, to no avail. He looked at his pocket watch, and then up and down the street.

Jim watched the proceedings from a side street a safe distance away. Behind him he could hear George talking to himself, and turned to shush him.

"Found a cat," George whispered.

"Just keep quiet," Jim said.

He turned to look back at the Inspector, who again glanced up and down the cramped street and checked his watch. The shop looked dark and dilapidated, dirty windows partially obscuring the interior. Taking hold of George's hand again Jim crept closer, wanting to take a better look at the shop sign hanging lopsidedly over the door, when Behrends was joined by another man. He wore a long black overcoat and a black, chimneystack hat. For some unaccountable reason, Jim shuddered at the sight of him.

He shrank back as the man let Behrends into the shop.

Suddenly he felt something snaking around his ankles, sending a cold, tingling sensation running up his spine. He looked down and saw a black cat rubbing itself against his ankles, twisting and turning between his legs. Jim picked up the cat, cradling it against his chest. It scrutinised him for a second or two, the deep green of its eyes momentarily sending a shiver through him, and then began purring loudly. Jim gave the cat back to George.

"There you are," George said, tickling the cat under the chin. "I lost you, where'd you go?"

"What's this?" Jim said, tugging at a leather strap around the cat's neck, embellished with strange symbols and diagrams.

"Dunno," said George, tugging at the strap too.

The cat began to fidget and struggle, extricating itself from Jim's arms and climbing up onto his shoulders. George giggled as its tail swished past his face, tickling his nose.

A figure stepped silently from the shadows behind them, large, gnarled hands reaching out for the two boys. The man grabbed Jim and George by the scruffs of their necks and hauled them towards him, the cat leaping from Jim's shoulders and running away.

"'Ello, lads."

Jim looked up at Marlow Crimps, his weathered, liver-spotted face leering back down at him. A large, black eye-patch covered his left eye and strands of greasy hair lay plastered against his forehead. Jim already felt faint from the stench of booze and rotting meat on Crimps' breath.

He struggled free from Crimps' grasp, gasping for air.

"Crimps," Jim said. "What are you doing here?"

Crimps cuffed Jim around the head.

"That's Mr Crimps ter you, yer cheeky sod."

"Sorry."

"An' I expect old Marchek'll want to know what yer doin' 'ere, playin' with the cute little pussycat, when yer should be out thievin'!"

"We were just—"

"Ah, don't bother," Crimps said, waving a dirty hand in dismissal. "S'trouble with you kids these days, no respect for yer elders. When I were your age I would've got a good beatin' just for breathin' out of place."

He looked at the two brothers for a while, probing the inside of his mouth with his tongue. Finding a remnant of half masticated food stuck between his teeth he began chewing.

"Hunh," he grunted. "Maybe I should give the two of yer a good wallopin' anyway, just for the 'ell of it."

"But we have been thievin'," Jim said, producing the morning's takings and presenting them to the filthy old man.

"Aahhh, good lads, good lads," Crimps said, scooping the money out of Jim's hands and hiding it away in secret pockets within his tattered, old waistcoat. "Marlow Crimps, 'e knew yer wouldn't let 'im down, 'e did that. C'mon lads, old Mulready's 'spectin' me down at The White Swan, I'll take yer both with me an' we'll show 'im what good lads yer've been, eh?"

He planted his dirty great hands on Jim's and George's shoulders and began guiding them back up the narrow street. Jim glanced back at the shop, at its dirty windows and crooked door, and the chipped, wooden sign hanging above it.

A single word had been scrawled in black paint across the dirty wood: Magick.

Chapter Four
Federith MacPherson and the Heptameron of Arcanity and Pacts

The sound of Inspector Behrends' shoes echoed around the vast corridor as he walked through the African Associaton's headquarters. Beside him walked Sir Samuel Egerton, beneath the vast vaulted ceiling decorated with elaborate chandeliers and past ornate doorways leading to rooms packed with the spoils of decades of African exploration. Along the walls and between the broad marble columns hung oil paintings, portraits of the Association's intrepid explorers: Daniel Houghton, killed searching for the source of the Niger, Mungo Park, Major Dixon Denham, Rene Caillie, discoverer of Timbuktu, David Livingstone and Henry Morton Stanley.

"Stanley is in the heart of the Congo as we speak," Egerton said, indicating the oils with a casual wave of his manicured hand. "Of course he's working now for that Belgian Leopold, and I doubt we shall see any benefit whatsoever from his latest trip."

"And all of these men explored Africa for the benefit of the African Association?" Behrends said. He had no real interest in the subject, but felt compelled to ask the occasional question for the sake of social niceties.

"My dear Inspector, no! These great and courageous men all explored the savage heart of Africa for the sake of scientific knowledge, to bring civilisation to the wild African, and to convert him from his paganism to the Christian religion. Many of these great men have died in pursuit of that great ideal; that every man, woman and child of the world's farthest reaches should bow the knee before Christ."

"I see," Behrends said. They had stopped walking now, and as he looked around at the display of fantastic wealth the Inspector could not help but feel that the Association had done very well out of the greatest missionary expedition ever. "And you said Mr Tempest was lecturing where?"

"Oh, just through there," Egerton replied, pointing to a set of dark oak double doors, from which came the muted sound of a lone voice. "I believe he's lecturing on a relatively unknown Scottish explorer of the Dark Continent, Federith MacPherson. He was never a member of the Association, something of an individualist I believe." Egerton chuckled. "Mr Tempest always has some very interesting titbits of information to entertain us with when he graces us with his lectures, but nothing of great import, it has to be said."

"Is Mr Tempest a member of the African Association?"

"Alas no, like MacPherson he has always been somewhat of an individualist. Still, he has explored the furthest reaches of Africa and always entertains us with accounts of his adventures. One has to admire his courage and tenacity, and he is indeed a very popular speaker."

Behrends felt he detected a note of regret in Egerton's voice, as though he would be happier if this particular individualist was less popular and therefore given less chance to air his nonconformist views.

The Inspector thanked Egerton for his time and stepped into the lecture hall. Every seat had been taken and Behrends had to stand at the back along with others who had arrived late. Tempest stood in front of a simple wooden lectern and spoke without notes.

"MacPherson tells of a strange episode in his travels," Tempest was saying, "when he was deep in the heart of the Congo, and he came across a village plagued by terrible swarms of insects. Exhausted to the point of death, MacPherson decided to brave the insects and rest, but he found the only way he could keep from being continually bitten and stung was to build a large fire, and sit in the clouds of smoke as much as his lungs could stand. Eventually one of the local people, part of the Fulanji tribe, took pity on him and invited him into his hut. MacPherson was in for quite a surprise. In an attempt to keep the clouds of insects at bay the villagers had built larger than normal huts, the interiors of which were made up of several interconnecting chambers, the central one being the living area, and the only place where anyone could find release from the insects. Now, this is the really interesting part. As guest of honour, MacPherson was introduced to the Chief, sitting in the centre of the largest hut with the Fulanji witch doctor at his side. The witch doctor was a haggard, ancient crone dressed in dirty hyena skins. In her lap she clutched a large, heavy book. Unable to believe that a tribe in the heart of the Congo could read and write Macpherson approached the witch doctor for a closer look. Besides being an explorer, Macpherson also had a fervent interest in the occult, and recognised the book immediately."

"The Heptameron of Arcanity and Pacts," someone called from the audience.

"Exactly!" shouted Tempest, thumping the wooden lectern. "A book of occult inscriptions and incantations and reputedly the only book to exist which not only acknowledges the existence of the Council of Seven, but lists each of their names."

"Isn't the Council of Seven a myth?" someone else said. "A story we tell our children before bed to keep them quiet, like the stories of old of vampires out hunting at night? We live in an age of enlightenment Mr Tempest, when many of the old superstitions and religious mythology are proving to be just that, myths and lies. If, as you say, MacPherson found this important book of the occult, a book which you have yourself in the past equated in its importance with the Bible, then why has nobody else seen it? Where is it?"

"You would do well not to dismiss so lightly the superstitions and stories of old, especially those involving vampires," Tempest replied. "There is evidence that the vampires you dismiss so readily are hunting again. Ask the Inspector if you don't believe me."

Behrends shifted uncomfortably as every eye turned upon him.

"A series of admittedly brutal murders committed over the last few months are no evidence of supernatural entities," replied the speaker from the audience, "and you still have not explained why nobody else has seen the Heptameron of Arcanity and Pacts, Mr Tempest."

"MacPherson kept many detailed records of his journeys, but no one has been able to retrace his steps to this village of insects, despite many attempts. It is now considered that the explorer was suffering delusions brought on by fatigue and malnutrition, and imagined the whole episode."

"But you believe differently?"

"Yes, I do."

"What happened to MacPherson?" somebody else asked. "Did no one ever believe him about the Heptameron, and the village of insects?"

"No," replied Tempest, "and a few years later he set off on his travels again, and then disappeared. No one ever found out what happened to him."

"Do you think he might still be alive?"

"No. MacPherson disappeared more than forty years ago, and he would be in his eighties by now. I still believe that we might be able to find the Heptameron, indeed that it is highly important that we find this most highly prized of occult books. If it were to fall into the wrong hands the consequences would be very serious indeed. Therefore, and to come to the point of my lecture, I have come here today Gentlemen of the Association, to ask for funds to organise an expedition to the Congo and retrieve the Heptameron of Arcanity and Pacts."

The refined atmosphere of the African Association was shattered as everyone began talking at once. Men stood up to make themselves heard above the tumult, but did nothing more than add to the cacophony of raised voices. Chairs scraped over the tiled floor and the chairman could be heard banging a gavel and shouting for order.

"I've never heard such rot in all my years!" someone shouted.

"And he expects us to fund a wild goose chase into the Congo!"

Men began leaving, pushing past Behrends as they pulled on expensive great coats, muttering about the lunacy of the modern age.

The hall emptied quickly and, after conversing in hushed tones with the chairman, Tempest joined the Inspector.

"Let us take a walk outside, Inspector," Tempest said, taking Behrends by the arm and guiding him through the doorway and down the vast hall past the portraits of the Association's intrepid explorers into the savage heart of dark Africa. "I think I may have outstayed my welcome within the halls of this venerable institution."

New Oxford Street was filled with hansom cabs, ladies wearing the latest Parisian fashions and men conferring together on street corners. Tempest lit a pipe, his face shrouded in wreaths of blue smoke for an instant before they were snatched away by the chill wind to reveal once more his piercing eyes and stern jaw.

"So, Inspector," he said, "you now see the difficulties I face as I seek to warn the world of the dangers it faces."

Behrends said nothing; he always felt a little uncomfortable in Tempest's presence. He perhaps shared more of Samuel Egerton's dislike of the individualist than he realised.

"Come, Inspector Behrends, what did you find out this morning? Good news, I hope?"

"I visited several antique and curio shops across the West End, but no one could shed any light on what the murderer might be after, or why he would drain his victims' bodies of blood."

"Inspector, you have no need to trouble yourself on that detail of the murders, it is obvious to me that Talos and his horde of bloodsucking fiends are abroad once more. What we need to know is what they are after, what they are seeking, and why."

The Inspector harrumphed at being interrupted, and then continued. "I visited one dirty little shop in a back street off Bedford Street shortly after we parted. There is a sign above the door with one word scrawled on it; Magick, spelt with a 'ck' at the end. Most unusual, as is the unpleasant-looking proprietor. He told me there is an American woman who frequents the opium dens in the East End who might be able to help us. In fact, he seemed most certain that she could be of help."

"Does this woman have a name?"

"Denver McCade. Apparently she is hiding from someone, and may be a little reluctant to talk."

"And did the proprietor of this magic shop say how he came by this information?"

"He said only that he has many contacts in the world of the occult and gathers snippets of information in his days tending shop. Personally Mr Tempest I see no reason to trust him, but then we have no other leads to follow."

"Quite the opposite, my dear Inspector, I have two fellows working for me right now following the trail of slaughtered antiquarians and their specialist stock from New York to Paris to London. Once we find out what, if anything, has been stolen from their shops then we should have a better idea of Talos' intentions."

"I see, I see," the Inspector said, not sure that he saw at all.

"Believe me, Inspector Behrends," Tempest said, halting and turning on Behrends, his face wreathed momentarily again in a cloud of blue tobacco smoke, "this is the work of vampires. We need to be on our guard, especially at night-time. I feel their presence in the city; they are hidden amongst us, perhaps closer than we think. It won't be too long before they make their presence known."

Chapter Five
Billy Rackitt Escapes

Billy Rackitt hung from the spiked iron rail that surmounted the top of the wall surrounding Newgate Gaol's exercise area. His brown trousers and tunic were badly ripped where the iron spikes had torn at him as he clambered over the rail, and small, dark patches of blood seeped through his prison uniform. He looked down at the ground twenty feet below him and then swiftly back up, momentarily closing his eyes and holding his breath, waiting for the sensation of vertigo to leave him.

But he couldn't afford to wait long; his hands were slippy with blood from the many lacerations caused by the spikes he hung onto, and he was losing his grip.

"C'mon Billy, yer silly sod," he whispered to himself. "If yer don't get movin' soon yer gonna fall, an' a couple o' broken legs ain't gonna stop 'em from keeping yer appointment with the hangman later on today, that's fer sure. Murderers don't get a second chance, Billy, yer should know that by now."

Ignoring the pain, he continued working his way along the wall; the iron spikes cutting into the flesh on his hands at each movement. When he judged he was in the right spot, he looked down and saw the roofs of the guards' quarters below him.

He hung silently, contemplating his next move. His daring escape from Newgate Gaol, on the morning of his proposed execution, had so far gone entirely unnoticed by the prison guards. A couple of other convicts had seen him, but they weren't going to tell anyone; thieves' honour would count for that.

No, all had gone well so far, but then shinnying up the wall in the exercise yard in the fortuitous few moments when he had been left alone, and then climbing over the serrated spikes at the top of a twenty-foot wall, hanging from the other side and making his way to the guards' quarters where he knew he could safely drop onto the roof without risking breaking a leg, well, that had all been the easy part.

Now for the difficult bit; landing on the guardhouse roof was going to give him away, no question. As soon as the guards heard the loud thump as Billy hit the roof they would be out to investigate. Only one thing to do then; as soon as he landed, he had to be up and running across the guardhouse roofs for the outer perimeter prison wall. He could easily shin over that and then it was a short drop onto the roof of the nearest terrace backed up against the prison and he was free.

"This is it then Billy, lad," he said, by way of encouragement. Taking a deep breath and closing his eyes, he let go of the iron railing and dropped onto the tiled roof. His battered prison shoes crunched against the slate tiles and he stumbled slightly.

But by the time he heard the commotion beneath him he was up and running, straight as an arrow for the prison wall, for freedom. Laughing heartily as he listened to the outraged shouts from below and behind him, he forgot about climbing over the wall and instead cleared it with a single bound, landing on the sloped roof of a row of terraces butted up against the prison. He instantly fell on his side and began sliding down the dirty slate roof. Scrabbling furiously at the grey, cracked tiles, Billy tried to halt his descent, swearing at himself for being too cocky and not shinnying over the wall as originally planned. Before he reached the edge, he managed to halt his fall and pulled himself back up to the top of the roof. With a single glance behind him he turned his back on Newgate Gaol and began gingerly making his way along the apex of the terraced roof, away from his enforced confinement of the last few months, and away from his appointment with the hangman later that afternoon.

He was only half way along the terraced roof, coughing in the clouds of filthy black smoke that billowed from the many chimney-stacks, when he heard the policeman's whistle.

"Damn and blast!" he cursed, his round white eyes staring from his soot-covered face. "My lucky stars ain't shinin' down on me today, that's fer sure."

But just as he said this, he heard the clip-clopping of a horse's hooves on the street below him, and the neighing of the horse, startled by the sudden commotion.

Looking from his vantage point from the top of the roof, Billy could see the rag and bone man directly below him, sitting on his cart, his horse standing in front of him, shaking its head and straining against its reins.

He could also see two policemen running down the street, blowing their whistles, and followed by a small contingent of Newgate Gaol's finest, intent on recapturing their escaped convict. With a loud oath, Billy started a precarious slide down the tiled roof and leapt from the edge, landing in the rag and bone man's cart with a sickening thump, and startling both horse and man.

Within a second Billy was scrambling to his feet and pushing at the old man on the front of the rickety wooden cart, sending him tumbling to the cobbled street shouting curses on the thief who was stealing his horse and cart.

"Sorry mate," said Billy, grabbing hold of the horse's reins, "but I'll see you right an' sure enough if I gets away from them lot that wants to slip a noose around my neck."

With a well-aimed kick at the horse's rear end, and a mighty shout, Billy Rackitt began his escape from the advancing policemen as the horse bolted away. They hurtled through the narrow, cramped alleyways and streets of inner London, the old wooden cart creaking and groaning alarmingly, and threatening to fall apart under the strain at any moment. Billy began laughing helplessly, just about enough strength left in his body to hang on to the cart, his skinny backside bouncing up and down on the hard wooden seat as they clattered over the cobbled streets.

Men, women and children, cats and dogs, and anything else that got in his way, all had to leap from his path as the horse galloped along, pulling the rickety cart behind it, the rapid staccato clack of its hooves filling the morning air.

After a short spell of frenzied running, the old horse began to visibly tire, and so Billy reined it in a little, and let it walk along at a much more sedate pace. He needed to get out of London now, before they got too many peelers on his case, but he didn't think that the best way of doing it was by horse and cart.

Not this horse and cart, anyway. The cart looked as though it might fall apart at any moment, and the horse, well the horse looked good for nothing more than the knackers' yard.

Besides all of that, Billy looked nothing like a rag and bone man. In his prison uniform, he looked just like what he was; an escaped convict. And up here on the cart, everybody could see him. No, he needed to get rid of the horse and cart, get some new clothes, and then get out of the city.

After guiding the horse down a dim, dingy alleyway, Billy pulled the animal to a halt and climbed from the cart. The horse was an old, chestnut coloured brewer's nag, and it looked at Billy now with a sad, mournful look, its nostrils quivering with each breath it took.

Billy scratched the animal between the ears, and gazed back into its large, dark eyes.

"Yer a good ol' boy," he whispered. "Yer did Billy right, an' that's fer sure. I owe you one, I rightly do, but I ain't that convinced our paths are gonna cross again, mate, so I have a feelin' the debt's gonna remain outstandin'."

The horse snorted softly and rubbed its head against Billy's hand, enjoying the attention.

The screech of a policeman's whistle echoed through the cramped street, and Billy realised he had been discovered again. With one last pat on the horse's head, he set off at a run, deeper into the dim, narrow alley.

Rounding a bend he saw some steps leading up to a doorway to a tiny little theatre set back in the wall. The sign above the entranceway read, 'Le Theatre du Grand Guignol.' The theatre was disused and the entrance had been boarded up, but one of the boards at ground level had come loose, and Billy could see a gap big enough for him to crawl through.

Getting on his hands and knees, he wriggled through the tiny gap, ripping more of his tunic in the process, and pulled the loose board up behind him as best he could. In the cool, dim interior he sat and waited, and sure enough he heard the policeman's booted feet running down the narrow, cobbled street, and heard him blowing his whistle. Billy held his breath as he heard the copper pause outside the theatre, but then he carried on running, and when Billy could no longer hear him he let out his breath in a long whoosh of air.

Billy took a moment to look around him now; on his right stood an empty ticket foyer, a poster on the wall behind it advertising what must have been the last performance the theatre ever held. The poster depicted a woman in the foreground, sitting on the floor and looking behind her, her hand to her open mouth, obviously screaming. Behind her loomed the Devil, stretching out his hands to take her. The title read, 'In the grip of Satan'.

Billy pulled himself to his feet and walked deeper into the foyer. Thin but overly ornate pillars interrupted the wall space, which was decorated with carved, masked faces. More posters littered the floor.

Billy picked up one of them and unfolded it, reading the title, 'Le Masque de la Bête'.

He let the poster flutter to the floor and shivered slightly in the cool of the building. Billy inspected his hands, registering the pain in his palms now that he was no longer preoccupied with his desperate escape attempt. The cuts still bled a little.

"What next then, Billy lad?" he said, a little startled at the sound of his voice breaking the silence of the building, bouncing off the damp walls in a faint, mocking echo.

Best to lie low, maybe, at least for a couple of hours, he thought. It would be dark soon, and he would have a better chance then of getting as far away from this miserable city as he possibly could.

His eyes having grown used to the dim interior, he now noticed a flight of carpeted stairs in front of him, leading down into the depths of the building. He stood at the top of the steps and looked down into the darkness.

"What the hell," he said. "I might as well have a look around while I'm here."

He walked down the richly carpeted stairs and pushed through a set of thick wooden, double doors at the bottom. The subterranean space he walked into was the theatre, closely packed wooden benches filling the room and facing a simple wooden stage.

Billy walked further into the room, intrigued by this place he had never come across before. Billy had never been to the theatre before in his life, but he had a fair idea of what the experience might be like, and what he saw before him came nowhere close. Where he would have expected ornate design, comfort and artful craftsmanship, he saw a cramped, dirty and dingy little room. He could not imagine respectable people coming here for a night out, for an evening of refined entertainment.

No, this place had an aura of sensation, of shock horror and cheap thrills.

Of murder and mayhem.

Billy turned at a noise behind him, in the shadows; something being scuffed or kicked.

"Who's there?" he said, turning around in a full circle. "C'mon, I heard yer, there's no point hidin' now, is there?"

Silence greeted Billy's challenge. A cool breeze whispered against his cheek.

Maybe he imagined it. He was seeing and hearing coppers everywhere now.

Billy stepped onto the stage at the front of the tiny theatre. The floorboards were pitted and stained, and bits and pieces of scenery had been left scattered about. At one end of the stage sat a French guillotine, its blade caked dark with blood.

Fake blood, he hoped.

Billy picked up a knife from the wooden stage floor and pressed the tip of the blade against his thumb. It felt loose. He pushed a little harder and the blade disappeared into the handle.

A prop, nothing more. You could easily pretend to stab someone with this, and make it look very real.

Again a sudden noise made Billy turn and peer into the dimness of the low, cramped room. There was someone in here with him, he was sure of that now. But where? There was nowhere for them to hide in this tiny room.

He dropped the prop knife on the stage floor; it would be useless in a fight.

Maybe it was time to leave; this place was giving him the creeps.

Sensing a movement behind him, Billy turned, his fists up ready to fight, but he was too late. The thing slammed into him hard, pushing him to the wooden stage floor and pinning him down before he had chance to resist. Hot, rancid breath rasped against his face as the thing hissed its displeasure at him.

"What are you doing here?" it said.

Billy said nothing, too stunned at what he saw to speak.

The thing that held him pinned to the old wooden stage floor looked like nothing he had ever seen before. Its grey, pallid flesh was stretched tight over its prominent cheekbones, and its red eyes bulged from its head. Its nose was upturned and flattened like a bat's, and pointed, dirty fangs protruded from its thin lips.

Billy struggled against the thing's hold on him, but its grip was too powerful. It sat on his chest and held his wrists against the floor. Leaning forward until its upturned nose was touching Billy's, its fangs dripping hot saliva onto his face, it said again, "What are you doing here?"

"Don't kill it," said another voice, similar to the first.

The thing that held Billy pinned to the floor looked up, and Billy followed its gaze. Another, similar monstrosity stood beside them, crouching on the floor and looking at Billy with much interest, its head cocked quizzically to one side.

"Why not?" hissed the first. "It refuses to speak and tell who us who it is, and it's a Hell's age since I last feasted on the fresh blood of one of its kind."

The thing beside them shuffled closer, looking intently at Billy.

"The master will want to see it," it said. "The master will want to know how it found us."

Billy swallowed nervously as the thing on top of him fingered the collar of his prison tunic, stroking the flesh of his neck with its dirty fingers. Then it lifted one of his hands to its face and licked at the blood on his palm.

"And then the master will let me drink its blood, as a reward," it said, looking up at its companion.

One of the monstrosities lifted a hatch from the stage floor, revealing a tunnel shaft beneath the stage, which dropped vertically into complete darkness. They hauled Billy to his feet and pushed him over to the hole in the ground.

He had a single, fleeting moment to look down into the inky blackness before he plummeted head first into the tunnel entrance.

Chapter Six
Paddy's Goose

George jumped off his chair and crawled under the table just in time. The empty bottle flew across the room, passing through the space he had occupied only a moment before, smashing against the wall, and showering a group of sailors with shards of glass. One of their number, a colossal bear of a man, his skin sunburnt from many months spent at sea, clambered to his feet, brushing slivers of glass from his clothes. With an unintelligible roar he charged the man who had thrown the bottle, sending them both crashing into another group of drinkers.

"Stupid Russians," Mulready snarled, tossing back the last of his drink. "Should know better'n comin' round 'ere."

"Ah, they're alright," Crimps said. "At least they're better than those filthy, thievin' Jews. Steal the coat of yer back, they would."

The other drinkers ignored the fight at the opposite end of the pub. Although called The White Swan, the pub was known locally as Paddy's Goose, and was notorious throughout the East End as a hangout for elements of the London underworld. The police tended to avoid the pub as much as possible, despite the fact they could have solved half the cases on their files in one visit; but they knew the rough treatment they would be afforded upon entering, and so stayed away.

If, however, an enterprising officer of the law were brave enough to visit Paddy's Goose, and then survived the inevitable mauling he would receive upon entering the pub, his next problem would be how to identify his quarry through the pall of thick, heavy tobacco smoke that hung permanently in the long, low-ceilinged room. Then he would have to penetrate the masses of squalid, swarthy bodies, packed together in groups around the rickety old tables, discussing 'business' and trading stories. Among these groups drifted fat, middle-aged women, faces dull and bestial, eyes puffy and red with drink. Occasionally one of them would sit down next to a man, inviting him upstairs, looking for easy money for her next drink.

There was a bar, the top of which was scarred and stained from countless broken glasses and spilled drinks. Behind the bar there used to be a large mirror, but it had been smashed so many times the present landlord refused to replace it. Instead, in the place of the ill-fated mirror, there were shelves of brightly coloured bottles containing, for the most part, evil tasting spirits and cheap beer. The landlord himself had been a notorious career criminal once, but confessed to being tired of the life, and even more so of the hard labour he had served at Her Majesty's Pleasure, and so took up a respectable business. At the opposite end of the pub there burnt a miserable fire, tended to by a wizened old crone. Some people said she was the landlord's mother, but nobody knew for sure, and nobody asked. The fire never produced enough heat to keep the place warm in winter, but the old woman tended to it every night, as though her life depended on it.

Besides the criminal society of Paddy's Goose, there was also a second society of men, made up of many nationalities. These were the sailors on shore leave, and between jobs; the black, muscular African, fighting his friends with much shouting and laughter; the Chinese, small and wiry, chattering away in their own groups; the bronzed, handsome men from the Pacific Islands; the tough, weather-beaten men from the Arctic seas.

And beneath them all, beneath the rotten floorboards that supported them, seethed a teeming mass of vermin. The rats could be seen occasionally, darting through one of the many holes in the floor for a scrap of food, and then disappearing back into their subterranean lair.

Jim slid off his chair and joined George under the table. Down here they could hear the rats scuttling around underneath the crumbling floorboards, devouring their scraps of food.

"Did he take all the money?" George said.

"Yeah," Jim said. Crimps had pocketed the money they had swindled with the help of the match seller that morning, but had not shared any of it with Mulready. The old man had searched Jim's pockets for loot when he had arrived at the pub with Crimps, and then cuffed him around the head for not having anything. A warning glance from Crimps had encouraged him to keep his mouth shut. He knew that he would get far worse than a slap around the head from Crimps if the old man found out that Crimps was holding money back from him.

"How are we ever gonna get enough money to buy a barrow, Jim?"

"I dunno," Jim said. He had hoped that last night he could steal enough to pacify the old man for a while, maybe even run away with, and buy that barrow he kept promising George. The last thing he had expected was to find the owner of the shop lying in a pool of his own blood, and the police at the front door.

Jim closed his eyes and saw the pools of blood, the mutilated corpse, his fleshy, waxen features, frozen in a grimace of fear.

They say he's killed people everywhere, all across the world. Always antique collectors, and people selling curios and artefacts, like. And they say the victims' bodies are always drained of blood.

"I wonder who he is?" Jim said.

"Who?" said George.

Jim looked at his little brother and smiled. He hadn't realised he had been thinking aloud.

"The man who killed the shopkeeper, that's who. Why did he kill him?"

"I dunno," said George. A large, black rat had poked its head out of a hole in the floorboards and was now looking at George, twitching its nose. George looked back at the rat.

"I wonder what they were doing today. I wonder what's in that shop the peeler went to." Jim said. "Maybe there'll be another murder soon . . ."

"Ah, sar, you are looking to be very clever man, indeed," said a high-pitched voice above him, interrupting his thoughts. From underneath the table Jim could only see the legs of the newcomer; the faded yellow trousers, the once exotic, colourful shoes, now dirty and ripped beyond repair. There was a clattering noise on the tabletop above his head.

"I am tinking you are two very clever-looking men indeed, and tinking dat my little bet will be of interest to you both."

Jim pulled himself back up off the floor and onto his seat to look at the speaker. He was a small, thin Indian man, dirty and dishevelled, and cunning looking. On the table he had placed three egg cups, upside down, in a line, and a small cork ball.

Placing the ball under the middle of the three egg cups, he said, "You must keep your eye on de cup wid de ball in it."

He began shuffling the egg cups around each other. Intrigued, Crimps leaned forward, his one good eye following the Indian's hands as he shuffled the cups around and around.

Finally he stopped and said, "Now sar, you must be telling me which of dees cups has de ball in it, and if you are right I be buying you a drink, but if you are wrong den you be buying de drinks, yes?"

"Hunh," Crimps grunted. He lifted a big, meaty hand and picked up the middle one of the three egg cups. It was empty.

He looked at Mulready, and then at the Indian, and scowled.

"I am tinking you are owing me a drink," said the little man, lifting up another egg cup to reveal the cork ball underneath.

"Do it again," Crimps said.

"Oh no no no, not until you are buying me de drink dat you promised me."

"Do it again," Crimps snarled.

The little Indian man, deciding that Crimps was not to be argued with, placed the cork ball under the middle egg cup once more, and began shuffling.

"Slower," Crimps snarled.

The Indian slowed his movements down, and finally stopped. Crimps leaned across the table and lifted the egg cup he thought contained the ball. It was empty.

Again he scowled at the dirty little man in front of him, and then glanced at the barman and gave him a nod. Within a few moments three glasses of 'blue ruin' had been placed on the table.

"I am tanking you very much," said the Indian, and threw his drink back in one.

"Do it again," snarled Crimps.

Jim watched with growing apprehension as the man repeated his trick several more times, Crimps growing more agitated every time he picked up the empty cup. George was watching too, his eyes wide with astonishment. Every time Crimps lost, he indicated to the barman to bring them another 'blue ruin' each. And then, after throwing his drink back, he always said, "Do it again."

The dirty little man became increasingly drunk as he repeated the trick over and over, becoming ever more careless. Mulready and Crimps both watched the Indian, their heads mimicking the movement of the egg cups as the little man shuffled them round and round.

And then Jim saw it; saw the careless little movement revealing how it was done. He glanced up at Crimps, sick with fear.

Crimps had seen it too. He leaned forward and grabbed both the Indian's tiny hands in his one big one, and held on to them. With the other he lifted the egg cups off the table one by one.

They were all empty.

The little Indian man cried out in pain as Crimps tightened his grip on his wrists, squeezing and squeezing, a grim smile revealing his yellow, chipped teeth. The Indian opened up his hands and the tiny cork ball fell onto the table, rolling away until it fell to the floor, to be stolen by a hungry rat.

"You lyin' little cheat," Crimps snarled.

Mulready started laughing, banging the table with his fist.

"Oh no, no, sar, I not be lying to such a gentleman like you, sar, no sar indeed."

"Shut up!" Crimps roared. With his free hand he reached down behind him and pulled out a knife, pressing it against the Indian man's face. The knife was six inches long; wide and flat, the blade caked dark with rusted blood, it curved to a vicious point at its end. It had a serrated edge, once used perhaps for gutting large fish, or cutting open carcasses at the slaughterhouse. Nobody ever asked Crimps what he used it for.

The Indian man's eyes bulged from his head as he tried to look down at the blade pressed against his cheek, sweat dripping from his face. A tiny pinprick of blood appeared at the point where the tip of the blade pressed into his cheek, and then ran down the length of the rusty knife.

Mulready laughed even harder, banging the table some more with the flat of his hand, the empty glasses jumping in the air.

"Please sar, if you be letting go of my hands den I can be repaying you for all de drinks dat you were so kind to be buying me tonight, sar!"

Crimps scowled, and thought about this for a while. Having mulled it over, he came to a decision, and let one of the Indian's hands free.

The little man scrabbled around in his pockets with his free hand and scattered a handful of coins across the tabletop. Mulready scooped them up and began counting them.

Crimps leaned over the terrified Indian, a little rivulet of blood now running down the rusty blade. With a powerful roar, Crimps pushed the little man backwards off his chair, slicing at his face with the knife. The Indian crashed to the floor, clutching at the gaping red wound across his cheek. Howling in pain and fear he leapt to his feet and ran from the pub.

Several of The White Swan's customers laughed as he ran past them and out into the night.

Crimps wiped the blade of his knife on his trousers and placed it on the table in front of him. He laughed quietly, downing the last of his drink, and wiped his mouth with the back of his hand.

"That showed 'im," he said.

Mulready used the Indian man's money to buy more drinks. Settled back in his chair, the entertainment over with, Mulready's gaze settled on the two brothers.

"Useless pair o' toe-rags," he said. "What were yer thinkin', comin' round 'ere wi' no money? What use 'ave I got fer yer, if'n yer ain't gonna steal no more?"

Mulready turned to Crimps. Pointing at the two brothers, he said, "Who took 'em in when they were out on the streets? Who were it who 'elped them, in their 'our o' need? If it weren't for me, they'd be in the workhouse now. An' how do they repay me?"

"No respect fer their elders, that's the trouble with kids these days," Crimps said, tossing back another shot of the cheap gin. "No respect fer their elders, that's their trouble."

Jim and George had been sitting in The White Swan for several hours now, watching Crimps and Mulready drink the day away. The two men had alternately berated the brothers for their lack of respect, and then ignored them. Now Mulready was looking at the boys with barely disguised contempt.

"S'time," said the old man, slurring his words, and looking at Jim. "S'time yer were back out on them streets, thievin'. S'time yer wer provin' to me that yer still got what it takes."

Jim sat up a little straighter.

"I ain't got no use fer yer, sittin' round 'ere all day, when yer should be out thievin'. I ain't got no time fer yer pathetic excuses 'bout blood, an' dead bodies, an' peelers."

He took a swig of his drink and slammed the glass back down on the table.

"Ain't got no time fer bloody peelers," he said. "G'warn with yer, and don't come back empty 'anded tonight, or I'll give yer a bloody good 'idin', that I will."

He waved his hand dismissively at them.

As the two brothers stood up to go, Crimps reached out a hand and took George by the arm, pulling him close.

"Don't forget," he said, "wherever yer go, whatever yer up to, Crimps got the all-seein' eye. Ol' Crimps, 'e always got 'is eye on yer."

Slowly Crimps peeled back his eye patch. The empty eye socket stared at George, a sunken hole of scaly, scarred, blood red flesh. Crimps pulled a filthy rag out of his pocket and gave the hollow eye socket a scrub, the rag almost completely disappearing into its depth. When he pulled it back out it was red with blood.

He laughed and let George go.

The two boys ran out of the pub and down the street, their feet splashing through the river of filthy liquid that overflowed the gutter and ran with them. George ran hard to keep up with his brother, who seemed to have no regard for him tonight, not checking on his progress, not slowing down to let him catch up.

Jim was thinking, thinking hard. He needed to bring something back for the old man tonight; he knew that if he could just bring some loot back he would be in the old man's favour again, and things would be okay, for a while at least. He just needed a little while longer, just so as he could hide away a little more money. They needed money, not just to buy a barrow and stock it, but money to live on for a while. He'd seen the other costermongers around town, listened to their stories, knew that it wasn't the easy life that he painted it for George. Sure, some of them made a success of their business, enough that they could then go on to open up a proper shop, but not all of them. The life was a hard one, almost as hard as living on the streets.

Just need a little more time, Jim thought. Just enough to put away a bit more loot, enough to move on, get out of this life.

Enough to start living like normal people do.

Chapter Seven
The Fight in the Opium Den

At about the same time that Jim and George ran from The White Swan, and only a few streets away, in the same, run-down and dangerous borough of London, walked a Chinaman. He walked with a certain athletic grace; he was tall and slim, and dressed elegantly in a dark blue waistcoat and trousers. He looked to be in his early thirties, he was very handsome, and his short black hair was perfectly combed and styled with a little oil. There was no hesitation in his stride. He did not look to the right or to the left, did not stop to talk to the dolly-mops on the street corners who invited his attention, or the drunken halfwits begging for money. He appeared so graceful and cultivated, projected such a powerful, lithe presence, that people passing him would sometimes stop what they were doing and turn to look, wondering where he was going and what he was going to do when he got there. But the Chinaman ignored them and just kept walking.

The air was turning cold and a mist was beginning to roll in off the Thames, creeping through the narrow streets, now turning into a fog that would soon shroud almost the whole of the city in its clammy grasp. The staccato clack of the Chinaman's expensive shoes on the pavement soon became muffled by this encroaching, all-enveloping fog.

But the Chinaman walked on, paying no attention to the fog, until he found the road that he wanted. He soon turned off that road and into a cramped side street. The Chinaman walked slowly down the narrow alleyway, glancing periodically up at the rotten windows that overlooked him, more cautious now than he had been. He walked into the tiny courtyard at the end and examined the three doors that led off it, now just about visible in the thick fog. Over one of the doors hung a tiny wooden sign with a couple of Chinese characters painted on it.

The Chinaman presented himself at the rickety, rotten door of Moon Lee's Opium Den, and was met by Moon Lee herself, a tiny, wrinkled, old Chinese woman. She cackled to herself at the sight of the impeccably presented Chinaman, but did not bother to tell him what amused her so, and stepped aside to let him enter. The doorway was small and narrow, and the Chinaman had to stoop as he walked through it and into the cramped, cold hallway.

Grimy and featureless, the hallway was completely bare apart from a ladder in the middle of the floor leading up to an open hatch in the ceiling. A dirty yellow light spilled from the hatchway, illuminating the hall.

The Chinaman looked at Moon Lee, who indicated that he should ascend the ladder first. She nodded and smiled, and cackled to herself some more.

The Chinaman walked over to the ladder and placed a hand on a rung. He looked up through the open hatch in the ceiling, at the swirls of smoke visible in the room above him. He crinkled his nose at the dry, burning smell, and then began to climb the ladder.

The Chinaman pulled himself up the ladder and into the room. He stood by the hatch and swiftly looked around him. Although lit by greasy, yellow oil lamps, which gave off foul, black fumes, his view was obscured by a thick fog of smoke. This heavy, acrid smoke, which filled the room, stung at his eyes and nose, and the back of his throat. The Chinaman knew the odour well. After only a moment or two in the confined space he could already feel its narcotic effects; the throbbing in his temples, a slight light-headedness. He knew he had to conclude his business here swiftly, before the stupefying influence of the opium drug overcame him completely.

The Chinaman blinked his eyes and looked around him again. Various bodies reclined on low benches scattered around the room, some of them sharing an opium pipe, others smoking the drug in hand-rolled cigarettes. These customers of Moon Lee's were of many nationalities and social classes, but they all shared a craving for opium, a need to escape their lives for a few hours at least, in a comforting blanket of forgetfulness and bliss.

The Chinaman moved among them, looking closely, searching for someone. Occasionally one of the somnolent bodies would lift a head and look up at the Chinaman with glassy, unfocused eyes, and then lay his head back down again, or return to sucking on the pipe being passed around the room. Many of the men were thin and wasted, any money they earned going to satisfy their body's need for the drug, rather than food.

The Chinaman continued his search around the room, until suddenly stopped in his tracks by a lone female voice. The voice of the very person, he was certain, he had come here looking for.

"Well, I'll be a raggedy old donkey's scrawny behind, if it ain't the Chinaman," the woman drawled from the gloom.

Johnny Chen turned in the direction of the voice, and said, "Miss McCade? Is that Denver McCade?"

Denver McCade leaned forward, revealing herself from the darkness of the corner in which she had been reclining. Between the forefinger and middle finger of her right hand she held a burning cigarette. She lifted the cigarette to her lips and sucked on it, closing her eyes while she held the smoke in her lungs for a few blissful seconds.

Then she sighed, and the smoke billowed from her mouth, partly obscuring her face.

"'Course it's me, Johnny Chen. Who in the hell else were you expecting? It's me you were looking for, after all."

Denver McCade sat on a long, low bench, legs astride, her arms resting casually on her knees, and looked up at Johnny Chen. She wore a pair of fustian trousers and shirt, and a brightly coloured rag loosely knotted around her neck. But for her long, blond hair, roughly tied into a ponytail, she could have been mistaken at first glance for a man.

"I mean, why else would the mysterious Johnny Chen be hanging around an opium den, unless he was looking for someone?" she said. "An' me not bein' one to blow my own trumpet an' all, but I don't expect you'd be lookin' for anyone else in here. Am I right?"

"Miss McCade . . . Denver, I am not here under my own authority. Mr Tempest sent me here to find you."

"That ain't one whole hell of a surprise, Johnny. I suppose he expects me to come back with you, an all, don't he?"

"Mr Tempest believes you can be of help with a certain . . . problem he is investigating."

"I'll bet he does." Denver took another drag on the opium cigarette.

"Mr Tempest would very much like it if you were to come back with me, Miss McCade."

For a moment Denver said nothing, head tilted up slightly, her eyes closed, and then she expelled the smoke from her lungs with a deep sigh.

"How did you find me?" she said, opening her eyes and fixing Johnny Chen with a cold stare. "And why, what possible use could I be to the great and mighty Caxton Tempest?"

Johnny Chen said nothing. Behind him he sensed, rather than heard, movement: two men, approaching him, stealthily. He tensed, ready.

"Easy boys," Denver said, holding up a hand in a placatory gesture. "This here's Johnny Chen. Ain't you never heard of him?"

Johnny Chen looked behind him. Two young, muscular Chinese men stood just either side of him, their bodies like coiled springs ready to explode. One of them cracked his knuckles repeatedly. The other one had a scar running diagonally across his face from his forehead, across his nose, and down his cheek onto his neck.

"Don't pay them no heed, Johnny," Denver said. "They've kinda taken a shine to me since I got here. I guess they kinda see themselves as my guardian angels."

Johnny Chen turned back to Denver, his hands, by his sides, balled up into fists.

"Mr Tempest asked that I find you and bring you back with me, Miss McCade. He did not discuss any other options."

"I'll bet he didn't. I'll bet Mr Caxton Tempest is used to getting his own way, ain't he?"

Denver took another drag on the opium cigarette. After holding the smoke once more in her lungs for a few, long seconds, her eyes narrowed down to slits, she said, "I'm sorry, Johnny."

She clicked her fingers.

Johnny Chen heard the tiny whoosh of air; saw, in his mind's eye, the fist heading towards his lower back, about to deliver a disabling punch into his spine. He sidestepped the fist and grabbed hold of the man's wrist, using his own momentum against him to propel him head down onto the floor. Before the scar-faced man had even finished ploughing face first into the rotten boards, splinters of wood piercing his cheeks and gouging at his mouth, the knuckle-cracking man had leapt onto Johnny Chen's back. He wrapped his left arm around his throat and raised his right arm high, a shiny stiletto knife in his hand. Again Johnny Chen used his attacker's own momentum against him, doubling over and sending him crashing on top of his companion.

The two Chinese men jumped to their feet, the first one clawing at the bloody slivers of wood piercing his face, adding more scars to the first. With a single, united roar of anger, the two men charged Johnny Chen.

He was ready for them.

He had already seen the rotten ceiling above them, revealing the wooden supporting beams, and leapt, arms outstretched. The Chinaman hung from the ceiling, lifting both his feet, and delivered a stinging kick into the Chinese men's faces, sending them reeling backwards.

He dropped silently to the floor and crouched, hands in front of him ready. The three men slowly circled each other for a few moments, ever watchful with wary eyes.

Scar-face wiped at the blood dripping from his face.

Suddenly, knuckle-cracker lunged at Johnny Chen, making a long, swift slashing movement with the stiletto. Johnny Chen knocked the knife out of the way and inflicted a punishing punch to the man's face. He staggered backwards and shook his head, sending globs of snot and blood flying from his broken nose.

Meanwhile scar-face charged, head down, at Johnny Chen, striking him in the stomach and sending them both crashing into a group of men sharing an opium pipe. They all went down, mixed up in a tangle of arms and legs.

The bloodied thug was up first, searching for his opponent in the mess of bodies below him. He saw him, still extricating himself from the mass of dirty, groggy bodies, and lifted a booted foot to stamp on Johnny Chen's head.

Johnny Chen's arms and upper body were still obstructed by the other bodies on the floor with him, but his legs were free. He lifted his knees up into his chest as the Chinese man's foot came down and kicked his legs out, hitting him in the stomach and sending him back crashing down onto the floor.

Johnny Chen freed himself from the mass of bodies and looked for a window. The opium fumes were making him groggy, slowing down his reflexes; he needed to take the fight outside.

He saw a window and leapt for it, just as the two Chinese men charged him again. Without touching the sides, Johnny Chen sailed through the open window and outside, suddenly immersed in a blanket of clammy, wet fog. For a moment or two he experienced a sense of weightlessness, totally free of any sense of orientation within the cloak of white mist. But he knew that the laws of gravity still held true, and that he was plummeting to earth, that within an instant of leaving the window he would hit the ground, hard. So he tucked his knees up against his chest, performed a perfect somersault, stretched out his legs and landed silently on his feet instantly ready to fight any opponent who approached him.

Enveloped in this impenetrable cloak of white a normal man would have been seriously handicapped by his loss of vision and the muffling effect of the fog upon his hearing. But Johnny Chen was no ordinary man. Now he was in his element, his every sense fine-tuned to detect and locate the slightest movement.

He could hear the two men grunting and scuffling as they helped each other climb out of the window and down the wall. He waited patiently.

With all of his senses focused upon the two men in front of him hidden by the fog, he did not notice, until the very last moment, a third man sneaking up on him from behind. The man held a broken chair back, and brought it down in a vicious arc; but Johnny Chen felt the disturbance in the air and turned at the last moment, bringing up his arm in a protective gesture.

The wood splintered across his arm, breaking in half, and the Chinaman continued turning on the spot, lifting one foot high and cracking the heel of his expensive shoe against the man's jaw. The man staggered, senseless; but, before he could fall, the Chinaman grabbed him and lifted him above his shoulders. Holding the man high above his head he turned, as scar-face and knuckle-cracker rushed towards him, their bodies appearing suddenly through the fog.

Johnny Chen threw the man's unconscious body at the two running figures. The big, heavy body smashed into their chests, and the three of them hit the floor hard.

He walked over to the three fallen men, scar-face and knuckle-cracker struggling under the weight of their unconscious ally. Without any sense of pity or hesitation, Johnny Chen kicked each man in the head, sending them both into an instant oblivion, deeper than that of any opium pipe.

The Chinaman then turned and ran back inside, past Moon Lee, climbing the ladder up to the opium den. Inside it was business as usual, dirty, groggy figures bending over shared opium pipes, or sitting in the gloom smoking a cigarette. It was as though the fight had never happened.

Johnny Chen searched every corner of the opium den, despite knowing it was pointless.

Denver McCade was gone.

Chapter Eight
The Thing in the Trunk

Jim dropped from the loft hatch and landed silently on his hands and knees on the richly carpeted floor. He coughed and spluttered a little, choking on the filth he had had to crawl through in the loft space. Looking up he saw George's pale face peering down at him.

The two boys had run hard through the night-time London streets, eventually finding themselves at the shop they had seen Behrends visit earlier that day. Jim had peered through the shop window, but could see nothing in the darkness. Impelled by curiosity, and certain that there were many valuable items inside, much like the antique shop where they had found the corpse, Jim decided they would break in. An empty house, three doors away down the terraced row, was their means of entry. Inside the house they climbed into the loft, which was one long, continuous space above the terraced row, and began crawling through the filth and muck until Jim was certain they were above the shop.

Wiping the sweat from his forehead with his shirtsleeve, he looked around. Shrouded in darkness, the hallway was illuminated only by a pale, flickering yellow light emanating from underneath a closed bedroom door. Two more doors led off the hallway, but no light shone from underneath them. There was a staircase at the opposite end of the hall leading downstairs.

Above him large swathes of the intricately patterned wallpaper hung in mildewed curls, peeling from the damp walls and revealing rivulets of moisture running down the bare plaster. Long strings of dirty cobwebs, suspended from the ceiling and thick with dust, swayed slightly in a cool, clammy draught.

Beside Jim stood a large, heavy chest of drawers topped by a bookcase, and crammed full of antique, leather-bound books, all covered in a deep layer of grey dust and ancient cobwebs. Many of the books' spines were cracked and ruined, some of their pages hanging from them, slowly decaying in the damp atmosphere. Another bookshelf stood further down the hallway, similarly stuffed full of ageing, rotting books.

Still on all fours, Jim suddenly realised that the carpet beneath him felt wet and sticky. He lifted his hands and rubbed his thumbs and forefingers together. They were slick with a gooey, gelatinous liquid. Slowly, carefully, he drew his hands up to his face and sniffed at them.

He recoiled in a wave of nausea.

They smelt of blood.

Jim stood up and looked at George above him, hanging from the loft hatch. Before he could signal to him to stay where he was, his younger brother had dropped beside him, slipping slightly on the wet carpet. Jim grabbed at him to steady him, and then signalled to him to remain completely and utterly silent.

He could just about see his brother's grubby face in the dim, dingy light of the hallway; enough to see his eyes widen in terror as Jim simultaneously felt a cold chill of fear spread from the pit of his stomach and out through his arms and legs, to pinch at the skin of his face.

A long, low, almost inaudible moan could be heard from behind the door of the lit room, an abject wail of utter misery and pain. Jim thought the cry would never stop, it carried on for so long. But finally it did stop, fading away into a dull nothingness. Jim and George remained frozen, staring at each other in horror, hating the silence almost as much as they had hated the sound of the moaning. But then the dreadful silence was interrupted by the sound of something heavy being dragged across the floor, followed by the dull, muffled scrape of metal upon metal.

Again Jim motioned his brother to stay silent and pointed to the staircase behind him. George remained frozen, not looking where Jim pointed, not moving at all.

Slowly Jim turned George around to face the staircase and gave him a gentle push. George took a hesitant step toward it, and then another, encouraged by the occasional prod from his brother. In this tentative fashion they began to make their way to the top of the stairs.

They both stopped dead in their tracks when they heard more sounds from behind the bedroom door. This time the something, whatever it was, slithered across the floor; no longer being dragged, but moving under its own awful willpower.

Jim forced his limbs into movement, prodding at his brother again to get him moving too. As the brothers walked slowly along the landing to the stairs, their feet made wet, sucking noises on the blood-soaked carpet.

At the top of the staircase, George froze.

"C'mon," Jim hissed into his ear, "get a move on."

And then he felt it too.

And had to clamp his mouth shut before a scream of absolute terror escaped from him.

Something warm and lithe snaked between his ankles, coiling itself around his legs.

Suddenly he heard George giggling with relief.

"It's a cat," he whispered.

George bent down and, just able to see the jet black cat in the darkness by the flash of his green eyes, picked him up and cuddled him.

Jim looked at the cat closely and saw the collar of strange symbols around its neck.

"Ain't that the same cat we saw earlier?" he said.

"Yeah, I think so," George said. "Maybe it lives here."

"Put it down," Jim said.

"Why?"

"I don't like it, it's giving me the creeps."

George and the cat both turned their heads to look at Jim. The cat blinked its large, round eyes at him, and began purring loudly.

"I ain't putting it down," George said.

The cat purred so loud that Jim feared the thing in the bedroom would hear and come out to investigate. He decided to let George keep the cat, at least until they were outside.

"C'mon," he whispered. "We've got to get down these stairs."

Little by little, they made their way down the stairs, the soles of their shoes still sucking at the blood-drenched carpet with each step they took. They hugged the wall as they made their descent. Occasionally Jim's shoulder would knock one of the ancient oil paintings hanging there, and he would be showered with the accumulated dust and filth of years of neglect that lay on their frames.

George carried the cat all the way downstairs.

At the bottom of the flight of steps, Jim stopped to look around. He felt sure they were on the ground floor now, and in a corridor of some kind. The light was too poor to see much of anything down here. He was certain that the corridor must lead to the shop at the front, and from there they could escape into the foggy night. Jim had intended to explore the shop, to find out why Behrends had come here, and met the stranger who let him in.

But right now all he wanted to do was get out of this place as fast as he could.

The cat jumped out of George's arms and disappeared into the darkness.

"Keep close to me," Jim said, and began moving down the corridor, still hugging the wall, an arm outstretched in front of him, his fingers cautiously exploring the gloom.

They came across a closed door, and Jim felt for the door handle.

Slowly, ever so slowly, he opened the door.

A large, bay window allowed the fog-enshrouded street lamps to cast a dull, yellow light over the room, dimly revealing its time-ravaged contents. Heavy, red velvet curtains had once hung in front of the window, but now lay on the floor, torn and trampled upon. More paintings hung at crazy angles underneath ornate plaster coving and beside the brass lamps, which were dull and misshapen, as though they had been mangled by someone of incredible strength. Broken-backed dining room chairs, and larger easy chairs, lay on their sides scattered throughout the room. Beside the large stone fireplace sat an imposing grand piano.

But strewn throughout the destruction of the once magnificent living room were boxes, and crates, and old sea chests. Some of them lay open, and others remained closed. And there were more books; mountains of ancient, leather-bound books, faded and yellowing, many of them falling apart at the seams. Over everything lay a thick layer of dust. And between the boxes and the books could be seen many footprints in the dirt on the floor, tracking repeatedly backwards and forwards.

Impelled by curiosity the two boys took a few cautious steps into the room.

Jim came upon the first of the open crates and, without touching it at all, looked inside. A large, African mask stared back at him with bulbous eyes, the mouth open and showing off a perfect set of vicious, sharpened teeth. Around its head, underneath a covering of bright feathers, lay a circle of skulls.

Jim reached a trembling hand into the crate and lifted the mask from its bed of shredded paper and twine. It felt heavy in his hand, and cool to the touch. He looked up to say something to George, but he was no longer standing beside him. Jim looked around, and saw his young brother was exploring further into the room, threading his way between the boxes and crates.

Jim looked back at the mask, at the blank, lifeless eyes, and then at the skulls. Such tiny, human skulls, much smaller even than a baby's. What race of people could be that small? And had they been killed simply to decorate this mask? Jim seemed to remember stories of African cannibal tribes who chopped the heads off their defeated enemies and then shrunk them, and kept them as trophies.

Jim placed the mask back in the wooden crate, trying to replace it in the exact position from which he had taken it.

He walked deeper into the room, towards George who was standing by the grand piano, examining a small trunk placed on its top. He had his ear to the trunk, his arm wrapped around the sides as though hugging it, and he was listening intently.

"What is it?" Jim whispered.

"Dunno," said George, still pressing his ear against the side, a look of intense concentration on his face.

Up close the trunk looked to be covered with some kind of stiffened leather, faded and tatty in places, with rusty iron reinforcements at the edges and the corners. The latch was down, but there was no padlock securing it. A cylindrical piece of wood had been hammered through the latch, holding it in place.

Jim put his ear against the side too.

At first he heard nothing, and was about to give up, thinking that they should open the trunk to find out what was inside, instead of just listening to it.

But then he heard something.

A scratching, scraping noise, so faint that Jim thought he might have imagined it. But the look on George's face told him that he had not imagined it; that George had heard it too.

"What do you think it is, Jim?" whispered George.

"I dunno, what do you think it is?"

George pressed his ear against the trunk once more, and so did Jim.

Again there was a long period of silence, long enough for Jim to become bored and realise that he had imagined the noise in the first place. Just long enough for him to think about opening up the trunk once more.

And then the scratching started again.

And this time it was louder, more persistent.

The two boys snatched their heads away from the trunk and looked at one another in disbelief.

"There's somethin' in there," said Jim.

"Do you think it wants to get out?" said George.

"Dunno," said Jim. "But I ain't letting it out."

"Me neither," said George.

They both looked at the battered, old trunk again, perched on top of the grand piano. The scratching noises grew louder, more insistent. There was a scuffling inside the trunk now, as though they had woken something that lived in there, and it did indeed want to get out.

Jim and George looked at each other, and Jim put his finger to his lips, motioning George to keep quiet. He knew that whatever it was that lived in that box had heard them, and he did not want to disturb it anymore.

As the scratching and scuffling inside the trunk grew more and more frenzied, Jim took a step backwards, motioning for George to follow him.

And trod on the cat's tail.

The cat shrieked in pain and fled back into the darkness, and the two boys jumped, emitting their own shrieks of terror. Jim overbalanced and fell, his arms flailing wildly. He crashed into the grand piano and knocked the trunk off the top, sending it tumbling to the ground.

Jim leapt from the grimy floor as though it was on fire, and began slapping at his body, and wiping his hands, trying to clean the dirt and dust from him.

"I hate this house," he said.

"Jim . . ."

He slapped at his clothes some more, clouds of dust billowing from them.

"I don't care if we don't nick nothing . . ."

"Jim . . ."

". . . we're not stopping here any longer."

"Jim!" George hissed.

"What?" Jim said, looking at his agitated little brother.

George pointed into a dark recess of the room, his hand shaking slightly.

"The box is open," he said.

Jim walked over to the fallen trunk, lying on its side in the filth, its lid wide open.

It was empty.

Suddenly, on the periphery of his vision, he saw a dark, amorphous shape scuttling across the far side of the room. He whipped around, but the shape had gone, and then there it was again on the edge of his vision, scurrying behind the fallen furniture, emitting a high-pitched squeal.

Jim turned again, trying to locate it, just catch a glimpse of it, even. Occasionally a chair or a box shifted slightly as the thing dashed past it, and Jim would turn towards the source of the sound. But just as he thought he had located it, it would disappear from his vision, back into the gloom, an indistinct blur.

Sometimes the squeaking, scuffling noises were far away, sometimes they were much closer. And sometimes wet, snuffling noises, and low, guttural grunts interrupted the high-pitched squeaking.

"C'mon," Jim said, grabbing hold of George, "let's get out of here."

They began threading their way through the destruction of broken furniture and boxes and crates, looking around as whatever it was scurried throughout the room, snuffling and grunting and squealing malevolently.

Just got to get to the door, Jim thought. Get to the door, and shut this thing in here, and then they could get out through the shop front.

And then, with a tremendous bang, the door slammed shut.

From upstairs came shuffling noises, footsteps, and the sound of a door opening. Whoever, whatever, was up there was coming down to investigate the noises.

They had to get out, and quick, before they were discovered.

But before Jim could act on that thought, George began screaming and flapping his hands at his head.

"Get it off me, get it off me!" he shouted, thrashing about, grabbing at a small, dark blur of motion fastened to his scalp. Before Jim could even respond to his brother's cries for help the thing had gone, disappearing back into the darkness of the room.

"C'mon, c'mon," Jim said, "we've got to go, c'mon."

"But I'm bleeding," George said, touching his scalp and pulling his hand away to reveal his blood red fingertips.

Jim grabbed hold of his brother's hand and dragged him towards the closed door. He felt something scuttle over his feet, sending a shiver through his body, impelling him to the door, impelling him to get out of this place.

He took another couple of steps, and then he heard the grunting and snuffling again, much louder this time; and then the thing was on his shoulders, its sharp claws digging into his flesh, its hot, putrid breath on his face. Jim reached behind and grabbed at the small, scaly body as it writhed and squirmed, emitting its high pitched squeals and clawing at his back and shoulders. He tried to get a grip on the wriggling body, but could not get a hold of it. He could feel warm blood running down his back now as the thing slashed at his shoulders. Screaming in anger and pain he threw himself forcefully onto his back, landing hard on the dirty floor, and the thing leapt off him and disappeared back into the darkness.

Jim struggled to his feet, panting heavily.

His mind screamed two words at him, over and over again.

Get out! Get out!

He knew it was too late, though.

He could see the light growing in the gap underneath the closed door, the flickering yellow lamplight drawing ever closer. He could hear the footsteps come to a stop outside the door; he could see the handle turning, turning.

Jim found George's trembling hand and held on tight.

The door opened.

Chapter Nine
The Fallen Angel

The tall, stooped figure stood in the open doorway, holding the oil lamp out in front of him, casting its yellow light across the room.

That was the first thing that Jim ever remembered about him, this tall, skeletal, bent over figure, holding the dirty oil lamp. The second impression Jim had of him was his long, blackened fingernails and his bony, crooked hands. The next was his clothing; shabby, grey shirt and trousers, stained with dried blood and hanging loosely from his gaunt frame.

The bile only rose in the back of Jim's throat, threatening to choke him with disgust and fear and utter loathing, when he finally saw the man's face; the haggard, pallid features, the thin wisps of hair trailing across his head, the skin stretched taut over the skull, and threaded with fine, blue veins.

The man's sunken, hollow eyes glittered with baleful pleasure when he saw the two frightened boys standing before him.

"Aaaahhhh," he whispered, as he took a few steps towards the brothers, casting the flickering yellow light of the oil lamp over them, to see them better with.

Jim squeezed George's hand hard, keeping a tight hold on him.

Just let him come a few steps nearer, thought Jim, just a few steps nearer, and then we'll run round him, and out the door. Just a bit closer, just a bit . . .

As if reading his mind, the man reached out a gnarled hand and pushed the door shut behind him. And then he whipped his head round at the sound of grunting and squealing as a dark shape scurried past them.

He looked back at the two boys and said, "You've been naughty boys, haven't you? Meddling where you shouldn't, no doubt, as naughty boys are wont to do."

The man lifted the glass of the lamp and blew out the light. In the sudden gloom Jim just about saw the man squatting on the floor, and scratching his long fingernails on the filthy carpet.

Suddenly, with much squealing and grunting the thing from the shadows leapt at the man's hand, but in a flash he had pinned it to the floor, and then lifted it high as he stood up. The thing wriggled and squirmed violently in his hand, but he held on tight.

"You've been fortunate indeed," whispered the man. "Devil's Imps don't usually leave their prey so long before killing them. But this little one is out of practice. Too long boxed up in a cramped old trunk, eh my pretty?"

Snarling and grunting, the thing sunk its teeth into the man's hand.

"Aaaahhhh, yessss, bite away my pretty, do your worst, before I pack you away again." He reached out a dirty hand and gently stroked its head.

The man walked past the brothers to the fallen trunk, and, kneeling down, placed the squirming, struggling Devil's Imp back into his prison.

Still holding on tight to George's hand, Jim took a step toward the closed door.

Before he could take another the man had turned on the spot, an arm outstretched to point at him.

"Stay right where you are!" he hissed. "I haven't finished with you two boys yet."

He turned back to the trunk, making sure to fasten it securely.

"Wh . . . who are you?" Jim said.

Slowly the man rose to his feet, his back to the two brothers.

"My name is Murmur," he said. He turned slowly and looked at Jim, and then George, his gaze lingering over each of them. His tongue snaked out of his mouth and wet his thin lips. "And now, my lovely little creatures, it is my turn to ask, who are you?"

"My name's Jim, an' this is George, my brother. It were my idea to break into your house, Mister, not George's. If'n you're gonna call the peelers . . ."

"Sshhhh . . ." Murmur said, waving his long, bony fingers at the boys. "Nobody's calling the police, oh no."

George tugged fitfully at Jim's hand.

Jim swallowed hard, even though his mouth was as dry as parchment. Despite the cool of the room he was sweating profusely.

Murmur shuffled closer to them, reaching out a hand and stroking Jim's cheek with one of his long, dirty fingernails.

"Such handsome little boys," he whispered. "Such beautiful, fair skin, such delicate features."

Jim's flesh flinched involuntarily at each touch of the old man's fingers. The stench of death lifted from the man's dry, cracked skin and filled Jim's nostrils. His stomach turned over as he struggled to keep his breathing under control.

Murmur reached out another hand, sliding it around the back of George's head, slipping his skeletal fingers through his tousled hair. Slowly, inexorably, he began to draw the young boy's head toward him. In a display of pleasurable anticipation, he bared his teeth and sucked in his breath, bubbles of spit glistening on his withdrawn lips.

64

"I . . . I saw you today," Jim said, in a desperate bid to distract the old man. "I saw you . . . with Inspector Behrends."

Murmur turned to Jim and dropped his hand, suddenly ignoring George, who staggered backwards and sat on the floor with a thump.

He stayed where he was, his eyes unfocused and glassy.

"What do you know about Behrends?" Murmur hissed, drawing closer now to Jim.

"I . . . I saw you with him," Jim repeated, a tremor creeping into his voice.

"Yesss, yesss, you already told me that, you pathetic dribble of snot. Tell me what else you know, quick before I scoop out your innards and chew on your guts."

Jim felt that at any moment now he would lose control of his bladder, a final humiliation to suffer before this thing killed him and ate him. He closed his eyes for a second, blotting out the hideous features that were now only inches from him, but unable to ignore the freezing, stinking breath that blew across his face.

"I know he's investigating a murder, that he needs help and he asked Caxton Tempest."

"Caxton Tempest, eh? And what do you know about Tempest my pretty little thing?"

Jim struggled hard to think, to come up with something to say just to keep this monstrosity distracted until he could think of a way to escape.

"Well come on then, my handsome little creature," Murmur hissed, crouching like giant, black spider over Jim and reaching a clawed hand out to stroke Jim's cheek. "Tell me what you know before I suck your eyeballs out of your skull."

"I don't know," Jim whispered, "I just know that he helps the coppers sometimes, an' that he's worried about these murders, said it were serious."

Murmur pulled back, and Jim coughed and gasped for air, grateful to be free of the man's stinking breath.

"Serious indeed," Murmur said, thoughtfully. "The angels in Hell have waited for just such a moment as now approaches for aeons, and they are eager. Oh, yes. They are eager."

Jim took a step back, willing himself to stay focused, to not let the fear overcome him so much that he lost his grip on the situation, on the hope of getting free.

If I can just get him talking, he thought. Maybe we can distract him, gain ourselves some time.

"I . . . I thought angels lived in Heaven," Jim said.

Murmur clacked his dirty, brittle fingernails together, making a dry, rattling sound, as though a coffin full of bones were being shaken around.

"You know nothing, boy, I can see through your pathetic little ploy, just stalling for time. Still, let me humour you and tell you the truth, for the truth shall set you free."

He reached out a hand and tenderly wiped the beads of sweat off Jim's forehead. Jim watched with an overwhelming sense of disgust and horror as Murmur then sucked the sweat off his fingers.

"Don't you read your Bible?" he whispered. "Don't you know about the great war between Satan and his army, the rebel angels of Heaven, and God and the archangels? I was part of that war, that terrible battle. In his great wrath God defeated us and cast us out of Heaven, and we fell for nine days. For nine terrible days we fell, until we reached the awful place beyond time and space, beyond the reaches of Heaven."

"You . . . you're a demon?" Jim whispered.

"Yesss, that's what they say we are, we the fallen angels of Heaven, cast out of our rightful kingdom by a jealous and vengeful God. We once formed a third of Heaven's hosts. And now they call us demons."

Murmur shuffled closer to Jim and pushed him to the floor, where he sat down next to George, who stirred only slightly. The demon leaned across the boys, drawing in ever closer. His body emanated a terrible cold, which chilled the brothers to the bone.

"Once you would have been compelled to approach me for the answering of questions. In the twilight world of death, between Heaven and Hell, I would have compelled you to answer questions about your conduct in this life, to justify your actions and your non-actions."

Murmur placed a hand under Jim's chin and tilted his head to face his, their noses only inches apart. Jim looked helplessly into the demon's eyes and saw an infinite blackness, a void.

"For who knows where our actions take us," he whispered, "the decisions delayed with consequences unknown, the choices we make, the chances lost. What compelled you here tonight, was it a greater power, part of some omnipotent being's great plan, or was it pure chance, the curious workings of your simple little mind?"

He sighed, a rasping, diseased sigh of infinite sadness and weariness.

"Once I was a duke, a great leader of thirty legions of infernal spirits, who waited on my every command."

Suddenly he turned and walked away. Jim grabbed hold of George's hand, ready to jump to his feet and run to the door.

Before he could act, Murmur turned back to them, and said, "But what use authority, what use even thirty *million* legions of spirits at my command, when trapped in Hell for the rest of eternity? Here is where I belong now, free to pursue my own plan of mischief and mayhem, free to provide a service to those seekers of knowledge who know of me. Free to suck the precious life spirit of those who cross my path, and know me not."

"Seekers of knowledge?" Jim said.

Murmur strode towards them and lifted the two boys off the floor by their collars. He swung them around so that they were facing the room, the piles of books, the trunks and crates, scattered before them.

"Yesss, seekers of knowledge, they come to me for wisdom, for truth, for comprehension of the dark arts. See these books, ancient books, grimoires, books of black magic and pacts with evil spirits. Books of forbidden knowledge, long forgotten, forbidden knowledge, which humans were never meant to know."

"What . . . what's in the . . . the boxes?" Jim said.

"Talismans, amulets, sigils, collections of shadows from the darkest parts of the earth, the essence of evil, the instruments of iniquity. Come, come with me, and see . . ."

Still holding them by the backs of their collars he dragged the two boys deeper into the chaotic room, past the boxes and books, disturbing the deep layer of dust and filth that settled over everything. He dropped them by a small, battered crate, marked with strange symbols.

Murmur prised open the top of the crate and reached inside, pulling out a clay bottle with a stopper in the top. Carefully, gently, an evil smile creeping across his wizened features, he pulled the stopper from the bottle.

An awful stench, more powerful than anything Jim had ever experienced before, penetrated the room; a rotting, putrid smell, sickly sweet beyond all comprehension. Beside him George turned and stuffed his face into Jim's side, burying himself into the folds of his shirt. Jim began to cough and gag, helplessly.

"Please," he said, "please, stop it, stop it . . ."

"It's a poison," Murmur whispered. "The essence of the secretions of ten decomposing corpses, mingled together, and distilled into this single, small decanter. A few more days and the smell will go, and then a single drop of the tasteless liquid placed within a drink, or dropped into food, or onto the tongue of the peaceful sleeper, will kill a man before the hour is ended."

He replaced the stopper on the bottle, and placed it back in the crate.

Jim's flesh crawled as he saw a dark, indistinct shape creeping from behind the wooden box, its eyes flashing at him as it drew nearer. He tensed himself, ready for another stinging attack from the Devil's Imp, ready to fight off its fearsome, savage claws.

Drawing closer to them the dark shape became the cat, prowling around Murmur's ankles, purring as the skeletal figure stooped to stroke the animal with his bony, begrimed fingers.

"Have you met my friend, Lucifer?" whispered the demon. "He's never far from my side."

The cat began twisting and turning between Jim and George, snaking between their legs, its purring growing louder. Jim reached out a trembling hand and began stroking the cat.

"Wait there," Murmur said, holding a wizened, bony finger up before them.

He left the brothers where they were and shuffled deeper into the room, searching for some other instrument of the black arts to show them.

"George," Jim whispered, pulling his brother's face out from his side. "George, are you okay?"

His little brother looked up at him, his eyes round and wide with fear, tears rolling down his pale face.

"I'm scared," he whispered. "I'm scared he's gonna kill us, and boil us up and turn us into poison."

"Remember what I told you; I ain't gonna let nothing happen to you, okay? Nothing. There ain't nothing can hurt the Kerrigans, we're gonna get out of here, we'll be alright, okay?"

Murmur returned, holding a cracked, yellowed skull in his hands. On the skull's forehead was engraved a symbol. He held the skull carefully, as though it was a precious memento.

"This is the skull of the fool who summoned me here. He thought he could control me, use me for his own ends and then send me back to Hell when he had finished with me. But I was too strong for him, too powerful. I inhabited him for a few years, but he was sick when he invited me here, so I had to discard him eventually, discard him for the body I now inhabit. This one is growing old now, and soon I must throw it away and find myself a new host. Perhaps a young boy, with many healthy years ahead of him, eh?"

Murmur placed the skull to one side, the dry rustling of his bloodstained clothes the only sound in the cold, damp room. He gazed at the two boys for a long, long time, his skeletal fingers scratching compulsively at his sides. His grey, wet tongue snaked from his mouth and across his thin, white lips, his open mouth revealing, just for the briefest of seconds, his chipped, rotten teeth.

"Yesss," he exhaled slowly, the word dripping like poison from his mouth. "Yesss, young, healthy boys."

Every muscle, every tendon and fibre, in Jim's body tightened up, ready to run, to fight, with all the energy he had. Murmur was going to kill them now; there was no more putting him off, no more stalling for time.

Murmur's fingers stopped their compulsive scratching.

He's getting ready to pounce, Jim thought.

A second later Murmur lunged at the boys, his arms outstretched in a deadly embrace, his mouth open and dripping mucky yellow strands of saliva.

But Jim was ready for him. He grabbed hold of the cat and threw it, screeching in anger, at Murmur's face. The demon fell backwards, howling with rage, the cat scratching at his face.

Jim leapt to his feet, pulling George with him. They ran for the door, and Jim grabbed at it, but his hand slipped off the doorknob, his palms slippery with sweat. He glanced behind him.

Murmur was gathering himself off the floor, staring at them, baring his teeth in a low, angry, bestial growl.

Jim gripped the door handle with both hands and managed to turn it, opening the door and fleeing into the dark corridor, pulling George behind him.

"He's coming Jim, he's after us," George whispered.

The two brothers ran down the gloomy corridor until they reached a second door. Behind him he heard the other door slamming shut, heard Murmur's rasping breath, his footsteps shuffling closer to them.

Jim turned the door handle and pulled helplessly at the door. It refused to move. He pulled again, and again there was no movement in the solid oak door.

"Quick Jim," George hissed. "Hurry, hurry!"

This time Jim pushed at the door and the door opened. The boys fell over themselves into the room, skidding across a cold, flagstoned floor. They scrambled to their feet and looked around.

Surrounding them were shelves and shelves of ancient books, and bottles, amulets and talismans, skulls, candles, every conceivable element of the paraphernalia of black magic.

They were in the shop at the front of the building. The shop that Jim had seen Behrends visit earlier that day. The shop that Jim had intended ransacking for Mulready.

No time for that now, Jim thought. Got to get out of here, quick!

He could see the shop window now, the thick fog hiding the street outside. He could see the shop door. He could see freedom.

And then he felt the clammy, vicious grip of Murmur's fingers on his scalp, pulling him back by his hair, dragging him to the floor.

"Stupid, pathetic little boys, thinking they could run from Murmur," hissed the demon, his black eyes momentarily alight with a malevolent glow.

He lifted Jim and George from the ground, holding them both aloft by their hair. Their feet paddled helplessly in thin air, and they both held on to Murmur's wrists, trying to lessen the pain on their scalps.

"Aaahhh, which one shall I eat first?" Murmur whispered, blowing flecks of spit into their faces. "Which one shall I eat first?"

With an absent flick of his wrist he threw Jim crashing into a set of shelves, the contents smashing to the ground around him.

Jim tried to struggle to his feet, but got no further than his hands and knees, as he shook his head and tried to clear his vision, and the deafening roar in his ears. His sight clearing now, he saw Murmur pinning a helpless, terrified George to the floor. Still dizzy from the fall he watched as, like some giant, monstrous spider, Murmur crawled over his brother, blocking him from Jim's view.

All he could see of George now was his hand, reaching out in a silent plea for help. And as he watched, helpless with fear, he saw the skin on his hand shrinking and growing tight over the bones beneath.

Chapter Ten
Denver McCade

Denver McCade stood on the rooftop of the Grand Hotel, her hands on her hips, beads of sweat glistening on her forehead despite the cold night air, and looked across the fog enshrouded cityscape below her. Directly in front of Denver, rising proud from the blanket of white fog lying over Trafalgar Square, stood Nelson's Column. Denver looked at Nelson, and Nelson gazed implacably back at Denver.

"Hey, there's no need to look so smug," she said. "You think you had it rough at the Battle of Trafalgar, you should try walking around in my skin for a while. I tell ya, if I ever get myself out of this freakin' mess I'm in, they'll put a statue of me up here too, right by your side. And then we can both look smug together."

Denver looked out beyond Nelson. The fog stretched as far as she could make out under the night sky. In the distance she could see Big Ben, and the rooftops of the Houses of Parliament; dark architectural mountains, jutting out above the dirty white cloud of fog which covered much of the city, and muffled any sounds of life there might be down there.

The Grand Hotel had been easy to climb, the cornices and outcrops on the face of the building giving her numerous hand and foot holds. Denver had learnt how to climb on the trips she took to the Santiago Mountains with her father and brother, in the endless summers of her childhood back home in Texas. Climbing trips she had once thought she would take with her own children one day, once she had settled down and married.

But marriage never came, and neither did the children. Instead Denver's life had been turned inside out the day she had watched helplessly as her whole family was slaughtered before her eyes.

Now, standing on top of the Grand Hotel, with only Vice Admiral Nelson for company, and a thick covering of fog hiding her from the rest of the city, she felt safe, free.

Invisible.

But not for long. She could not spend the rest of her life living on the rooftops of London; sometime soon she would have to get back down to street level. There was a big problem with that, though. Somewhere down there Johnny Chen was still looking for her.

And if she stayed in one spot for too long he would find her.

Denver had known for some time now that it would come to this. That soon she would be confronted by her past, that there was only so long that she could spend hiding in the opium dens of London, trying to obliterate every last sense of the person she had once been.

"But I didn't try very hard, did I, Horatio?" she said to the statue. "Hell, I'm not even that sure any more that I didn't want to be found."

After all, there were plenty more obscure parts of the world she could have chosen to hide out in other than London. Plenty more places around the world she could have found opium dens to frequent, to live that half life of drug-addled stupefaction and dimly remembered forgetfulness.

"I could even have gone back to Texas," she said.

But no, there were too many bad memories there; too many ghosts to run from.

And so she chose London. And why London in particular? Especially when she had to travel halfway around the world to get there.

"Hell, that ain't a difficult question to answer," she said. "There's only one reason I came to London, and it weren't to stand here looking at your ugly phizog, that's for sure. It was Tempest."

Caxton Tempest. A man she had never met, had no connection with at all. But *they* had talked about him, *they* had been obsessed by him. She had first heard the name Caxton Tempest on their lips and had ultimately come to detest it, for mention of that name meant the questions would begin again, and the pain. And so when she had escaped she had run to London; the one place in the whole, wide world where you were sure of running into Tempest if you stayed put long enough.

But why Tempest? Why risk encountering the one person who would help her remember what she had spent so long trying to forget? Surely the point of the opium was to help her forget, continue that process of amnesia that had begun that fateful night in that dark underworld of evil that Kralik had foolishly led her into, to prolong it for as long as possible? Already, her mind clearing in the cold night air, the memories were flooding back, searing her brain with the images and sounds of the uncontrollable, demonic fury that Kralik unwittingly unleashed. Maybe living here was just her unconscious way of not prolonging the inevitable. After all she would have to face her past at some point.

Those murders she had heard about, surely the work of Zedekiah Kralik. Was he looking for her, too? Did he even care now, if she were alive or dead? No; surely she was nothing to him now. At best she would simply be in his way, and he would pay her the briefest of attention as he wiped her off the face of the earth.

But how had Johnny Chen known of the connection between her and Kralik, and how had he known where to find her? Denver already knew the answer to that, had known something like this would happen eventually when Murmur stepped back into her life one murky night a few months ago, in Moon Lee's Opium Den. Lost in her own fog of oblivion, lost in a literal fog of opium fumes swirling around her, she had seen him. Of course he had swapped bodies by then, someone she did not know; but still, he was instantly recognisable. They always were.

Murmur had seen her, too, she was sure of that. He had shown no reaction, no flicker of recognition passed across his ravaged face; he just took another drag on the opium pipe and closed his eyes, lost in a moment of blissful forgetfulness.

But he had seen her.

Strange, that even a demon should seek the oblivion of opium. What was it that possessed him so, what awful memories haunted his life, tore at his very being until he could bear it no more, that he needed to forget, needed to erase them from his mind for a short while at least?

Denver followed him that night, through the deserted London streets, back to his run down shop in the heart of the West End, with the faded sign hanging above the door, one word scrawled carelessly in black paint upon it: Magick.

At first Denver was convinced Murmur was here to kill her. He had tried to kill her once before, after all. But as the nights, and then the weeks, wore on, she realised that was not his intention at all. She was nothing to him now. Whatever plan he had, whatever scheme he was hatching, she was no part of it, no obstruction to it.

Until now.

It was no coincidence that Tempest, Kralik and Murmur were now together in the same city at this point in time. Things happened for a reason, Denver believed that. Their fates were linked. Whatever was going on, whatever train of events was now in motion, they were all destined to meet again.

"So I guess, if I want to stay ahead of the game, I'd better make the first move," Denver said. "Maybe it's time I paid a visit to Murmur."

Vice Admiral Horatio Lord Nelson said nothing.

Denver smiled at herself for talking to a statue.

"Carry on like this, girl, and they'll be carting you off to Bellevue."

Denver began her descent of the Grand Hotel, hanging from awnings and jumping onto ledges, then finding her way to more handholds, and again hanging and jumping and climbing, until finally she reached the ground.

She moved swiftly through the fog, running down well-travelled streets, finding her way when others would have been completely disoriented. Occasionally dark shadows appeared in front of her – nocturnal citizens of the city, pursuing their own secret business – and then stepped aside to let her pass. Peals of drunken laughter rang out from the fog around her, but Denver ignored them. Sometimes a whispered entreaty for money passed her ears, but she paid it no heed, and continued on her way.

Soon she had found the street she wanted; and in it the run down shop with the dirty windows and faded sign above the door.

Here, Denver was sure, lay the answer to the evening's mystery; how Tempest had known to send Johnny Chen to Moon Lee's Opium Den to find her.

Denver wiped at a filthy pane of glass and peered inside.

She could see movement.

She could see . . .

All Jim could see of his brother was his hand; clawed, rigid with pain and fear, reaching out to Jim in a silent scream for help, as the demon Murmur sucked the life from his body. The flesh covering George's slight frame seemed to be shrinking, drying out, before Jim's eyes.

Jim's senses screamed at him to do something, *anything*, to pull the monster off his brother. But he could hardly move. His head was still pounding and his vision swimming from being thrown into the shelves by the demon.

Suddenly, the shop windows exploded inwards, shards of glass and slivers of wood showering Murmur. Before the demon had a chance to react a shadowy figure leapt at him, delivering a vicious kick to his head, snapping it back and sending filthy gobbets of spit flying from his mouth. Another kick to his stomach, and the demon was thrown from George and landed heavily on his side, hissing and snarling.

Jim crawled towards his brother, lying lifeless on the floor, and tugged at his arm. George stirred slightly.

Murmur jumped to his feet, baring his teeth and growling his anger at being deprived of his victim. The demon stood astride the two brothers, his long, bony fingers twitching compulsively.

Jim looked up at the newcomer, facing the demon down without a trace of fear in her face.

Jim thought she was the most beautiful woman he had ever seen.

"Leave them alone," Denver said.

"What use are their pathetic little lives to you, Denver McCade?" hissed the demon. "You should have stuck to smoking the opium, obliterating what little you have left of your miserable existence."

"Seems you have a taste for the stuff yourself, Murmur. Got something you need to forget? A guilty conscience maybe? Or perhaps there's still the tiniest little bit of humanity left in that poor old body you inhabit, and it needs to find some kind of escape from you, no matter how brief that might be?"

"You know not what you talk of, Denver McCade. But still, you should have known better than to come here. Now I will have to suck the life from *your* body before I continue with my feast that you so rudely interrupted."

"Seem to remember you tried that trick once before. Didn't work then, and it won't work now."

Murmur's fingers stopped their compulsive twitching. Jim knew what was coming next.

But Denver was way ahead of him. With a gunslinger's flourish she pulled a large revolver from behind her and pointed it at the demon.

"Easy, fella," she said. "You just stay right where you are. This here's a Colt .45 Peacemaker, once used by Bat Masterson when he was sheriff of Ford County. It can blow a hole right through your chest, or in your case, your host body's chest. So while it might not kill you, it'll send you back to Hell where you belong, and that's good enough for me."

Murmur said nothing, his skeletal fingers beginning their uncontrollable twitching again.

"Hey, you two kids," Denver said, glancing briefly at Jim and George. "Now might be a good time to leave, you know what I mean?"

Jim said nothing and made no move, too stunned to do anything but hold on to George.

"Go on, skedaddle!" Denver shouted.

Jim pulled his young brother to his feet and half carried, half walked him to the shattered front window. George was shaking violently now, and his legs trembled underneath him, making him difficult to manoeuvre.

As they climbed through the empty window frame, Jim glanced back at Denver, who was giving him a strange look.

And then she was lost from sight as Jim disappeared into the all-enveloping embrace of the fog.

Jim pulled at his brother and shook him and prodded him, anything to keep him from slipping back into the comatose state he had been in before. But this proved difficult, and their progress through the streets was painfully slow. Sometimes George collapsed onto the filthy ground, shaking uncontrollably, and Jim had to haul him back onto his feet, and get him walking again.

"S . . . s . . . so c . . . c . . . c . . . cold," George said, his teeth chattering noisily.

"We're almost there," Jim said. "Just keep walking, we're almost there."

Jim's intention was to get back to the doss, retrieve his money from its hiding place and then run as far as they could. Mulready would be incandescent with rage that they had not managed to thieve anything again, and Jim was not prepared to take any more beatings off him. They did not have enough money saved up yet, but they could manage, Jim was sure of that. Anything was better than the life they were now involved in.

And besides, George needed a doctor, something Mulready would not be prepared to allow. Jim had seen many of the other kids at the doss die from lack of medical care.

Soon they reached the Seven Dials, and the two boys made their way down the narrow alleys and streets to their doss. Jim sat George down outside while he crept into the decrepit old building and glanced around for Mulready.

He was nowhere to be seen.

Jim hauled George inside and sat him on the floor.

"Wait here, while I go upstairs," he said.

George said nothing, just clasped his arms around his body, still shivering violently.

Jim set off up the rickety stairs, taking the steps two at a time, until he was on the top floor. Each of the rooms in the slum dwelling held a family, sometimes more than one. Mulready owned the building and charged a rent for each room, but did nothing in the way of upkeep or repairs. Families of four or more were packed into these tiny rooms, and shared the toilet and water facilities with the rest of the square. Right now the women and children would all be asleep, while the men were in the taverns, spending what little money they had earned on drink.

In a darkened corner at the end of the top floor corridor there was a loose panel in the rotting wall. Jim prised the panel away and slowly reached inside, mindful of the rats that scuttled about inside the wall partition. Hidden here was his money, tied up in an old bag and stuffed out of sight until the day he needed it.

He stretched as far as he could, his entire arm disappearing down the length of the wall. Just a little further, just a bit more, and then he would have it.

Jim strained, his fingers stretching out as far as he could make them, feeling with his fingertips for the familiar touch of the rough cloth.

There was nothing there.

The money was gone.

Hot tears of frustration stung at Jim's eyes.

Surely he had made a mistake, started searching from the wrong spot?

The money was there.

It had to be.

Jim pulled his arm out from the wall partition, now covered with filth and dirt. The cloud of dust he had disturbed made him cough.

Slowly, carefully, he inserted his arm back through the gap in the wall, but from a slightly different point this time. But already he knew this was wrong, that he would find nothing.

Already he knew that somebody had been here before him, had found the money and taken it.

Jim pulled his arm out and punched the wall in frustration, powerful sobs convulsing through his body. He leant his back against the wall and slid to the floor, and began crying softly.

What now? Without the money they had nothing.

Nothing.

As Jim sat there, wretched and miserable, he became aware of a pain in the back of his shoulders. An intense, fiery throbbing, where the Devil's Imp had slashed at his flesh.

Slowly, gingerly, Jim reached behind him and touched his back. He winced at the sharp stinging pain shooting through his shoulders. He pulled his hand away. His fingertips were dark red with blood.

The hurt, the blood, gave him something fresh to think about, something new to fight. As he sat in the dark hallway, looking at the blood on his fingers and feeling the pain in his back, a grim sense of determination rose within him.

"C'mon Kerrigan," he said to himself. "Get yourself moving, this ain't no time to be sitting around on your arse. Remember, there ain't no one can hurt a Kerrigan. No one."

Jim pulled himself to his feet and started the descent of the stairs.

They had to leave before Mulready came back. After all this time at Paddy's Goose, he and Crimps would be insanely, murderously drunk. One look at the two brothers would send them into a violent rage.

Jim leant against the walls as he made his way down the stairs, which seemed to shift and sway underneath him. Occasionally he had to stop altogether and sit down for a few moments, until the seesawing motion stopped and his vision cleared.

"Keep moving, c'mon, keep moving," he said.

He dragged himself upright and began his descent of the stairs again, trying to ignore the drunken swaying the steps and the walls made.

Finally he made it to the ground floor.

He paused for a moment, taking a while to register what his eyes told him.

George was nowhere to be seen.

Chapter Eleven
London under London

Billy Rackitt closed his eyes, but the sight before him was burned onto his retinas forever and would haunt him for the rest of his life. Unfortunately for Billy, the rest of his life did not look like it would be lasting very much longer.

Billy had fallen for a short but sickening moment down the tunnel shaft, his hands scraping against the hard, rocky surface, trying to gain purchase and halt his descent. He had hit the ground hard enough to explode the breath from his lungs in a sharp cough, and he lay dazed and senseless until the two monstrosities that had caught him threw themselves down the dirt shaft and landed on top of him. They seemed to be very excited now and made strange clicking, chittering noises, and pawed frenziedly at him, until he thought they might forget about taking him to their master, but just kill him there and then.

Suddenly, as if making up their minds and overcoming their primitive urges, they took hold of Billy and pushed him on, along the narrow dirt tunnel in front of them.

Billy could see none of this; they were in utter, pitch black, not a chink of light anywhere to illuminate his surroundings. The things that pushed him on did not seem to have any problems finding their way, moving quickly and goading him on with every step they took, prodding him and hissing threats in his ear whenever he paused.

Billy scrambled quickly along, but as carefully as he could; he was unused to being deprived of his vision and held his arms out by his sides, to feel the tunnel walls as he moved. Sometimes the walls disappeared, at a junction with another tunnel, and he would fall over only to be pulled to his feet again and prodded onwards. Sometimes the things directed him down one of these intersections, and very soon Billy knew he had not the slightest chance of ever finding his way out of this seemingly vast labyrinth of catacombs that lay under London City.

On and on they pushed Billy relentlessly, sometimes pushing him down low and forcing him to scramble through the low-ceilinged tunnel, at other times dragging him upright so that he could stumble blindly through the dark, and all the time the tunnels took a downward slope, taking him ever deeper underground. Just as Billy thought he could take no more, that he would fall to the ground and lie helpless in a faint, no matter what they did to him, he was suddenly plunged into a vast, lit cavern.

Shielding his eyes against the light, Billy was pushed into a corner where he lay quietly. He could hear movement and whispering noises, and he had a feeling of being surrounded. Tentatively he opened his eyes once more and then quickly shut them again.

He felt sick to his stomach by what he had seen; and very, very frightened.

Completely hemming him in on every side, and trapping him in the corner of the cavern where he had been thrown, were gathered a multitude of things similar to the two that had caught him. The grey-skinned, skeletal figures that approached him were clothed in little more than dirty rags. They stared at him through hollow eyes, their cheeks sunken and their dirty fangs protruding from lips pulled back in a permanent sneer of hunger, and they whispered excitedly among themselves, pointing at their captive.

Billy struggled up into a sitting position, looking around at his surroundings. Behind the cadaverous monstrosities that surrounded him, he could see the cavern walls were studded with burning oil lamps, which were the only source of light. The cave disappeared into darkness above him, so that he could not see its ceiling.

Billy started as one of the things made a lunge for him, and he pressed himself up tight against the cave wall.

"Leave it," one of them hissed, and he recognised it as the one that had caught him in the theatre. "The master will want to question it. And then he will give it to me and I will feast on it."

Billy swallowed nervously. Death by hanging suddenly seemed an attractive proposition compared to the fate that now awaited him. He was beginning to regret ever having conceived his escape plan.

The thing that had caught him originally now grabbed at his prison tunic and lifted him from the rocky ground. It seemed stronger than the others, healthier somehow, if the word health could be applied to these corpse-like monsters. Dragging him along, it led him down another tunnel, but this one was well lit and wider than the first. Many more passages, also lit by yellow oil lamps, led off this main artery, but the thing ignored them all, walking straight on until they reached an elaborately carved wooden door at the end of the passage. Here it stopped and knocked, and soon the door opened and they were ushered in.

The interior of this section of the tunnel complex was a different story to the rest. The space was large, like the first, but here the resemblance ended. A vast banqueting table occupied the far end of the room, decorated with bouquets of lilies and orchids. The table was set with polished silverware, as though a meal was about to be served at that very moment, and surrounded by grand dining chairs. At the opposite end of the cavern a great marble fireplace had been set into the wall, and a fire roared in the grate, casting heat and a yellow, flickering light across the room.

Oil paintings hung from the walls, and valuable looking vases filled the corners. The room was lit by many candles in silver candelabras, wax dripping down their stems and gathering in pools at their bases. Sumptuous easy chairs were scattered around the room, and the rocky floor was covered with an expensive Persian rug.

In one of the chairs reclined a woman, who looked at Billy with barely concealed distaste.

"What's this?" she said, her low, husky voice thick with disgust.

"We found it in the theatre," hissed the thing behind him. "We thought the master would want to speak to it."

Slowly, languidly, the woman rose from her chair, and laughed.

"Thinking now, are we? My, how you elevate yourself above your station. Leave him here, Talos will return soon and decide what to do with him."

The thing turned and scurried away, pulling the door to behind it with a dull thud.

Billy Rackitt contemplated the woman before him with a certain amount of wary curiosity; she certainly looked human, that was for sure, and her low cut, figure-hugging dress showed off her voluptuous body to devastating effect. And there was something tantalisingly familiar about her, an indefinable feeling that he knew her somehow.

Then he realised she was doing the same to him; looking him up and down, her initial disgust replaced with curiosity.

"Who are you?" she said. "And what do you think you're doing here?"

"It weren't my choice, believe me," Billy said.

"No, I don't suppose it was," the woman replied. She walked over to the banqueting table where a bottle of red wine and two cut crystal glasses sat on a silver serving tray. She poured herself a glass and then looked over at Billy.

"Would you like a glass?" she said.

Billy hesitated, unsure of what to say.

"I would if I were you," the woman said. "It's likely to be your last."

"Yeah, okay then," Billy said, nodding.

The woman poured a generous serving of the dark red wine into a glass, filling it almost to the brim, and brought it over to him. Billy took a long gulp of the alcohol, hoping it would steady his nerves.

"My name is Mina," said the woman. "And yours?"

"Billy," he said. He turned and looked nervously at the door. "What the bloody hell are all those things outside? I thought they were gonna kill me."

"They are vampires," said Mina, "and you are right to think that they might kill you. None of them have fed for quite some time now, and I am surprised they showed the restraint they did."

"But you . . . you're not . . ."

"No, I am not a vampire, I am all human." Mina reclined once more in her chair and gazed at Billy for some time. "Underneath all that dirt and blood you are quite handsome really, aren't you?"

Billy shuffled his feet, not knowing what to say.

"Oh please, sit down, before you fall down. Enjoy your drink; my husband will be back soon, and then you may never have the chance to enjoy anything ever again."

Mina stretched out an arm and curled her index finger at him, indicating that he join her on the chair. Ignoring the invitation, Billy perched on the edge of a chair opposite her, and took another deep swallow of the wine.

"Where am I?" he said. "What's goin' on here?"

"You are in the other London now, Billy," Mina replied, still observing Billy carefully from beneath hooded eyelids. "The London under London, that teems with a life all its own, a life of darkness and death and blood. Occasionally the two Londons converge, especially when the vampires are particularly hungry and desire to drink blood. Cats and dogs will only suffice for so long, and when their desperate desire to slake their unholy thirst drives them to it they might dare to take a small child, or suck dry the old and the infirm where they lie in their sickbeds."

A powerful shiver coursed through Billy's body, and he struggled not to spill any of the wine. When the shivering had passed, he looked up at Mina and saw that she was gazing piteously at him.

"I almost feel sorry for you," she said. "Fear not, your ordeal will be over with soon. Some people say that once bitten by a vampire you become one of them, a vampire yourself, cursed to live out the rest of your days feeding on others' blood. But don't worry, that's not true. Once you have been bitten and bled dry you will be dead, and your torment will be at an end, forever."

"I don't know about that," Billy muttered. "I ain't intending to hang around here long enough to find out what happens after I've been bitten by one of those fiends outside, that's for sure."

"How bravely you talk, such bravado masking your fear."

"It ain't bravado, no it ain't. I've already escaped from one prison today, and I don't reckon it's impossible to do it again."

Mina threw back the last of her wine and walked over to the grand dining table, filling her glass once more. She looked at Billy and held the bottle up, silently offering more of the dark red liquid.

Billy shook his head.

"And what crime did you commit that forced the keepers of the law to put you in prison, Billy?" she said.

"I went down for murder," Billy whispered. "Today were my appointment with the hangman, but I decided it were an appointment I wanted to postpone for as long as possible."

"Who did you murder Billy? What base impulse drove you to perpetrate that most terrible of acts?"

"I said I went down for murder," Billy said, looking up at Mina, still lounging by the table, drinking her wine. "I didn't say I were guilty."

Mina carried the bottle of wine over to Billy and filled his glass once more. Billy took a long gulp of the deep red liquid and said, "I were out with my girl one night, out on the town. First time in my life I were actually flush, could afford to treat us both to a good time. I'm a con artist by trade, a chancer, always ready to swindle some unsuspecting dupe out of his money. But I'm what you might call an honest con artist. I only swindle those who have enough money that they won't notice the bit I con them out of. I have my principles, and I stick by them. It's my principles that got me in prison, not murder. We were down by the docks at the end of the night, looking at the full moon, and me intending to be all romantic like, and propose marriage to my girl, when we heard a scream. Now the London docks ain't exactly deserted, whatever time of night you go down there, but people these days they tend to mind their own business, an' ain't that the truth. Unfortunately that's not my style, never has been, always sticking my nose in where it don't belong. There were this girl, a proper dolly-mop, and no more than fourteen or fifteen at the most, being given a right good hidin' by a gentleman slummer. Well, like I said, I'm not one to stand on the sidelines, so I laid in with my fists like, intendin' to give him some of his own medicine."

Billy paused, and took another long gulp of the wine. He could feel it going to his head now.

"Bloody peelers came out of nowhere, all over me they were, and I looked down and this toff were lying on the floor, dead like. Well, my luck weren't in that night, were it? Turned out this geezer were someone important, with lots of connections. My girl stood up fer me in court, and so did the dolly-mop, bless her, but it weren't no good, they sent me down fer murder."

Billy tossed back the last of his wine and looked at Mina.

"It matters not, Billy," she said. "Soon the world will come to an end, and the darkness will reign forever. Drink your fill of the wine, and embrace death when it comes. It will be but a short respite before you are dragged screaming from your grave once more."

"I don't understand."

"No, neither do I," Mina said, and sighed. "Talos says he will protect me, that we will be king and queen in a new age of evil, of eternal night. But sometimes, just sometimes, I like to see the sun, to feel it on my face, on my bare arms. And sometimes, just sometimes, I even crave the companionship of ordinary people, dull and slow witted though they are."

Billy jumped as, behind him, he heard the door open and then close with a loud thud. Every nerve fibre in his body screamed at him to run, to fight, to do anything but look at whatever had just walked through the door.

But slowly, slowly he turned his head, and looked anyway.

A man stood in front of the door. He stood tall and powerful, and his dark, empty eyes blazed at Billy with a fierce, unholy light. For a moment Billy thought that he looked almost . . . human. Almost.

"Who is this?" he said.

Billy flinched at the sound of the man's voice; it cut through him like an ice-cold knife.

"He was caught prowling in the theatre," Mina said, stifling a yawn. "They brought him here. They thought you might want to . . . question him."

Talos walked over to Billy and stared down at him. His lips parted slightly, and Billy could see his white, pointed teeth, but no fangs like the vampires had. He was dressed in an evening suit, and Billy wondered why there were no scuffs or marks on it from where he had made his way underground through the dirt tunnels.

Unless there was more than one route to the surface; an easier, wider route.

"Why would I want to question this pathetic specimen?" said Talos.

Grabbing hold of Billy's collar he hauled him to his feet and shook him like a dog might shake a rat. Billy dropped the empty wine glass and it fell to the rock floor and shattered. Talos stopped shaking the terrified Billy long enough to regard with him utter contempt, before turning and dragging him along the ground to the door, where he threw him into the tunnel.

The door slammed shut behind him, and Billy lay for a moment on the stony ground, breathing hard. Before he had a chance to gather his thoughts he felt more hands grabbing at him, pulling at him.

"You're mine now," hissed the vampire, spitting flecks of saliva into Billy's face. The thing grabbed at his hands and began snuffling at the blood and licking at his wounds. Billy felt a wave of repulsion flow through him, and with it a new determination that he was not going to finish his days here underground, at the hands of this monster.

Curling his knees up underneath him he shoved at the vampire with his feet, pushing it from him. The monster hit the tunnel wall, dazed for a second, but a second was all Billy needed. He jumped to his feet, grabbed the vampire by the neck and punched it in the face; once, twice, and then on the third time a fountain of blood spurted from its nose, splattering across Billy's arm.

Leaving the thing squealing in agony, Billy pulled an oil lamp from the wall and ran down a passage chosen at random. Behind him, he could hear more of the vampires coming to investigate.

"C'mon Billy, run, run," he whispered to himself as he bolted down the dark tunnel, the lamp his only light now. He found another tunnel, intersecting with the one he ran down, and entered that one, the ground beneath his feet slowly sloping ever downwards. He could hear a commotion behind him as the vampires chased him, fighting with each other to be the first in line to drink his blood.

Billy kept running.

He needed a weapon. If only he had some kind of knife, or club, he stood a chance of fighting them in this confined space. But without anything to fend them off, they would overpower him within seconds.

On he ran, his boots crunching on the rocky ground, and his breath coming in short, sharp bursts. It was hot in this subterranean space, and Billy's face dripped with sweat.

How much longer he could keep running he did not know, but he knew that the moment he stopped running he was dead.

Suddenly the tunnel opened out into another large space, this one not lit like the last one, but empty and dark. Billy stopped in the middle of the cavern and held his lamp up high, looking around him. More tunnel entrances led away from the main space, but Billy hesitated in choosing one.

Hearing a noise, Billy turned and saw the vampires had been gathering behind him. They huddled together in a group and kept their distance, whispering among themselves.

"Well, come on then!" Billy shouted. "Let's have yer! You're gonna kill me anyway, so let's see how many I can take down with me. What's the matter, yer scared all of a sudden?"

As one, the small band of vampires rushed the defenceless Billy Rackitt who, unable to think of anything else he could do, held up his burning oil lamp, ready to throw it at them in one last, futile gesture of defiance.

But he did not need to throw the lamp. With a shriek of agony, the vampire in front of the others fell backwards on the floor, clutching at an arrow sticking from its chest. It writhed in pain for a few seconds, making a high-pitched squealing noise, and then lay still and silent.

The other vampires stood motionless, looking at their dead companion. Then they all looked up at the figure walking from a shadowed corner of the cave.

Billy was shocked to see his rescuer was a young girl, no more than twelve or thirteen years of age at the most. The scraps of rags loosely tied to her skinny body were her only clothes, a mass of long, curly red hair cascaded wildly over her head, and her defiant face was almost obscured by the dirt which covered it. But the thing that made the greatest impression on him was the crudely made bow and arrow she held, and which she was currently pointing at the group of vampires.

She glanced up at Billy and said, "You ain't one o' them."

Before he could answer, she had loosed her arrow and another vampire fell squealing to the ground. The rest of the vampires turned and ran back into the tunnel.

"You gotta get them in the heart," the girl said. "If yer don't get them straight in the heart then they just keep comin', an' they never stop. But a shot straight in the heart, that does for them."

With that the girl turned and walked away, back to the shadowed corner from where she had come.

Billy stood where he was, too dumbstruck by what he had seen to do anything but stare at his unlikely rescuer.

The girl stopped walking and looked back at him.

"If yer stay there they'll come back and kill yer," she said.

Billy followed the girl.

Chapter Twelve
Emma

"Jim!" a voice said. "Quick, over here, come in here."

Jim turned in the direction of the voice. Slum Lassie Sal stood in the open doorway of her room, beckoning him in. She looked drawn and tired, more so than he had ever seen her look before.

A large, ugly bruise marked her left cheek, and her left eye was swollen and red.

"I've lost George," Jim said.

"He's in here. Come on, quick, before they come back."

Jim dragged his tired, aching body into Sal's room, and she closed the door behind him. George sat on a battered, wooden chair by an open fire, a thin blanket wrapped around him, the powerful trembling still convulsing his body.

Looking at him, Jim felt scared. Even in the warm glow of the fire, his brother looked deathly pale.

"What's wrong with him?" Sal said, putting her arms around George, and rubbing his hands between hers.

"I dunno," said Jim.

"You poor lamb," Sal said, pressing her face against George's, hugging him tight. "You're absolutely freezing. Where have you been? What have you been doing?"

Jim said nothing. In the corner, on the table, was his bag of money.

Glancing up, Sal saw where Jim was looking.

"It's yours, isn't it?" she said.

Jim nodded.

"I knew it. I thought to myself when I found it, there's only one lad in this place with enough gumption to hide away money, to save it up for the future. That's what you were doing, wasn't it? Hiding away bits of money, until you felt you had enough to get away from this place."

Jim nodded again, his eyes fixed on the worn, old bag sitting on the table.

"Don't worry, nobody knows about this but me. And I'm not going to steal it from you. It's yours."

George moaned slightly, a series of even more powerful shivers coursing through his body.

Sal hugged him a little tighter, rubbing his hands again.

"Oh, you poor, poor lamb. Even this fire isn't warming you up, is it?"

She looked up at Jim.

"He needs help, he needs care and attention, more than he can get here. He probably needs a doctor, but he's not going to get that here, is he? I know someone who can help, he belongs to the Salvation Army . . ."

"The Kerrigans don't need no one," Jim said. "I'll look after George. He'll be alright."

"Will he? I don't think so. Look at him, he's sick."

Ignoring Sal, Jim walked over to the table and picked up his bag of money. He opened up the bag and looked inside.

"It's all there," Sal said, a careworn look of pity passing across her face. "You don't trust anyone do you, Jim? It's a hard life when you've got no one you can trust, no one to confide in. Can't say I blame you, though, the life you've led."

Jim said nothing, just looked at his money. He wanted to count it, check it was all there, but he had no idea how much he had in the first place; no idea really how much money he needed to leave this life for the better one he kept promising George.

As if reading his mind, Sal said, "Have you got enough, Jim? Do you even know how much you need, how long the money you have there will last you?"

"We're gonna buy a barrow," Jim said, quietly. "We're gonna be costermongers."

"Oh, Jim, Jim," Sal said, her eyes glistening with tears. "There's not enough money there to buy yourselves a barrow. Do you have any idea how much they cost? The money you've got there's not enough to last you a week, even. Where would you live? What would you eat?"

Jim could not bring himself to look away from his money, to look at Sal. He felt foolish, an immature little child who knew nothing.

"Please Jim, you need help, both of you do. You won't bring any shame on the Kerrigan family name if you accept a little help right now, just this once. Everyone needs a helping hand at least once in their life. Even the Kerrigans."

Still unable to bring himself to look at Sal, Jim took a deep, ragged breath.

"Okay," he said.

"Good," Sal said. "That's good. This man I know . . ."

"How do you know him?" Jim said.

"He's an old friend. I met him when I was in the Salvation Army."

"You were in the Sally Army?" Jim said.

"Yes, didn't you realise? I thought everyone knew. I thought the nickname was a dead giveaway."

"Slum Lassie Sal."

"My real name's Emma. Emma Harris. I come from a nice middle-class family, never wanted for anything when I was growing up. When I was a teenager, I started coming into the city with the Salvation Army to hand out food and sing songs. I was always amazed at the welcome we got; the first time I went in a doss house I thought we would get thrown out."

"Everyone knows there's no coppers' narks in the Sally Army," Jim said.

"That's right, we were trusted, and that felt special. I know you won't understand this next bit, Jim, but I was kind of drawn to the life. Don't ask me why, because I don't really know myself, but I'm not the only one, you know that. It happens to others, sometimes."

"Yeah, the gentlemen slummers."

"But I'm not like them, Jim. Their reasons aren't my reasons, I promise you."

George let out a low, miserable moan, and squirmed in Sal's arms.

"Let's go now," she said. "Let's go and find my friend, he'll help us, I know he will. He'll get George a doctor and make him better. And maybe then we can all find a way out of this life."

Jim looked down once more at the money in his hands. He felt lighter now, as though a great weight had been lifted off his shoulders.

This is it, he thought. We can do it, we can find ourselves a new life, we can get out of this doss hole.

And then his life caved in on him, and nothing was ever the same again.

"What the 'ell's goin' on 'ere, then?" Marchek Mulready said, standing in the open doorway, blocking their route to freedom, to the new life Jim had promised George.

Instinctively Jim hid the bag of money behind him, but he was too late. Mulready noticed the movement.

He stepped inside the room and slowly closed the door behind him.

"This boy needs a doctor," Sal said, still holding George in her maternal grasp.

"Shut it," Mulready said, not bothering even to look at Sal.

The old man walked over to Jim, never letting him out of his gaze for a second, his yellow eyes narrowed down to thin, tight slits.

"Well?" he said, his voice dropping to a hoarse, dusky whisper. "What did yer get fer me, lad? What thievin' did yer get up to, tonight, eh?"

Mulready's flesh oozed the stink of booze, and cigarette smoke, and dried sweat. When not speaking, he worked his jaw relentlessly, as though chewing on something. A brown trail of dried spittle stained his stubbled chin.

"Nothing, sir," Jim said.

"Sir? Sir?" Mulready said and cackled. "Who're yer callin' sir? Eh? Tryin' to butter me up, is that what yer doin'?"

Jim looked down at the floor, avoiding Mulready's gaze. The bag of money behind him felt heavy in his shaking hands.

In a ridiculous, high-pitched voice, Mulready said, "Nothing, sir, nothing sir."

Then he grabbed at the money bag behind Jim, snatching it from his hands. He held it under Jim's nose.

"Then what the 'ell's this then, eh?" he said. "Tryin' pull the wool over old Mulready's eyes, weren't yer? After all I've done fer yer, yer'd do this to me. Yer nothin' but a useless little snot rag, Kerrigan."

Mulready pushed the bag into Jim's face, holding the back of his head with his other hand, and began stuffing the money bag into his mouth. Jim struggled and began coughing and gagging. He lifted his hands and tried to push the old man away, but he was too strong.

The money dropped out of the bag and scattered across the floor.

"Leave him alone!" Sal shouted.

"Ah, shut it, you silly little bitch!" Mulready snarled, letting go of Jim and turning on Sal.

For a moment or two, the old man trembled with barely checked rage, his lower jaw working furiously, spittle oozing from the corner of his mouth. But then his anger subsided as the stupefying effects of the alcohol took over once more.

Forgetting the others for the moment, Mulready shuffled over to the fire, sitting down next to Sal and George. He picked up the poker and began tending the fire, stirring the white-hot embers around and around. The rhythmic working of his lower jaw slowed down now, and his eyelids began to droop, no longer tight slits of anger.

Jim looked at the door, at freedom. He could make it, he knew that for sure. He could be out on the street and hidden in the fog before Mulready even knew what was happening.

But not George and Sal; they had no chance. They were too close to the old man; George was too ill, too slow.

Catching Jim's attention, Slum Lassie Sal put a finger to her lips and nodded towards Mulready. Jim looked closely at the old man from his spot across the room. He had stopped tending the fire, leaving the poker sticking in the flames, and was sitting back in the chair, his head beginning to droop on his chest.

Sal silently gestured to Jim to have patience, to wait while the old man fell asleep. But a knot of urgent anxiety was burning in Jim's stomach.

Surely Marlow Crimps was not far behind Mulready? The two men were practically inseparable. And once Crimps arrived he would act as the fuel to Mulready's anger, and then they would not stand a chance.

Jim balled up his hands into fists and began tentatively walking towards Sal and George. Sal shook her head, mouthing the word NO, but Jim kept walking.

They had to get out now, before Crimps arrived. They had to take the chance that Mulready was already in a deep enough sleep that he would not be disturbed by their movement.

Suddenly George let out a pained, anguished howl, as he was gripped by a powerful seizure in Sal's arms.

Startled from his sleep, Mulready jumped out of his chair and looked at Sal holding on to the boy's body, as the terrible convulsions passed away.

"What the 'ell's wrong with 'im?" he said, and then turned to see Jim behind him. "And you, yer up to somethin', ain't yer? It's written all across yer ugly little face, yer up to somethin', I can tell."

"No, I'm not," Jim said. "I'm worried about George, he's sick."

"Sick? 'E's a waste o' bloody space, that's what 'e is."

He shuffled closer to the trembling boy in Sal's arms and, reaching out a gnarled, nicotine-stained hand, turned George's face to look at him.

"What's wrong with yer, boy?" he said.

"S . . . s . . . so c . . . c . . . c . . . cold," George stammered.

Mulready waved a hand of dismissal in George's face and turned away, looking once more into the fire.

"He need's a doctor," Sal said.

"Don't tell me my business," Mulready said, his voice a low growl, still staring into the dancing, yellow flames. "He don't need a doctor. He needs a good thrashing, that's what he needs."

"That's your answer to everything, isn't it?" Sal said. "If the poor things aren't earning you any money, give them a beating. And if they still aren't earning you any money, then get rid of them, before they start *costing* you money. You're a callous, cold-hearted old man, Marchek Mulready."

"An' what of it, Slum Lassie Sal?" snarled Mulready, turning on Sal. "What of it? There ain't no one forcing yer to stay 'ere, ain't there? But yer stop anyway. Like a bit of rough, don't yer? Always did, way I've 'eard it. But if it's getting' a bit too rough fer yer now, then yer know what to do. Bugger off back home to yer nice family in their flash, big house in the country. Be bit of a job explainin' what yer bin doin' slummin' it in the Dials fer these last couple o' years, though, won't it?"

"C . . . c . . . c . . . cold," George said, squirming in Sal's arms.

"Need warmin' up, do yer?" Mulready said. "Well, I've got just thing, I 'ave. Just the thing."

The old man turned back to the fire and grasped the handle of the poker. Slowly, deliberately, he pulled the poker from the fire and held it in front of him, its red-hot tip only inches from his face.

"Just the thing," he whispered, his eyes narrowing down into tight little slits, the red glow of the hot metal giving his face a hellish, demonic look.

"No, no," Sal said, struggling to her feet, still holding on to George.

"Out o' the way, Sal," Mulready said, turning on her, and raising the hot poker above his head. "I ain't afraid to use this on yer to get to 'im, I'm tellin' yer now."

Sal bundled George to the floor behind her, standing between him and Mulready.

"If that's the way it has to be, then so be it," Sal said, a slight tremor in her voice the only sign of her fear. "But I'll die before I let you lay a finger on this poor child."

"Have it your way, Sal," Mulready said, taking a step towards Sal, bringing the red-hot poker down in a ferocious arc.

"Stop it, stop it!" Jim screamed and, head down, charged at the old man. He collided into Mulready, his fists flailing wildly at his body, pummelling him with all his might.

Jim was dully aware of the old man staggering backwards, and then the two of them falling. He clung on to Mulready with all his strength, his face buried in his filthy, sweat-stained shirt, and arched his back, waiting for the red-hot poker to come smashing down and sear his flesh.

Instead, Mulready suddenly screamed, a high-pitched, agonising scream of utter and complete agony.

Jim pulled himself upright and then fell back on his bottom. Recoiling in shock, he began scrabbling backwards, trying to get as far away as he could from the horror before him.

Still holding on to the poker, his right arm engulfed in flames, Mulready pulled himself from the fire. The flames licked greedily up his arm and onto his back, and then spread rapidly across his shoulders, setting his hair alight.

"Help me!" he screamed at Jim. "Help me!"

He began thrashing around, still holding on to the poker, and screaming as the flames consumed his body. His entire torso was now on fire, the flames advancing rapidly as though the old man's flesh were covered in lamp oil. His shirt hung in burning tatters from his bony frame, and the fire began spreading down his legs.

Jim looked on silently, frozen in horror at the freakish spectacle before him, the room filled with the awful sound of Mulready's high-pitched screaming.

And then he stopped screaming, and looked at Jim, who suddenly became aware of the sound of Mulready's skin crackling and popping under the intense heat, and the smell of roasting flesh.

For a long, long time, Mulready held Jim's gaze, suddenly oblivious to the intense pain. As Jim watched, the skin on the old man's face blistered and burned, falling away in patches to reveal his skull underneath.

Jim fancied he could see the flames burning deep in the old man's eyes, a fire just as fierce burning in his soul as the one consuming his body.

Mulready, now a human ball of flame, leapt at Jim, wildly swinging the poker in front of him. Jim jumped to his feet and ran to the opposite side of the room, putting the table between him and this fiery, devilish monster.

Mulready roared and again charged Jim, leaving scraps of burning skin on the floor behind him. Jim dived under the table, scrabbling through the dirt and the filth, and out the other side. He gagged at the stench of burning flesh, gasping for air in the heat of the room, and turned to look for Mulready.

The old man was turning this way and that, his arms flailing wildly, as he roared his anger and pain, his body now almost completely invisible within the flames. He dropped the poker and clawed wildly at his face, before dropping to his knees and then finally falling on his front.

Jim crawled over to Sal and George, huddled together in the far corner of the room, and hung on tight to them both. They watched as Mulready's body, lying lifeless before them, continued burning.

Sal ran a hand across Jim's face, wiping away the sweat from his forehead.

"Jim," she whispered. "Jim, you've got to go, you've got to run, now."

"No, I ain't goin' nowhere," Jim said.

"Oh, Jim, please, you've got to go, now, before you're discovered. If Crimps finds you here now, he'll kill you."

Already they could hear movement outside the door, voices on the stairs as people came to investigate the noise, and the smell.

"I ain't goin' nowhere without George," Jim said. He looked up at Sal. Her face was lined with streaks of tears.

"I'll look after George," she said. "Don't worry about him, I can look after him, but I can't look after you. I can't protect you if Crimps finds you here. Please, you've got to go."

And then she bent her face to Jim's and kissed him lightly on his cheek.

"Please. Oh, Jim. Please go. Run. Run now as hard as you can. I'll look after George, I promise. You can find us later, when it's safe. Ask for us at the Salvation Army headquarters. They'll know me. They'll know where we are."

Still Jim could not move, paralysed by uncertainty.

"Run, run now!" Sal screamed, sobbing, and pushing at Jim with all her might.

Suddenly, his mind made up, Jim jumped to his feet and ran for the door. He came to a sudden stop when he opened the door, as the hallway was full of children and their mothers, curious to know what was happening.

Jim pushed his way through the bodies, heading for the front door, for freedom, ignoring the questions of the women around him, ignoring the screams and gasps of horror as they looked into Sal's room and saw the smouldering body lying on the floor.

Suddenly Jim collided into a man's body, and the man placed his immense, meaty hands around Jim's arms, trapping him in his grasp.

Jim looked up at his captor.

Marlow Crimps looked back down at him.

Chapter Thirteen
On the Run

Sir Robert Horsley-Montague of 38 Grosvenor Place, a recently retired magistrate, poured himself a small glass of port and downed it in one. He was a stout, well-dressed gentleman of advancing years, his red, veined cheeks betraying his fondness for rich living, and his well trimmed handlebar moustache his fastidiousness over personal appearance. After a lifetime of conscientious work, he was now looking forward to his retirement, indulging his favourite pastime of collecting unusual antique artefacts from around the world.

His faithful butler, Thomas Treadwell, having just arrived with the silver tray bearing the cut glass decanter of port and a single glass, hovered discreetly in the background for a moment.

"Will that be all, sir?" he said.

"I'm afraid not, Thomas," Sir Robert said. "I'm expecting a visitor any time now, a Mr Caxton Tempest. If you could show him up to the drawing room when he arrives, and perhaps you could open a bottle of the Portuguese red that arrived the other day. I've heard of this Tempest fellow, believe he has an appreciation of the finer things in life. Humph! Why in God's name he feels he needs to see me now, at this ungodly hour, I don't know."

"Very well, sir," said Thomas.

He turned to leave, but stopped when Sir Robert called him back.

"Sorry, Thomas, but perhaps you should ask Elsa to stop behind, too. It looks like a God-awful night out there, what with that blasted London fog, not safe for man nor beast to be out alone. If she could wait until Tempest has gone, perhaps you could walk her home."

"Yes, sir," said Thomas, and left the living room.

Sir Robert reclined in his favourite easy chair, and poured himself another glass of port, this time taking an appreciative sip of the dark, expensive drink.

So, what would the great and mighty, not to say mysterious, Caxton Tempest want with a retired magistrate? Especially so late in the evening, and at such short notice?

Sir Robert mulled over what he knew of the man, which was very little indeed. Up until about ten years ago, he had been known for his explorations into the heart of Africa, and that some kind of tragedy had befallen him. Now, he was . . . what? Some kind of policeman, perhaps? A private detective? A secret agent?

No, surely the point of secret agents was that their identities were secret. Whatever, whoever, Tempest was, he had many powerful connections and was prepared to use them. This was the second time today Tempest had requested an audience with Sir Robert, who had refused him the first time.

Then Sir Robert had received a telegram from a senior government official, requesting, in no uncertain terms, that Tempest should be given an audience.

A senior government official that Sir Robert felt compelled to not refuse.

Outside, in the hallway, the grandfather clock chimed 11:30.

Blast it! fumed Sir Robert, silently. What could be so important that it couldn't wait until the morning? And where the hell was the man? Sir Robert had expected him a good half hour ago.

He finished his glass of port and was contemplating a third, when he heard the door chimes announcing the arrival of his visitor.

At last, he thought, listening out for the familiar tread of Thomas's footsteps in the hallway as he went to answer the door.

Sir Robert looked at the port decanter and at his empty glass, and then quickly poured himself another drink and downed it in one.

One might as well get some enjoyment out of the evening, if one was forced to stay up beyond one's usual bedtime, thought Sir Robert.

Thomas entered the drawing room, a figure standing behind him in the hallway.

"Don't leave the man standing in the hallway, Thomas," said Sir Robert.

"I'm sorry, sir," replied Thomas, "but this is not Mr Tempest, although he claims to be here on urgent business."

"What!" shouted Sir Robert. "Where's Tempest, blast it? I'm not expecting anybody else tonight."

"Forgive me," said the man behind Thomas. "I'm an associate of Caxton Tempest, and it seems we may have come on the same business, not realising the other was also on his way. If you will permit me an audience with your good self, I can save you another visit from Tempest, and you may retire to your bed at a decent hour."

"Send him in, Thomas, send him in. And come in yourself, I'm sure it won't be long before we'll be finished, will we Mr . . .?"

"Kralik. Zedekiah Kralik."

"Ah, right, good. Well, come in, man, come in. Let's get this blasted mysterious business over with, shall we?"

96

Thomas stepped back to let the stranger into the drawing room. He was a tall, thin man of dark complexion. He wore a long, grey overcoat and held his hands clasped behind him. His eyes flitted restlessly around the room for a few moments, before settling on Sir Robert. The man had bleak, soulless eyes. Sir Robert blanched under their desolate gaze and wished fervently that they would begin their restless movement once more.

"So, what can I do for you?" he said, hoping to conclude their business swiftly.

"I am reliably informed that you have something, an artefact, in your private collection, that I . . . that is to say Mr Tempest and I, would be greatly interested in seeing."

"Yes, yes, man. What is it? Don't prevaricate old boy, get on with it."

Kralik tilted his head down slightly, a ghost of a smile passing across his face. When he looked up again he was deadly serious once more.

"I believe you purchased this . . . artefact, only a couple of days ago, from a shop in the West End, 'Antrobus Curios and Antiquities'."

"That's right, I did. Good God, the man was murdered in his shop the following day. Ghastly business, so I understand from the papers. Trying to find the murderer, eh? Bit of detective work, I suppose."

"May I see the item?" Kralik said.

"Treadwell," Sir Robert said, "go and fetch the packing case that was delivered the other day, will you?"

"Yes, sir," Thomas said and left the room.

"Haven't had chance to have a good look at it myself yet. Supposed to originate from biblical times. Once belonged in the Tower of Babel, so I'm told."

"Indeed."

"Bit of a collector, you see, a pastime of mine. Got to have something to while away the hours, eh? Fancy a drop of port?"

"Thank you, but no."

"Quite sure about that, old boy? Decent vintage, I can assure you."

"Once again, thank you, but no."

The two men stood in silence for a few moments, Kralik as still as a statue, his hands still clasped behind him, Sir Robert shifting slightly from foot to foot, his agitation growing as the minutes passed.

"Dammit, where is that fool of a man?" he exclaimed eventually, just as the door opened and Thomas returned with a small packing case, still sealed shut.

"Don't just stand there, Treadwell, open it up, open it up!" Sir Robert said.

Thomas set about prising the wooden casing open and pulling handfuls of straw from inside.

"Any idea who might have murdered dear old Archie?" said Sir Robert, craning his head to peer inside the packing case.

Kralik said nothing, waiting patiently for Thomas to finish his excavation of the wooden box.

Thomas lifted the precious artefact from the case and held it up to the two men for their inspection. It was a fragment of an ancient stone tablet, a strange design engraved upon its face.

"Know what it might be, old man?" Sir Robert said, glancing at Kralik, but trying to avoid making eye contact, lest he be caught once more under the man's desolate gaze.

"It is a fragment of a sigil."

"A what? What did you say it was, old boy?"

"A sigil. There are three more pieces like this one in existence, and together they form a whole, together they form the Sigil of Semjaza."

"Right, right, I see. Well, no, I don't see actually, don't see at all."

"I wouldn't worry about it," Kralik said, turning the full force of his unforgiving, malevolent gaze on Sir Robert. "In fact, you needn't worry about anything ever again."

"What did you say, old boy? What?"

Outside, on the street, a solitary pedestrian, hurrying home through the fog, might have halted momentarily, believing he heard a muffled scream, but then would have shaken his head and carried on his way, smiling at the flights of fancy his imagination was taking in the foggy night. But there was no one, and the short, anguished scream went unheard.

Denver McCade pulled herself out from under the wreckage of the collapsed shelving, brushing shards of wood and glass off her. Still holding tightly on to the Colt .45 Peacemaker, she looked wildly around her, fully expecting Murmur to lunge at her, his yellow teeth bared in a ghastly smile of hungry anticipation.

She fired off a shot into the depths of the shop, the gun kicking sharply in her hand.

"Easy, girl," she said, lowering the gun by her side, "get a grip on yourself, you're shooting at shadows."

Murmur was gone, she was sure of that now.

"Dammit!" she said. "What did your daddy tell you? Never look away, *never* look away!"

But she had looked away, just for an instant; but an instant was all Murmur had needed, and Denver had paid the price.

It was the boy she had looked at, climbing through the shattered shop window, his back covered in fresh, raw wounds. Denver recognised those wounds, knew there was only one kind of creature that could rip at your flesh in that particular way, and it was not any earthly kind of creature either.

It was a Devil's Imp.

Right now the Imp's venom would be circulating through the boy's system, invading his entire body, eating away at his insides and poisoning his mind.

How long did he have left? A couple of hours maybe.

And then he would be dead.

If he was lucky.

Jim looked up at Marlow Crimps. There were two of him, two ghostly versions of Crimps swimming in and out of focus, leering down at him with his one good eye, a battered cigarette dangling from his lips.

Jim felt sick, sicker than he had ever felt before in his life. His stomach turned over, threatening to spew its vile contents from his mouth at any moment.

Crimps looked at Jim, and then at the gathering crowd of women and children around him.

"Hunh?" he grunted, a look of confusion passing across his battered features.

"It's Mulready," someone said. "He killed him."

"Yeah," another voice said, "burnt 'im alive. Go an' see fer yerself, he's in there."

Crimps looked back down at Jim, his nose twitching now at the stench of burning flesh.

Jim threw up, a torrent of foul smelling, watery green vomit spewing from his mouth and splattering over Crimps' shoes. Crimps swore, and let go of Jim, stepping out of the way, trying to avoid the stream of steaming, stinking puke.

Jim took his chance. Still heaving and clutching at his stomach in pain, he turned and ran, pushing his way through the throng of bodies, searching blindly for an escape route. Hands reached out to grab hold of him, but he twisted and turned, writhing out of their clutches, biting at hands that came near him, scratching and punching at the bodies around him.

He had no idea where he was going until he took a step into thin air and then began falling, tumbling over and over down the cellar steps. Jim hit the cellar floor with a sickening thump and lay dazed, unable to pick himself up off the ground. He could hear Crimps at the top of the cellar steps.

"I'm gonna kill you, Kerrigan! I'm gonna rip yer stinkin' heart out of yer chest!"

Jim could hear Crimps running down the cellar steps, his boots crunching on the worn brick. More hands grabbed at Jim now, pulling at him, and this time he did not have the strength to fight back.

"This way!" someone hissed in his ear. "Quick, move, he's coming!"

Jim was plunged into an inky blackness, lying face down in damp, cold earth. He lifted his head and bumped it against brickwork above him.

He was in a tunnel. One of many escape routes dug out of the cellars of the rookeries and doss-houses of poor London. The tunnels all interconnected, forming a labyrinth of escape routes that only an exceptionally brave, or foolhardy, policeman would venture into in pursuit of his quarry.

Jim began crawling. He pushed with his elbows and his knees, scrabbling through mud and filthy pools of water. Behind him he could hear Crimps, still shouting for vengeance, pushing his way into the tunnel, all the while describing the terrible, horrific things he would do to Jim when he caught up with him.

Another wave of nausea swept over Jim and he had to stop crawling, his stomach seizing up with terrible cramps. He groaned, the pain surging outwards from the pit of his belly and through his chest, and then he threw up again, the stinking stream of sick splashing up off the ground and against his face.

When the retching and stomach cramps had passed he felt slightly better and began crawling again, trying to hold his breath as he crawled through the pool of sick. Behind him he could hear Crimps' laboured breathing as he squirmed his way through the narrow tunnel in pursuit of his quarry.

The darkness in here was absolute and Jim had to trust to instinct that he was not going to crawl straight into a brick wall, but kept scrabbling his way through the narrow confines of the tunnel. Jim's slender frame counted for him in the tight space of the escape tunnel, but Crimps, despite being bigger and heavier, was also more powerful.

Jim was sure he could hear him gaining on him all the time.

He kept crawling.

A faint flicker of light was the only warning Jim had before he was falling out of the tunnel and onto the dirty, damp floor of another cellar. Before he had a chance to register his surroundings he was grabbed by a number of hands and lifted to his feet.

"Peeler after yer?" someone said, propelling him across the cellar.

"Don't worry," someone else said, "we'll keep him busy."

And then he was pushed into another tunnel and began crawling again, the skin on his elbows and knees scraping off against the hard, sharp ground, wet with mud.

Behind him he heard a brief commotion as Crimps entered the cellar, and the two men attempted to fight him off.

Jim kept crawling.

On and on he crawled, the scuffling and laboured breathing behind him a sign that Crimps was hard on his heels.

Suddenly Jim was falling again, landing on the floor of another cellar. But no, this was more like a regular room, with a fire burning, and a table and chairs. A man and a woman sat at the table assembling matchboxes, a huge pile of them lying on the floor beside them. Two small children sat with the woman, thin and undernourished, a vacant look of abject misery on their faces.

Jim lay on the floor trembling uncontrollably. Another wave of nausea swept across him, and he retched silently, bringing up nothing more than a thin stream of yellow bile.

"Help me," he pleaded, his voice a hoarse whisper.

The man ran over to him and helped him to his feet.

"C'mon lad," he said, "quick, up the stairs."

With the man's help Jim began staggering to the steps, but then they both stopped at the bellow of anger behind them. They turned to see Marlow Crimps, his clothes wet and filthy, his face streaked with mud, brandishing his knife in front of him.

"Leave 'im!" shouted Crimps.

"You go on, lad. I'll deal with 'im," said the man, pushing the boy towards the stairs, and pulling a knife of his own from the waistband of his trousers.

Jim took the steps on his hands and knees, not trusting his body to stay on its feet. Behind him he heard the grunts of the two men as they fought, and then he heard the woman scream, and he knew that the man was dead and the two children sitting by their mother were now fatherless.

At the top of the stairs Jim collapsed again, another wave of nausea sweeping through him. A plump, middle-aged woman dragging a large bag of laundry across the floor saw him. She dropped her laundry and ran over to him.

"Please, please, don't let him kill me," Jim croaked.

The woman pulled the shaking boy to his feet and half dragged, half carried him to the front door, to the freedom of the foggy night.

"What's wrong with you, lad?" she was saying. "Who's after you?"

"Kerrigan!" Crimps roared, standing at the top of the cellar steps, holding the knife above his head, his shirt front stained a deep crimson. "I'm gonna kill you Kerrigan!"

"Run, run quickly," the woman said, pushing him towards the door.

Jim hesitated, looking back at Crimps, advancing slowly towards them.

"Don't worry about me," the woman said, rolling up her sleeves. "I'm fair 'andey with me maulers, I am."

Jim lurched outside and began staggering down the maze of alleyways and side streets. Occasionally his feet gave way beneath him, and he collapsed, only to pull himself upright and continue on his way. He could hardly see anything now; his vision was blurred and a red mist seemed to have fallen over his eyes. His stomach was continually seized by cramps, and the wounds on his back felt as though they were on fire.

Finally he left the cramped streets of the poor quarter and stumbled onto a main thoroughfare. As he staggered into the middle of the road the last of his strength left him, and he collapsed onto the ground, his arms and legs twitching uncontrollably.

This is it, he thought. I'm dying.

I'm dying.

He closed his eyes, ready to give up now, thinking, I hope George is okay. Hope Sal's looking after him.

Suddenly he heard a horse neighing, and the clatter of hooves on the cobblestones.

"Blimey, Guv'nor!" a voice shouted. "There's a boy lyin' in the middle of the road! Almost ran over the poor little blighter."

Footsteps now, as people climbed down from a hansom cab, and then a man speaking.

"Look at the wounds on his back," said the man, close to him, as though he was kneeling down beside him. The man's voice sounded familiar to Jim.

"A Devil's Imp," said another man, a Chinese-sounding man.

"We need to get him back," said the first man, "get those wounds treated, before he gets any worse. Johnny, you'll have to go on to Sir Robert's alone, and I'll take the boy back in the cab."

Jim felt strong hands lifting him, and placing him in the cab.

"Strange," the man said, "how on earth could this boy have been attacked by a Devil's Imp?"

As the hansom cab drove off, and Johnny Chen continued his journey on foot, a figure stepped from the shadows and looked at the departing carriage.

Marlow Crimps broke into a run, following the cab on its way.

One thought consumed his mind.

To kill Jim Kerrigan.

Chapter Fourteen
Safe at Last

Soft, warm sunlight filtered through the chinks in the heavy, velvet curtains and fell across Jim's serene face. Surfacing from a deep and peaceful sleep, his eyes still closed, he began stretching, pushing at the blankets covering him. He yawned and slowly opened his eyes, still too drowsy to register his strange surroundings and to wonder where he was.

It was the smell that prodded at his sleepy unconsciousness first, telling him that something was wrong; something was out of kilter in his world.

The smell was of clean, freshly laundered sheets; a spotless, airy room free of the stink of sweaty bodies and damp, mouldy surroundings.

Jim stretched again underneath the warm bedclothes, a slow smile of pleasure spreading across his lips. Had he ever enjoyed such luxury before? Did he care right now where he was or how he came to be there?

Suddenly the memories of last night's events came flooding back and he sat bolt upright in the bed, his hands clawing anxiously at the bed sheets. For a moment, in the shadowy recesses of the unfamiliar room, he saw Murmur, leaping at him, ready to devour him alive. Or was it Crimps, plunging his vicious, bloodstained knife down towards his chest, to cut out his heart and hold it up before his eyes closing in death?

But no, no, I'm safe now, he thought, his hands relaxing their grip on the bed sheets. I'm safe.

He looked around at his luxurious surroundings and thought, perhaps I'm dead, perhaps I died last night and this is Heaven.

But the bed felt real enough, the sheets soft and warm against his body. He looked down at himself; his tattered, filthy clothing was gone and he had been dressed in a pair of fine silk pyjamas. He slipped a hand underneath his top and felt for the wounds made by the Devil's Imp as it had slashed at his flesh. His shoulders were covered in bandages, and the pain was much less than it had been the night before. The nausea had gone too, and he felt stronger.

Jim swung his legs from the bed and placed his bare feet on the cold, varnished floorboards. Standing up, he felt suddenly dizzy and light headed, and sat back down on the edge of the bed again.

Okay, he thought, maybe not.

He remained seated for a few moments, gathering his strength and looking around him at his surroundings. The bedroom was huge, bigger than any room he had seen in a house before. The bed he was sitting on was a large, double bed. Across the other side of the bedroom stood an imposing, dark oak wardrobe and, by the window, a dressing table. Other than that the room was bare. Although clean, it did not have the feel of a bedroom used regularly.

Feeling a little stronger now, Jim stood up once more and padded his way across the cool floorboards to the door. He looked out into the deserted hallway, a hallway longer and wider than any he had come across before, richly decorated with dark, intricately patterned wallpaper and ornate plaster mouldings. He began walking down the hallway and then, hearing a noise behind him, turned suddenly.

A tall, slim, elegantly dressed Chinaman stood behind him, smiling.

"You are up, that is good," he said. "That means you are stronger now."

Jim eyed the Chinaman suspiciously. He had always been taught that the Chinese were a wily, deceitful race of people.

The Chinaman offered Jim his hand in greeting, and said, "My name is Johnny Chen, and you are most welcome in the abode of Caxton Tempest, Master . . .?"

"Jim Kerrigan," said Jim, his mind a riot of confusion.

He was in Caxton Tempest's house?

"Come," said Johnny Chen, "I'll take you downstairs to the kitchen, and cook can give you some food. I expect you're hungry after all your adventures."

Jim allowed himself to be guided downstairs, down *three* flights of stairs, his hand gliding along the polished mahogany balustrade, and into the cavernous, yet homely, kitchen, where he was introduced to a large, plump lady, with a jolly face and humorous, twinkly eyes.

"This is cook, Mrs. Mulligan," said Johnny Chen.

"Oh, go away with you laddie," said cook, waving a tea towel at the Chinaman. "How many times have I got to tell you, call me Mary, for goodness' sake?"

Jim sat down at the vast, pine kitchen table. The wood was worn away in places, and stained and pitted from many years' worth of use. A heavy, cast-iron stove filled the kitchen with a warm glow and the delicious smell of cooking. From the walls hung a confusion of pots and pans, chopping knives and skewers, and various other cooking implements.

"There you go," said Mary, bustling towards him at an alarming pace, "get that lot down you," and placed a large plate of food underneath Jim's nose. Eggs, bacon, sausages, mushrooms, toasted bread; all these aromas overloaded Jim's olfactory senses, and suddenly, overwhelmingly, he realised how hungry he was, and tucked into his breakfast with great abandon.

Once he had eaten enough that his stomach allowed him to divert some of his attention away from the consumption of food, he looked up at Mary, kneading dough at the opposite end of the table.

Noticing Jim looking up from his half-empty plate, Mary stopped her work and smiled warmly.

"Ah, you do look better for a bit of food down you," she said. "As thin as a rake, you are. Need building up, so you do."

With that, she took the frying pan from the oven and ladled out more sausages and bacon for him.

"Hey, does the kid get all the food, or is there any left for me?" a voice drawled from behind Jim.

He turned to see the woman who had rescued him from Murmur last night, and he reckoned she was still the most beautiful woman he had ever seen. She ambled across the kitchen, one thumb hooked in her trouser pocket, the other hand casually holding a cigarette by her side.

"Now, Denver," said Mary, taking the cigarette from between her fingers and extinguishing it in the sink, "I told you last night, there's no smoking in the kitchen. Not in Mary Mulligan's kitchen there isn't."

"Sorry Mary," Denver said, smiling lopsidedly at Jim and giving him a conspiratorial wink.

"And as for breakfast, well there's plenty. All you had to do was ask."

Mary ladled more of the fried food onto another plate and handed it to Denver, who sat down next to Jim and began devouring her breakfast, shovelling the food into her mouth as though she, too, had not eaten in an age.

Jim left the rest of his breakfast untouched, as he stared entranced at the beautiful Denver McCade.

Denver, briefly glancing up from her plate, noticed that she was being watched, and said, "Hey, what's the matter, kid? Never seen a woman with an appetite before?"

Jim looked down at the table and blushed.

"Most likely he's a might confused about where he is and how he got here," said Mary, kneading at the dough once more.

Denver paused, a forkful of egg and bacon midway between her plate and her mouth.

"Yeah, I guess you are, at that," she said. "You had a lucky escape last night, kid. By rights you should be dead now."

She shovelled more of the fried food into her mouth and said, "Ugg yurgg lugging goog, aahh mwav to shay."

"What?" said Jim.

Denver finished chewing and swallowed her food.

"I said, 'you're looking good this morning, I have to say.' You must have one helluva constitution to recover that quickly from an attack by a Devil's Imp."

"Who are you?" Jim said, feeling bolder now.

"The name's Denver McCade."

"And where am I?"

"You're in Mr Tempest's house," said Mary. "He found you last night and brought you here."

Jim felt at the bandages across his back again, aware still of the slight stinging sensation underneath them. The last thing he remembered was stumbling out into the main thoroughfare, Marlow Crimps close behind him, wielding his rusty, bloodstained knife. He remembered thinking that he was going to die.

"Don't play with your dressings kid, or your wounds will never heal," said Denver, pointing her empty fork at him. "You're gonna have enough scars as it is."

"You were there last night, too," said Jim. "You rescued us. How did you know we were there?"

"I didn't. I was just paying Murmur a friendly little visit. We go a long way back. Who was the kid with you?"

"My brother," Jim said, suddenly realising that he had forgotten all about George. How could I have forgotten about him? he thought. How could I?

"I've got to find him, I've got to see if he's alright," he said, standing up. He abruptly clung to the kitchen table for support as waves of nausea and dizziness engulfed him once more.

Denver reached out a hand and sat him down in his chair, saying, "You're going nowhere. You're still too weak from the poison in your system. You need to rest up."

"What poison?" Jim asked, still feeling sick, but willing himself not to throw up his breakfast in front of Mary.

"Devil's Imps have a poison that is secreted from their claws whenever they attack. All the time that thing was slashing away at your back it was poisoning you, too. The toxin is strong enough to kill you, but most people aren't that lucky. What usually happens is that your system fights off enough of the venom so that you survive, but you end up a zombie, a walking nightmare. The only thing that drives you on is an insatiable appetite for raw, red meat. And you don't rightly care where you get it from, either."

"How come I'm better?"

"You were lucky. Tempest found you, and from what I saw last night it appears there ain't a whole lot worth knowing that he don't know about

106

medicines and natural cures. Another hour, maybe, and you'da been gone, beyond anybody's help."

"I still need to find George."

Denver looked at Jim for a moment and said nothing.

"Okay, kid," she said finally. "We'll go looking for him later. Right now you need to rest."

Tempest stood grim and silent in the drawing room of 38 Grosvenor Place whilst Inspector Behrends struggled to open the curtains and allow a little grey daylight into the room. Johnny Chen stood in the hallway, comforting Elsa the maid who still trembled at the memories of the horror she had witnessed last night.

A policeman stood on duty outside on the doorstep.

Satisfied that he had done what he could with the curtains, the Inspector turned to face Tempest again. "Well, Mr Tempest, this is an ugly situation, is it not? Do you still think this is the work of your vampires?"

Tempest pointed at the body of Sir Robert Horsley-Montague lying on its back on the expensive Persian rug, glassy eyes staring at nothing and face fixed in a permanent grimace of fear. "And what else do you think could have drained these bodies of all their blood, Inspector?"

Behrends looked at Sir Robert. In the hall at the top of the stairs lay his faithful butler Treadwell. Both men had a savage wound to the neck from which most of their lifeblood had drained. And yet only a few drops of blood stained the exotic carpets.

"There will be an inquest, Mr Tempest," Behrends said. "And we're coming under a lot of pressure now from the Home Office. People are getting scared and the Home Secretary wants this villain caught as quickly as possible."

Outside in the hall Elsa sobbed and Johnny Chen put an arm around her shoulder and comforted her. Ignoring the Inspector's last comment, Tempest began pacing the perimeter of the room, studying the paintings and the ornaments gracing the sideboards and tables.

"And your man Chen saw nothing of this villain when he arrived last night?" Behrends said.

Tempest turned on the Inspector, his eyes flashing anger for a moment, causing Behrends to take an involuntary step back. "Johnny Chen is his own man, owned by no man and owing no one. No, he saw nothing, found the bodies exactly as you see them here."

"I see, I see," Behrends replied, fidgeting uncomfortably beneath Tempest's gaze. "And this girl Denver McCade, have you found her yet?"

"She came to my house of her own free will last night, where she is currently resting. We had rather a busy night, and I intend to talk to her later today."

Tempest continued exploring the corners of the grand living room, turning his back on the Inspector who was thankful to be free of the man's penetrating stare. The more he associated with the man, the less he liked him. Tempest certainly seemed to have some powerful friends though. Even the Home Secretary had called Behrends personally to ask him to give Tempest as much leeway as he wanted with the investigation.

But he also seemed to have some powerful enemies too. Only that morning the Inspector had received a telegram from the United States, asking him for help in an investigation. But it wasn't his American counterparts who had cabled him. Oh, no, if only it could be that simple.

"This is it!" Tempest said, turning and waving a slip of paper. He walked over to the Inspector and placed the piece of paper on a table between them, smoothing it out. Johnny Chen approached them, his arm still around Elsa by his side, who cried quietly.

"Looks like a receipt of some sort to me," Behrends said.

"A receipt from 'Antrobus Curios and Antiquities' dated the fifteenth, the day before yesterday," Johnny Chen said.

Tempest looked at Johnny Chen and the Inspector. "If Sir Robert took delivery of this item on the fifteenth and Antrobus was murdered on the night of the fifteenth, then I think we can assume that this is what the killer was after all along."

"Yes, I believe you're right," Behrends said. "Antrobus' book of invoices and receipts was missing. Perhaps the killer took it with him to trace the item he was after."

"And followed it here, to Sir Robert's house, where he murdered Sir Robert and his butler before disappearing with the artefact," mused Tempest.

"I am afraid we are dealing with more than one killer," Johnny Chen said. He looked down at Elsa who still trembled in his arms. "Go on, tell Mr Tempest and the Inspector what you told me."

"I saw it all," she said, her lip quivering as she struggled to hold back the tears which threatened to overcome her once more. "Mr Treadwell 'ad come down to the kitchen sir, and told me to not go 'ome on account o' the fog. 'E said 'e would take me 'ome after Sir Robert 'ad dismissed his visitor. Well I waited an' waited, but time were gettin' on like, an' I 'ad to be 'ome soon on account o' our Tommy an' his poorly chest. So I went upstairs, an' . . . an' . . . ."

"Take your time," Tempest said, gently. "What did you see, Elsa? What did you see when you came upstairs?"

108

Elsa's fingers fluttered over her lips and she closed her eyes and took a deep, ragged breath. Composing herself she continued with her story. "At first I could only see Sir Robert like. The door was open a little bit, an' I could see Sir Robert, an' he didn't look very happy. He looked scared, Mr Tempest, sir. He looked 'alf scared to death. I were thinkin' about goin' back down into the kitchen when I heard some scufflin' noises and then saw these *things* jump on Sir Robert. Then he screamed, an 'orrible blood-curdling scream like I ain't never 'eard before in all my life. Well I ran fer the stairs sir like all the 'ounds of 'ell were after me, and when I turned round fer a quick look behind me an' seen what were comin' out that door I realised they were."

Tempest leaned forward, fixing the maid with his penetrating gaze. "What was it, Elsa? What did you see?"

"I saw vampires, Mr Tempest, sir," Elsa said, her voice dropping to a whisper. "Two of them, on top of poor Mr Treadwell, leanin' over him and sucking at his neck, slurpin' at his blood like 'ungry dogs at their food. 'Orrible they were, sir, an' skinny, nothin' on 'em but skin and bones, an' filthy too, like they'd just crawled out the grave an' stinkin' o' death and sickness. An' I saw someone else, this tall figure leavin' the house while the vampires finished eatin.' He weren't a vampire though, he weren't one o' them. After I seen that I ran downstairs and hid in the cellar, didn't dare come out until today."

"Oh come now, girl," Behrends said, his face a tight, pale mask of fear. "There's no such thing as vampires. Just old wives' tales, stories to frighten the children with, that's all."

"Beggin' your pardon sir, but my mum and dad told me the stories about the old days, about when the vampires would come at night and knock on your door and tap at your windows until yer let them in 'cos yer knew there weren't no use in tryin' to keep 'em out. An' ain't yer noticed sir 'ow the wild cats and dogs are disappearin', an' 'ow there's more sickly babies an' poorly old folk than there used to be? That's 'cos the vampires are gettin' braver again, an' feedin' off the old an' the young, an the stray cats and dogs."

Behrends snorted and turned away from the young girl.

"Thank you, Elsa," Tempest said.

Turning to the Inspector Tempest drew him to the other side of the room. "I believe we have seen all we need here. I shall be in touch soon, Inspector, and trust that you will do the same if you receive any information of importance."

"But Mr Tempest, we still don't know what it was the killer was after. What was in that damned packing case that is so important to him that he murdered men in New York, Paris and London?"

"That is what I intend to find out, Inspector Behrends."

Tempest turned to leave, Johnny Chen and Elsa in front of him.

"Mr Tempest?" Behrends said. "What was the purpose of your visit last night, when the Chinam . . . erm Mr Chen found the bodies?"

"We had reason to believe that Sir Robert had had dealings with Mr Antrobus over recent years, along with other antique dealers and specialists in ancient artefacts. We had made an appointment to ask him some questions. It is a pity we had not arrived sooner."

Chapter Fifteen
Questions and Answers

Later that afternoon, Jim was awoken from a deep sleep, in the large guest bedroom, by Johnny Chen.

"Come, Master Kerrigan," he said. "Mr Tempest wants to see you, downstairs in the dining room."

Jim struggled fitfully from his slumber, rubbing at his closed eyes with his fists, and yawned. He felt sick again, confused and disoriented.

He opened his eyes and saw the Chinaman laying out a clean shirt and trousers on the bed.

"Please wear these for your audience with Mr Tempest," he said.

Slowly Jim's head cleared and he remembered where he was, remembered sitting in the kitchen earlier in the day, talking to Mary and Denver. He ran his tongue around the inside of his mouth. It felt sticky and still carried the aftertaste of his breakfast.

He looked up at Johnny Chen, who smiled at him. He had a warm, friendly face.

"You will feel better soon," he said. "And do not worry about Mr Tempest. He only wants to talk to you, to make sure you are well and fully recovered."

Johnny Chen left the room and Jim climbed from the bed and pulled the silk pyjama top over his head and let it drop on the bed. As he was dressing, he looked down at the pyjamas and noticed an embroidered monogram on the pocket. He reached down and traced the initials with his forefinger.

Jim had only basic reading skills, taught at the orphanage he and George were sent to after his parents died. He never stopped long enough for the skill to develop into a useful one. But he recognised his letters and sometimes he could put them together to form basic words. He traced the two letters with his finger many times, trying to make out the initials past the fancy curls and embroidery that masked them to his eyes. Finally he made out the letters 'HT'.

Johnny Chen came back into the bedroom, and Jim said, "Who do these pyjamas belong to?"

"Mr Tempest is waiting. You must hurry."

Jim finished dressing and walked back out to the long hallway and down the large staircase.

Outside the dining room door, Jim paused for a second.

Johnny Chen gently squeezed his shoulder, and said, "Come, Master Kerrigan, be brave; there is nothing to fear more than fear of the unknown itself."

Jim opened the door and stepped inside.

The room was dominated by a large dining table, covered haphazardly in sheaves of papers and maps, and books. The four figures sitting around the table, and deep in conversation, looked up as one at Jim as he walked into the dining room.

Jim saw Tempest first, sitting at the head of the table, obviously in charge of the meeting. Next he saw an aristocratic-looking young man, only a little older than Jim. He gave Jim a look of complete and utter disdain, as though he were a piece of dirt he had just scraped from the bottom of his shoe. Jim studied him for a moment, and realised he was not the fine example of the upper social classes that he had at first assumed. Certainly, from a reasonable distance at least he could pass as such, but up close he bore the unmistakable look of the shabby-genteel. His shirt, although clean, had aged such that it was no longer white, but just off-white enough to be considered grey; and his waistcoat, although giving the appearance of black, was turning white at the seams, a sure indication that the old and tired clothes had been 'revived'.

Next to him sat a bearded man. Large and rotund, he was dressed much better than his companion. He gave Jim the briefest of glances before returning to the papers on the table.

Finally, sitting next to the bearded man, at the opposite end of the table from Tempest, sat Denver.

"Come over here, young Jim Kerrigan," said Tempest, indicating to Jim to come closer.

Jim took a few hesitant steps further into the room, looking at the floor. He glanced up briefly at the people before him, and his heart leapt slightly as he saw Denver giving him a sly, friendly wink.

Suddenly he felt a little less alone.

The wounds on his back itched maddeningly, but he steeled himself against scratching at them. He felt it would be a sign of weakness.

"Come and sit with us," Tempest said, indicating a chair beside him.

Reluctantly, Jim approached the table and sat down on the chair next to Tempest.

Johnny Chen sat down opposite him.

"Do your wounds still pain you?" Tempest said.

"No, sir," Jim said.

"The Devil's Imp slashed deeply into your flesh, Jim. I'm afraid you will carry the scars of your hostile encounter the rest of your life. But still, you should count yourself fortunate indeed; there are precious few people alive today who can boast of an encounter with one of those Hell spawn, precious few people indeed."

"Yeah, you're one of us now, kid," Denver said.

Jim looked across at Denver. Smiling her lopsided smile, she lifted her left leg and swung it on to the table, her booted foot making a loud thump as it hit the rich, expensive wood. Rolling her leg sideways she pulled back her trouser leg up to the knee, revealing an intricate network of scar tissue across her calf, extending upwards until hidden by the cloth of her trousers.

"Dust devil," she said. "Took me by surprise one night out on the prairies, damn near chewed my leg off."

Johnny Chen, sitting next to Denver, smiled at Jim, and said, "We all have our scars to bear, Master Kerrigan."

He rolled his sleeve back, exposing the scarred flesh on his right forearm. "A werewolf did this. I underestimated its recuperative abilities and turned my back on it before I had finished it off."

Jim swallowed nervously and turned to look at Tempest once more. He had slipped a finger between his collar and his neck, as though he was a little too warm. Jim caught a glimpse of old, but deep, wounds disappearing beneath his collar. Tempest shifted position and he could see the scars no more.

"So, are you sending the silly little boy back to his room?" the young man said, looking at Jim and sneering.

Jim stood up, his hands balling into fists. Tempest placed a hand on his shoulder and pushed him gently back down onto his chair. "No, he shall stay here for the moment and hear what we have to say. I would remind you, Crosely, that you are a guest in my house, and that only by the recommendation of your mentor Mr Slavin. If your conduct displeases me in any way I shall not hesitate to eject you from this establishment and back to your dwellings in Miller's Court."

Oscar Slavin took no notice of this exchange and continued poring over the mounds of papers scattered before him on the table. Crosely looked down, his cheeks turning a deep crimson of embarrassment.

"Now Denver, you were telling us of your experiences with Zedekiah Kralik in New York?"

"Yeah," Denver drawled, reclining on her chair and casting an amused glance in Crosely's direction. "I don't know how Kralik might fit in to all of this, but I can tell you anyway. He was a good guy, the kind who would give you the shirt off his back if he thought you needed it more than he did, and it wouldn't matter if he'd only met you right there and then. We kinda ran together for a while, after he found me, after my parents were killed. And for a while there I was happy. We worked well together, you know? But then he heard about this cult, who performed demonic

113

summonings and then asked the demons questions and the demons had to answer. Whatever you asked them, they had to answer. And he got it into his head that maybe we could use this, we could attend one of these summonings and find out some stuff."

"I can do that," Crosely said, lifting his head, eyes aglow with excitement. "I could perform a summoning here, tonight, and we could find out whatever you wanted to know."

"It don't work like that, sonny," Denver said, her lip curling into a sneer. "These things summoned from the other side, they don't serve you; you end up serving them. You'd be demon food before you'd got past your first set of mantras."

"No, I can do it, I know I can. This is what I live for, the purpose of my existence."

Tempest ignored Crosely and silently regarded Denver for several long seconds.

"Why don't you tell us exactly what happened?" he said.

"Yeah," Denver replied. "Why the hell not?"

Chapter Sixteen
Denver's Story

The snow fell lightly, dusting the New York streets with a fine covering of white and lending the night a strange luminosity. Denver McCade rubbed her freezing hands together and stamped her feet, trying to ward off the cold that nibbled at her fingers and toes, and pinched the exposed skin on her face.

Where the hell was Kralik? He was a good half hour late now, and Denver was never happy about being stood up. Arriving late for a date was no way to treat a lady; but then Denver was the first to admit, she was no lady. She had never worn a dress in her life, at least not after the age of about seven, when her mother had given up fighting the wildcat that her daughter turned into any time she approached her with 'girl's clothes'. She did not possess the manners, or the bearing, of a lady. She could beat any man she knew in a drinking competition, leaving many a hardened drinker slumped across a table swimming in booze while she walked away, her reputation intact.

And she could fight, too. Oh yes, she could fight. In her earliest memories she was running screaming at her brother, fists flailing, the reason for her fury already forgotten. She was fearless, reckless, totally without any sense of self-preservation when anger took possession of her. Fortunately for Denver, she was strong too and could hold her own against most of the men she fought.

On the climbing trips she took in the mountains with her father and brother, her father taught them both the meaning of self-discipline and restraint. She learnt to hold her anger in check sometimes, to hone her fighting skills and channel her fury. And she also learnt that, no matter how hard and furiously she fought him, her bigger, stronger brother would always win.

Evan McCade was two years older than Denver and, despite their often tumultuous relationship, was very protective of his younger sister. And that night of the full moon, when the dark, evil things from the prairie lands came howling and scratching at the doors and walls of their cabin, Evan proved his love for his sister once and for all. Denver let the memories flood back, knowing it was useless to try and prevent them.

It was late in the evening, and fourteen-year-old Denver was preparing herself for bed, when they heard the wolves howling outside. Denver's father stepped out onto the porch with his rifle, intending to fire a couple of warning shots into the night air to scare them away. He quickly stepped back inside, his face an ashen grey.

The McCade's isolated cabin was surrounded by hundreds of wolves, prowling and circling hungrily, saliva dribbling from their gaping mouths. The McCades had never seen so many wolves before. Evan and his father began breaking open the rifles and loading them. Denver watched horrified as her father passed a loaded rifle to his wife. She had never seen her mother hold a weapon before, but she handled it like an expert.

Without warning, the wolves launched themselves at the cabin, howling and scratching at the doors, their bodies thumping furiously against the walls as they frantically tried to get inside. Then they began hurling themselves at the windows, finally crashing through the shutters. The three older McCades positioned themselves in the middle of the room, Denver between them, firing their rifles at the hordes of writhing, snarling bodies. Soon the carcasses of the wolves were piled high against the walls of the cabin, but still more came, howling and snapping their jaws at the trapped family. Realising that they were running out of bullets, that the hordes of wolves were never going to stop, Evan bundled Denver under the floor of the cabin, into a secret hiding place they had used as children. Through a gap in the floorboards she watched him fighting the prairie wolves, standing shoulder to shoulder with her father and mother as they fired their rifles into the endless torrent of marauding dogs.

But suddenly, just as Denver thought they would all die, the wolves stopped pouring through the windows, and the howling ceased, leaving in its place an ominous silence. Evan and his parents stood in the middle of their blood-soaked cabin, panting hard, their rifles hanging by their sides, surrounded by hundreds of wolf carcasses, unable to believe that they had survived this incredible onslaught.

But then things worse than wolves smashed their way into the cabin; hybrids of wolves and men, powerful, muscular, brutish animals standing tall on their hind legs and roaring their hunger at the family. It was only later that she learnt they had a special name: werewolves.

They rushed at the family who, as one, raised their rifles and fired the last of their bullets into the evil, savage pack of beasts.

Denver's mother was the first to be taken, her scream of terror forever scarred into Denver's brain, as she succumbed beneath the frantic, savage claws and teeth of the werewolves. Soon after that, Denver saw her father join his wife in death; overcome with rage and grief, he ran at the pack of hybrid men-wolves, roaring his defiance and throwing himself into their midst, beating at them with his bare hands.

That left Evan, smashing the butt of his empty rifle at anything that dared approach him. He beat at them with such fury that eventually it broke in half. Even then he refused to give in, but pulled his Bowie knife from his belt and slashed at the snarling, biting bodies surrounding him, until he was lost from Denver's sight in a maelstrom of insane fury.

Denver stamped her feet some more on the freezing sidewalk, not only to keep warm, but also attempting to dispel the memories that burned at her mind, that kept her awake at night, that led her on the path through life she now took.

After the carnage had finished, after the young Denver had lain beneath the floor of the family home for several hours in a terrified silence, her parents' blood dripping through the floorboards onto her upturned face, she had finally crawled out of her hiding space, convinced that she would be pounced on and ripped apart at any moment. But the werewolves had gone, and all that was left were the shattered, torn remains of her parents' bodies sprawled in pools of their own blood.

Of Evan there was no sight.

They had taken him with them, as a trophy perhaps, or a meal for their young.

One thing was for sure, though; Evan was dead.

Back in the present, Denver saw Kralik hurrying towards her, his hat pulled low, his shoulders hunched and the collar of his long, black overcoat turned up against the elements. She buried the memories once more, pushed them back into that dark recess of her mind where they troubled her unconscious mind, never fully letting her go, never allowing her rest from the events of that dreadful night.

"I've done it!" Kralik said, his eyes burning with excitement. "They're going to let us participate in a summoning tonight. I've got the address here."

He pulled a piece of paper from inside his coat and showed it to Denver.

"Hey," she said, ignoring the paper with the address, "doesn't a girl get a kiss from her man, anymore?"

"Sure, yeah," Kralik said, leaning forward and absent-mindedly kissing her on the cheek. "Now, are you ready to go?"

"I guess," Denver said, sighing.

"Well then, let's get a move on. We need to get uptown to East Fifty-sixth Street."

"Yeah? That's kind of an upmarket address for a bunch of wacko devil worshippers, don't you think?"

They were walking now, Kralik tugging at Denver's arm, pulling her along with him through the swirls and eddies of the tiny snowflakes.

"Yeah, that's right," Kralik said, occasionally checking his bearings as they walked. "They're all financial types, politicians and businessmen, you know. They have this secret society, totally unknown to most people, very, very exclusive. And no, the Order of Ahriman are not just a bunch of wacko devil worshippers, they're much more than that; they're the secret hub of power within New York right now. Actually, their influence probably spreads across pretty much the whole of North America."

"And these guys know all about the Council of Seven?"

"Maybe. That's what we're going to try and find out."

Denver stopped walking then and pulled Kralik up short.

"I don't like this," she said. "I've never liked this, not from the first moment you suggested it, and I'm liking it even less by the minute. You're telling me these guys, this secret society we're not even supposed to know exists, let alone how to find, are going to greet us at their front door and show us in, answer all our questions, and then let us sit and watch while they summon a demon?"

"No, it's not like that. It's all been arranged for us through my contact. They'll hardly even notice us, I promise you. This is our chance, Denver. This is the best chance we've ever had at finding out the source of all the evil around us, the evil that's touched both our lives, destroyed both our families, continues to destroy other families even as we stand here right now."

"Yeah, I see all that. I'm just not sure this is the right thing to do. Hell, we don't even know that the Council of Seven are real. They're just a legend for all we know, figments of somebody's imagination. And how do we know your contact's reliable? For all we know he's leading us into a trap, and the most we can hope to achieve tonight is that we finish up as demon food."

Kralik touched Denver's cheek, gently stroking her skin with his gloved hand.

"I would never let you come with me if I thought you were in any kind of danger, Denver. Never. You know how much I love you; more than anything else in this whole, wide world, I love you."

"Yeah, I know that."

"When I found you that day in the ruins of your cabin lying by the massacred remains of your parents, I knew you were a survivor, knew that you and I were alike. We've both lost people close to us, we both carry scars and yet we both fight on, not just for ourselves but others too. We've never been closer, Denver, never closer to finding out the truth about the Council of Seven. We've talked about this before; about how nothing ever happens without a reason, there are no coincidences, nothing is left to chance. We are meant to be here right now, tonight. Everything's fallen into place so perfectly these last few days, it has to be right."

"But still, I don't like it . . ."

"Dammit, Denver, forget it then, forget the whole thing, I'll do this by myself."

Kralik turned away from Denver and began walking again. After a moment's hesitation, Denver began walking too, quickly catching up with him.

"I'm sorry, I don't mean to shout at you," Kralik said.

Denver said nothing, and they continued walking.

For the fifth time Kralik checked the address of the mansion on East Fifty-sixth Street. Now that they were actually there, he was beginning to show signs of nervousness, the self-confidence visibly draining from his body the longer they stood outside, the snow gently settling on his shoulders and hat.

"Do you want to leave?" Denver said.

"No, we're here now. Let's get on with it."

He climbed the steps to the front door and pulled at the chimes. Within seconds, his call was answered by a grotesquely fat man, dressed in a butler's uniform. Kralik mumbled something Denver did not catch to the man, who then stepped back to let them inside.

The butler looked at Denver and Kralik for a moment through eyes compressed down to puffy slits by the fat on his face. His jet-black hair was greased back, and his forehead and upper lip were shiny with sweat. He took their coats and led them along the cavernous, wood-lined foyer, through an imposing set of double doors and into a large ballroom.

Denver shuddered at the sight before them.

An undulating mass of masked revellers, clad in outlandish fancy-dress costumes of varying degrees of immodesty, filled her vision. Waiter-girls, exotically dressed in colourful, body hugging costumes, mixed with the guests, constantly refilling their cut crystal champagne flutes from over-sized magnums, fuelling the drunken, hedonistic atmosphere.

An immense fire roared and crackled in a marble fireplace, casting crazy, drunken shadows across the ballroom, adding to the sinister, corrupt atmosphere. Chandeliers hung from the lofty ceiling, sparkling like stars on a clear summer's night. An orchestra played valiantly on the stage but could barely be heard above the cacophony of drunken laughter and shrieking.

They had stumbled onto one of the infamous masked balls of the New York *haute bourgeoisie*.

The obese butler beckoned them on, and they pushed their way through the crowd, Denver shying away from the semi-naked revellers. A hand reached out and pulled at her arm, but she shook it off. The man reached out again, his face hidden by a grotesque Punch mask. His trousers were emblazoned with the stars and stripes, but if he had worn a shirt at the beginning of the evening he did so no longer, and his bare, flabby torso was slick with sweat. He laughed drunkenly and pulled Denver to him.

Denver wrenched free of his grasp and, before he had chance to react, twisted his arm up behind his back and pushed him face down to the floor.

"Try that again and I'm gonna rip your arm off at the shoulder, okay?" she said.

Kralik pulled her off the man, saying, "Leave him. We don't want to draw attention to ourselves."

Denver laughed and said, "Are you kidding? Look around you. We couldn't have stood out more if we'd tried."

A loud peal of laughter drew Denver's attention up and behind her. For the first time she noticed the balcony running around the edge of the ballroom, filled with more guests. A woman in a black corset and suspenders, her eyes hidden behind a black leather mask, hung precariously from the edge of the balcony, her hand outstretched to take the bottle of champagne offered to her by a man riding on another man's shoulders above the sea of masked revellers on the dance floor. Just as the woman on the balcony grasped the bottle, the man lost his balance and fell. Emitting a terrified squeal, the woman lost her grip and fell into the crowd of men below, who greedily closed in on her, muffling her sudden, frantic screams.

Denver took a step toward them, but was restrained by Kralik's steadying hand.

"It's not our concern," he said. "We have more important business to attend to."

The butler led them on between the revellers and through a door into a quieter area. They descended a set of stairs and stopped at the door of a basement where the butler produced two long, black robes, which he indicated they should put on. Kralik took one of the robes and slid it over his head. It covered him from the neck down, draping across the floor. Around his waist was a gold cord, which he tied. Finally he pulled the hood of the robe over his head, which cast a shadow across his face.

Denver looked from Kralik to the obese butler, who silently offered her the second garment. Reluctantly she took the robe and slipped it on. It felt heavy and very cold, even through her clothes. She, too, pulled the hood over her head, covering her blond hair and disguising her feminine features.

The butler now opened the door to the basement and they stepped inside. The low, cramped basement had been painted a dark red and was illuminated by candles set in heavy black iron candlesticks scattered around the edges of the room. On the floor a large pentagram had been marked out in white chalk. Around the pentagram a circle of fat candles burned, spreading puddles of hot wax across the floor at their bases. Outside the circle of candles sat a circle of figures, cross-legged and all wearing black robes tied at the waist with a gold cord.

Spaces for two more people had been left in the circle.

Chapter Seventeen
Denver's Story Continued: The Summoning

Denver and Kralik took the places left for them in the circle, sitting cross-legged on the floor.

Surreptitiously, from beneath the shadow cast across her face by the robe's hood, Denver looked at the men opposite her. Their faces were hooded too, indistinguishable in the shadows of the black robes.

Apart from one man, sat directly opposite Denver. Dressed in the same black robe as everybody else, he wore no head covering, revealing his shaven head and the strange design he had painted in black on his forehead.

The butler returned and handed the shaven-headed man a strange apparatus: a bamboo pipe, about a foot and a half long, with an ornamented ceramic head and a jade mouthpiece. The man sucked on the pipe, holding the smoke in his lungs for a long, long time, before passing it on to the man on his left.

The pipe made its way around the circle, until it reached Kralik, who had no hesitation in drawing the smoke from it. He passed the pipe to Denver, who paused for the tiniest fraction of a second, before taking her first taste of opium.

For the longest of times, the pipe was passed around the circle of black-robed figures, Denver repeatedly sucking on the bitter, hot smoke, trying not to inhale too much of it, but striving to keep up the illusion that she had done this many times before. Soon she was feeling giddy and light headed. The opium pipe was regularly replaced with a new one, and Denver lost count of how many pipes they got through, how many times she sucked on the bitter smoke. The room began to swim before her, and her head was filled with the roaring of her blood rushing through her veins. At the point that Denver thought she could take no more, that she would rather break the opium pipe in half and stand and fight her way out of the brownstone than smoke any more opium, the shaven-headed man placed the pipe by his side. He stood up and walked into the middle of the pentagram, sitting cross-legged on the floor once more, still facing Denver.

Then the circle of men began chanting.

Nomeno Sancto Saday.
Nomeno Sancto Saday.
Nomeno Sancto Saday.

The shaven-headed man lifted his arms, the robe slipping down to reveal the same design tattooed on his arms as on his forehead.

Nomeno Sancto Saday.

Nomeno Sancto Saday.

Nomeno Sancto Saday.

Denver struggled to focus her eyes, to focus her mind; the opium had totally disoriented her, sent her to a place in her mind she had never fully been before. Sent her to the dark places, opening them up and setting free the foul things that lived there, that tormented her in the small hours of the night, that caught her when she was weak and tortured her with the images and sounds of her family being slaughtered before her helpless gaze.

Nomeno Sancto Saday.

Nomeno Sancto Saday.

Nomeno Sancto Saday.

Denver balled her hands into fists, digging into the soft flesh of her palms with her fingernails.

Get a grip, girl, she said to herself. Now's not the time to lose it.

As she focused back on the shaven-headed man, she became aware of another disturbance in her vision, a disturbance apparently outside of her control. Pale, ghostly figures were wandering around the inside of the circle of candles. Denver blinked several times, trying to dispel the image of the restless spectres, but still they flitted across her vision. They wandered without any apparent sense of purpose, always stopping at the circle of candles and then turning in a different direction to continue their aimless drifting.

Suddenly the chanting stopped.

His arms still raised, the shaven-headed man lifted his head and began speaking. "Te Gladi, trea Nomino Sancto, Murmur. Cados, Cados, Mono, Gladiorus, in omnium regnas negotia illos quem. Castellumque et alio contra omnium nonconspicuus praesidium. Armaros, Sariel, Ezeqeel, Araqiel, Semjaza, Gadreel, Kokabel, Sariel, Shamshiel, Baraqijal, Penemue, Azazel, vincinte resistant me quem res illos."

The shaven-headed man lowered his arms and let his head fall to his chest, and a heavy silence fell across the low, dark basement. Apart from the spectral figures still wandering purposelessly within the circle of candles, there was not a single movement to disturb the stale, smoky atmosphere.

A powerful, violent shiver coursed through Denver's body, and she realised that the temperature in the basement had dropped several degrees. She could see her breath billowing from her mouth in white clouds. The others felt it too, and some of the gathered men wrapped their arms around their bodies for warmth, or began rubbing their freezing hands together.

Denver turned to Kralik, ready to tell him they were leaving, and leaving now. But Kralik sat cross-legged still, unmoving as though impervious to the sudden cold.

A dull, wretched moan from the middle of the room drew Denver's attention back to the shaven-headed man. As she watched, the man lifted his head from his chest.

A shock of horror coursed through Denver's veins as she looked at the man's face. Although still recognisable as the same person, his features were different now, somehow twisted and contorted into something evil and malignant, all vestiges of humanity having been eradicated completely from his face.

And then he spoke in a harsh, guttural monotone, his voice thick with saliva.

"Who dares to invoke the names of the twelve Grigori to summon Murmur?" he snarled.

No one answered.

The demon sitting cross-legged in the middle of the chalk pentagram stared accusingly at the silent circle of hooded, black robed figures. As Denver watched, the strange design on his forehead began smoking and burning its way through the man's flesh.

"Well?" the demon hissed. "Answer me you pitiful carcasses of blood and mucus. Who summoned me?"

Several of the men in the circle had struggled to their feet now, backing up from the thing in their midst.

This is all wrong, thought Denver. This wasn't supposed to happen. They wanted to summon a demon, but not like this. He wasn't supposed to have this kind of control, this kind of freedom.

The shaven headed man . . . Murmur . . . struggled awkwardly to his feet, as though he were unused to the movement of his body, as though it were not his. Several more of the robed men broke from the circle, and Denver followed their example. She wanted to be on her feet and ready to run if that thing made a dash for them.

Denver shook Kralik, who had remained seated on the floor, and said, "Let's go. Come on. Let's go now!"

Kralik stirred slightly, as though waking from a deep sleep.

Suddenly the thing in the middle of the pentagram emitted a high-pitched scream and ran snarling at Denver. Before she had a chance to react, before she had a chance even to register someone shouting, "It's okay, he can't hurt you!" the demon stopped, abruptly, at the inside edge of the circle of candles. He took a step back, a look of pain and slight bewilderment passing across his demonic features.

125

"He can't get out of the circle," someone else said. "As long as the circle of candles remains unbroken, we're safe."

"Thank God," said Denver.

"What?" the man next to her said. He pulled back his hood, revealing a lined, middle-aged face topped by a shock of silvery grey hair.

His piercing blue eyes examined Denver for a long moment, before saying, "Say something else."

"I don't know . . ."

The man snatched back Denver's hood, her long, blond hair spilling out across her shoulders.

"Since when were women allowed within the Order of Ahriman?" he hissed.

Denver tried to pull away from the man, but he had a strong grip on her robe. Others of the Order began approaching, momentarily losing interest in the trapped demon.

"Let go of me," Denver said.

The man said nothing, tightening his grip on Denver's robe and drawing her closer to him.

"Not before you tell me how you infiltrated your way into our group and, more importantly, why," said the man.

Strong hands grabbed at Denver, pinning her arms to her sides, and as she looked around at the hooded figures closing in on her she knew she was outnumbered.

"Who are you?" the man snarled in Denver's face.

"She's mine," Kralik said, and struck him heavily across the head with a black iron candlestick.

The man dropped senseless to the floor, blood spraying from a gash in his scalp, and Kralik swung the candlestick at the other robed figures surrounding them.

"Stay back, all of you," he said.

They both heard the movement behind them, but Kralik was only turned halfway round before the hooded figure had thrown himself into Kralik, sending them both careering across the room. Kralik dropped his weapon, and the two men began pounding at each other with their fists.

More hands pulled at Denver, who struggled and squirmed, but was overcome by the sheer number of bodies. The black-robed figures closed in on her, hoods falling back to reveal the faces of respectable New York citizens twisted with hate and revulsion. Denver kicked and punched, lashing out in all directions, hitting anything she could, biting and scratching as she was pinned down by the men of the Order of Ahriman. She began to suffocate underneath the weight of the bodies, too many of them crushing the life from her, blotting out what little light there was in the basement.

A sudden scream distracted them, and lifted the weight of the mass of bodies off Denver enough to let her breathe freely once more. She struggled free from the men no longer pressing down on her, their attention elsewhere now; struggled free enough to see what they saw.

One of the fat candles forming the circle around the pentagram lay on its side in the middle, white wax spattered around it where it had been kicked over. In the middle of the broken circle now stood another figure besides Murmur.

Kralik.

It was Kralik who had screamed. One anguished, agonised shriek, cut short in his throat. Now he beat frantically at himself and clawed at his clothes as though thousands of tiny, crawling insects scurried across his body, biting and pinching at his flesh.

Ignoring Kralik, Murmur leapt from the circle at the nearest figure, snarling with demented pleasure as he dragged him to the floor. The man fought vainly to ward off the demon, his struggles growing weaker as Murmur overcame him, greedily sucking the life from him. When he had finished feasting, Murmur turned to eye the others, discarding the dried, cracked husk that was all that was left of his first victim.

The remaining members of the Order of Ahriman suddenly broke free from the fear that had held them paralysed, and descended into anarchy. Some of the men picked up the iron candlesticks as weapons, whilst others made a bolt for the door. Jostled and bumped by the bodies rushing past her, now forgotten as an impostor, Denver turned to look for Kralik.

He was gone.

The pentagram was empty and many of the surrounding candles had now sputtered out or been kicked over.

A robed figure pushed into Denver and she fell to the floor. Beside her lay a candlestick and she picked it up. It felt good and solid in her hand. Another scream rent the smoky air of the basement as Murmur claimed his next victim.

Okay, maybe it's time to get out of here, she thought.

Denver picked herself up off the floor and began pushing her way through the mass of bodies, swinging the heavy candlestick at anyone who stood in her way. She soon reached the door of the basement and ran up the steps and into the hallway of the brownstone.

The obese butler regarded her impassively from across the hall. He showed no concern about the events in the cellar, and made no move to stop her.

Denver ran past the butler, back up the stairs and into the ballroom. The frenzied, orgiastic mass of debauched pleasure-seekers ignored her as she forced her way through, until she was staggering from the mansion and into the freezing cold New York night.

The snow was coming down harder now, and the streets were deserted. Denver ran and ran, still clutching the black iron candlestick by her side. Her mind reeled with the things she had seen; the shaven-headed man possessed by the demon Murmur, and her last look at Kralik as he had beat at his body in a torment of agony.

Her run slowed to a walk, and then she came to a stop, gulping breathlessly at the freezing night air, her lungs turning into blocks of ice within her chest. The iron candlestick fell from her raw, lifeless fingers, hitting the ground with a soft thump.

She leant forward, placing her hands on her knees for support, and retched silently.

When the pain in her chest had subsided she looked up. She was standing by a large lake, frozen solid, and beyond the lake she could see a line of trees. She was in Central Park.

"Denver!" a voice hissed at her from the darkness.

"Zedekiah? Is that you?" Denver said, looking around her. It had sounded like Kralik.

And yet, somehow . . . not.

"Denver!" the voice hissed again, behind her and closer this time.

Denver swivelled around, desperately trying to locate Kralik, her uneasiness growing all the time.

"Please, Denver, help me," said the voice that was . . . that was not . . . Kralik.

Denver looked down at the ground, at the iron candlestick lying by her feet, already covered by a layer of fresh snow. She bent down and picked up the cold, heavy weapon.

When she looked up, Kralik was standing before her, less than a foot away. He had discarded the robe, and wore nothing more than a thin shirt and trousers, yet seemed oblivious of the cold. Fresh wounds lined his pale, drawn face. The long, jagged scratches were still bleeding freely. Denver glanced down at his hands and saw that the ends of his fingernails were red with blood where he had gouged at himself.

"I can't help myself, Denver," Kralik said, reaching out with his bloodstained hands and folding them around her head, pulling her closer to him, until their faces were close side by side, his freezing, bloodstained cheek pressed against hers.

"I can't help myself," he whispered. "There's something inside of me, Denver, something foul and degenerate, evil beyond all measure. You've got to kill me, kill me now, before it's too late."

His grip tightened inexorably around her head, squeezing at her face, his fingers pressing deep into her flesh, threatening to crush the bones in her skull. Denver tried to speak, to reason with him, but the words caught in her throat.

"Yes," said Kralik, his voice now a guttural, inhuman growl, "kill me if you can, Denver McCade."

Bright, multicoloured stars exploded across Denver's vision, mingling with the whiteness of the snowstorm, and a grey pall began to fall over her eyes, as Kralik's grip tightened and tightened. The heavy candlestick dropped from her freezing, useless hand once more. Denver grabbed feebly at Kralik's arms, trying to pull him from her, trying to release the pressure on her skull, but he was too strong. She could feel the bones of her skull creaking and scraping against each other. As she succumbed to the inevitable release into the oblivion of unconsciousness, her hands, with a will of their own, it seemed, fluttered and grabbed at Kralik's shirt, at his waistband, until they found what they wanted; a knife.

Denver took the knife, the knife that Kralik always boasted was more deadly in his hands than a gun in anybody else's, and feverishly slashed at his stomach.

Emitting the high-pitched shriek that Denver had heard in the basement, Kralik released Denver from his grip and clutched at his stomach, rivulets of blood seeping between his fingers.

Denver swayed and staggered slightly, her vision clouding over completely, her head pounding like a three-day-old hangover. She held the knife before her, held it tight. Around her the snow fell heavily.

Slowly her sight returned, the grey mist receding, and she saw that Kralik had gone. A vivid trail of scarlet splashes in the white of the snow led away, and was quickly covered over by fresh snow. The pounding in Denver's head grew stronger, and the grey mist fell across her eyes once more.

Denver fell to the ground in a faint, and her still body was swiftly covered over with a cold blanket of pure white. Moments later a figure approached her. He threw back the grey cowl covering his head and snow settled on his silvery hair.

Then he bent down and picked the unconscious Denver McCade up, casually slinging her over his shoulder. He turned and began walking, quickly disappearing into the white of the snowstorm.

Chapter Eighteen
The Council of Seven

Billy Rackitt chugged greedily on the pitcher of water for several long seconds, and then continued chewing on the greasy chicken leg as though he had not eaten for a week.

"This is good," he mumbled through a mouthful of the chicken, and eyeing the girl before him. "Where did you get it?"

"Stole it," said the girl, who had said her name was Maria. "The woman, she ain't a vampire, like the rest o' them. She needs proper food, which they steal fer her, and then I steal it from them."

Billy looked around him at the small, cramped cave in which they sat. The floor was littered with bits of rubbish; scraps of clothing, pieces of wood, old, worn shoes, broken crockery, rusted nails, mattress stuffing, pots and pans, and much more, mostly unidentifiable, bric-a-brac.

Billy picked up a roll of paper, dark with mould and damp, and unrolled it. He held it carefully, trying not to rip the fragile paper, and scrutinised it closely. It was one of the posters from the theatre, a crude illustration of a buxom woman screaming, while behind her a masked fiend raised a curved, gleaming blade over his head, ready to plunge it in her back. The title read 'Le Couteau Meurtrier de Paris'.

And now Billy knew why Mina had looked so familiar to him; she was the woman in the posters he had seen in the theatre. It was definitely her, a little younger perhaps, her hair a little longer, but most definitely Mina.

Billy let the poster fall from his hands and continued looking around the cave. A crude bed of boards and canvas bags lay in one corner, and in another was gathered an arsenal of weapons. There was another bow and set of arrows, a pile of sharpened stakes, a hunting knife, a small axe, once probably used for chopping firewood, a club, a policeman's whistle and a small handgun.

Maria saw Billy looking at the gun and said, "Ain't never used it. Ain't got no bullets."

"Where did you get all this stuff?" Billy said.

"Found it, mostly," said the girl, picking the flesh from an unidentifiable scrap of meat and placing it in her mouth. "When they bring people down here to kill them, they always leave the body where it lies for a while after they've finished. It's like they're drunk, or somethin', an' they can't do nothin' with the body until they've slept it off. So I always have a look myself, like, see if they got anythin' I can use. The whistle's the best; them bloody vampires can't stand it, they hate it, sends them mad."

And then she giggled, and Billy felt another shiver course through his body.

To compound the sense of horror he already felt, Billy suddenly noticed a large, grey rat peeking out from beneath a pile of dirty rags, and then scuttling across the floor towards him. At the last second it turned away from him and ran to Maria, climbing onto her lap and then up her body, disappearing into her mass of unruly hair.

Billy reached out a hand, ready to pull the rodent off the girl and kill it.

The look in Maria's eyes as she saw him approach made him think twice, and he retreated at once.

"Leave 'im alone," she said.

"Is he . . . is he your pet?" Billy said.

"Yeah," said the girl, chewing on her food once more. "His name's Jesus, like that feller in the Bible."

"You've read the Bible?" said Billy.

"Me Dad used to read it to me, told me Jesus were me best friend. Well, I don't know about that feller in the Bible being me friend anymore, but this here Jesus is me only friend down here."

The rat peeked out from the tangle of the girl's hair and observed Billy who, with an involuntary shudder of revulsion, could not help but notice the rat's tail curling around Maria's neck.

"What are you doing here?" he said. "Where are your parents?"

"Dead," said the girl, chewing on the meat, and tearing it from the bone with her teeth. "They're both dead, and them bloody vampires tried to kill me too, but I were too quick for them. I got away."

"But why do you stop down here?" Billy said. "Haven't you ever tried to find your way out?"

Maria stopped chewing on her food and looked at Billy between long strands of dirty, red hair. Her mouth glistened with grease. She had a defiant set to her chin, Billy noticed now, and a cold look to her eyes which made her appear older than her years.

"I tried a couple o' times at first, but it weren't no use. There ain't no way out now, not fer me, anyways."

"But how long've you been down here?"

"Dunno," Maria said, chewing on her food once more and losing interest in answering Billy's questions.

Billy wiped a hand across his mouth and sighed. He had no idea now whether it was night or day, or how long he had been underground. He knew that he had slept for a while, and that Maria had left him and returned a little while later with the food. And for a short time that had been all that had mattered.

But now that Billy was rested and had eaten something he began to contemplate his predicament a little more carefully. Billy was an optimist, but right now even he had to admit that things did not look too good. Pacing up and down the exercise yard of Newgate Gaol, waiting for his appointment with the hangman, even then he had not felt this despondent. Billy was a chancer, a trickster, a quick-thinking, smooth-talking con artist, always on the lookout for his next scam and never prepared to admit defeat.

Still, he'd never been trapped deep underground in the bowels of the earth, chased by a bunch of bloodsucking vampires and with nobody but a twelve-year-old girl and a rat called Jesus for company before.

Billy was not one for giving up that easily, though.

"There's got to be a way out," he muttered to himself. "There's got to be."

"What are you doing?" Jim said.

Oscar Slavin looked up from the mounds of ancient manuscripts, old, faded maps and dusty, leather-bound books which lay scattered across the table, and studied Jim thoughtfully for a moment whilst stroking his beard.

"Hmm," he said at last, "that might be an easy question to ask, young man, but I'm afraid that it is not quite as simple a task to answer it. I suppose the easiest way of replying to your question, and also perhaps supplying you with an answer that's closest to the truth, would be to say, I don't know."

Jim looked at Oscar, thinking that he had many more questions he needed to ask, but that if this was the kind of answer he was going to be given then he would be better off talking to somebody else.

But who? After Denver had finished telling her story, Tempest had received a message calling him away on urgent business. Johnny Chen had gone with him, leaving Denver and Crosely to argue over the merits of performing a demonic summoning. Losing her patience Denver had stormed out of the dining room and Crosely had left a few moments later.

Jim felt very alone again and increasingly uneasy. Denver's story about Murmur had brought vividly to life his experiences of the previous evening. Now knowing that there was another demon trawling the solitary, night-time streets of London, with his own mysterious, murderous purpose, gave Jim the chills. Then there was all the talk of werewolves and dust devils, secret societies and demonic summonings.

And yet it was also very exciting and mysterious. When Johnny Chen and Denver had shown him their scars, Jim had felt as though he was being initiated into some kind of private, and very exclusive, club; but a club about which he knew absolutely nothing.

Now everybody had gone, leaving him with no one to question but the studious and impenetrable Oscar Slavin.

Jim decided to try Oscar with another question. He seemed friendly enough, at least.

"Who are the Council of Seven?"

Oscar looked up from a filthy, tattered old book he had been engrossed in, and again observed Jim carefully.

"Well," he said, stroking his dark, full beard once more, "you're not the first person to ask that question, young man."

Jim sighed. This was not going to be easy.

"I ain't never heard of them before," he said.

"No, not many people have, and among those few, there is great debate as to whether or not the Council of Seven actually exist, or if they are just the stuff of myth and legend. But if they are real, then there is not a moment of your life that you can call your own, not a choice that you have made that was of your own free will."

"How do you mean?"

Oscar put down the book that he had been studying, giving Jim his full attention.

"It is said that the Council of Seven are the secret rulers of the world, that their influence extends everywhere throughout the nations and countries of the entire earth. Kings, queens, presidents, prime ministers, tribal chiefs, cruel despots, oppressive dictators, benevolent rulers, they all live under the authority of the Council of Seven."

Oscar paused for a moment, and then, leaning a little closer to Jim, said, "But none of them know it. The Seven extend their influence by stealth and cunning, never revealing their presence, but always working to shape the world for their own malicious ends, for their own pleasure and profit."

"But who are they?" Jim asked, encouraged now by the answers he was getting.

"Who knows?" said Oscar. "Are they even real, or just a rumour, a figment of the imagination, which has grown and become real enough that people search for them, and talk about them, and fear them."

"Do you believe they exist?" Jim said.

"Yes, I think I do," replied Oscar. "But what good does that belief do me? If the Council of Seven do exist, and their influence extends as far as I believe it does, then I only believe because they want me to believe. And if I don't believe, then that also is only because they don't want me to believe."

Jim sighed. He was getting his answers, but he was not entirely sure he understood them.

"It's complicated, isn't it?" Oscar said.

"And does Mr Tempest believe in the Council of Seven?" asked Jim.

"Tempest keeps his beliefs to himself, and only those closest to him know his thoughts."

"Do you know?"

Oscar smiled and reclined in his chair, saying, "So many questions, young man, so many questions. No, Crosely and I are not part of Tempest's inner circle. We are merely the hired help. I am here because of my knowledge of the history of the occult, its worldwide practitioners, its history, its hidden effect upon society. Crosely, well, I fear Tempest is beginning to regret me bringing Alex Crosely here. He lives a hand-to-mouth existence in a destitute lodging house in the depths of Shadwell, but he has the capability to become one of our foremost experts on the occult."

Oscar closed the book he had been studying and began tidying some of the aged manuscripts, attempting to place some order on the chaos before him.

"But you still haven't told me what you're doing," Jim said.

Oscar sighed and sat back in his chair again, leaving the mess before him.

"Whoever is murdering the antique dealers and specialists in ancient, religious artefacts is looking for something in particular. I am trying to find out what that might be by looking through the stock lists and invoices of those places where there has been a murder to see what might be missing." And then a light seemed to switch on in Oscar's eyes as he tapped a sheet of paper and looked at Jim. "And I think I might have found it. Using the receipt that Tempest recovered for me from Sir Robert's house, and checking it against Archibald Antrobus's stock, I do believe the murderer took off with a fragment of an ancient stone tablet containing the Sigil of Semjaza."

"What's a Sigil of Semjaza?"

"Sigils are magical symbols, used in the summoning of angels and demons. Every angel and demon has his own sigil. The symbol that Denver described drawn on the shaven-headed man's forehead is Murmur's sigil. The man probably copied it from a grimoire or book of black magic and pacts. The sigil that murderer is apparently searching for is the original stone tablet that was once stored in the Tower of Babel, several floors of which it is believed acted as a great repository for occult items, such as sigils and talismans. When God destroyed the Tower of Babel, and scattered mankind across the earth, everything held in the tower was also destroyed. But in the last few decades there has been great archaeological interest in an ancient site in Iraq, where it is believed that the Tower of Babel stood. Archaeologists and historians of many different nationalities have been sifting through the site for years now, competing with each other for that find of significant historical importance which will make them famous throughout the world. It is believed that all the fragments of the Sigil of Semjaza have been found, but they are scattered across the earth, a piece owned by a collector in one part of the world, another sitting in a museum in another part of the world. It seems that the murderer is trying to find all the fragments and piece them together, no doubt to summon the demon Semjaza. But what his ultimate purpose is, I don't know. That's what I need to try and find out, and if there are any more fragments of the sigil left and where they might be."

The door swung open then and Crosely walked in dressed in a long, grey flowing robe. Jim suppressed a laugh but Crosely saw the smirk on his lips and turned from him in a haughty gesture of contempt.

"If you would care to accompany me to the library, Mr Slavin, I am ready to perform the summoning," he said.

"The summoning? My dear boy, no," Oscar replied, his face a picture of anxiety. "You heard Denver's story, what happened to Kralik. I forbid it, absolutely forbid it."

"Then I will perform the summoning by myself."

"Crosely, once more I say that I absolutely forbid this foolishness. It is far too dangerous for one as inexperienced as yourself, despite your obvious talents and knowledge."

"You may forbid all you like, Mr Slavin, but this is my destiny, my very reason for living, and I shall perform the summoning with or without your permission."

Oscar sighed and stood up, knocking some of his papers off the table and sending them floating to the floor. "If I cannot dissuade you then I will accompany you, if only for all our safety. But I tell you now, if this goes wrong I will not accept any responsibility and you will have to face Tempest's wrath alone."

"Have no fear, within the hour we shall know all we need to and I shall be feted by Mr Tempest for my courage, my insight and my magical skills and knowledge, Mr Slavin."

They turned to leave and Jim stood up to follow them.

"Oh no," said Crosely, the contempt in his voice unmistakable, "you can stay here, little boy. I wouldn't want you to be frightened."

They left, Crosely closing the door behind him and leaving Jim alone in the dining room, the ticking of a clock the only disturbance in the silence that settled all around.

Chapter Nineteen
The Church

St James's church stood alone in a sea of desperate housing, its spire towering above the slum dwellings and rookeries of the poor dockworkers. In the dying rays of the late evening sun its red brickwork turned into the colour of blood, as though this house of God was sweating droplets of blood like Christ on the cross. The last orange rays of the setting sun illuminated the stained glass windows for a final few seconds. And then the grey of dusk cast long shadows over the gargoyles, transforming their stone countenances into grinning, living beings.

Tempest and Johnny Chen strode through the unkempt graveyard, past tombstones tilting awkwardly and covered in creeping ivy, and graves reclaimed by nature's relentless advance, almost hidden by long grass and weeds. The church stood silhouetted against the purple sky, one flickering orange light burning in the vestry window, like a single eye observing their approach.

The two men climbed the stone steps and Johnny Chen grasped the black iron ring in the centre of the huge wooden door and pushed. The door swung inwards, silent and smooth as though out of respect for the house of God it served. The two men paused in the chapel entrance. Three columns of pews ran the length of the church to the chancel, where stood the dais and the altar. Many candles had been placed around the church, the dancing light of their fluttering flames the only illumination in the hall. Shadows flickered in the corners, as though the stone gargoyles guarding the church had crept inside and now huddled in dark recesses, waiting for the moment when they could pounce on their victims. Cobwebs hung from the tapestries on the walls and a layer of dust covered the pews and the empty tables.

"Father Michael?" Tempest called, his deep voice echoing around the church's interior. Johnny Chen's eyes flickered restlessly around the church, probing the dark corners and looking up at the vaulted ceiling. A large, leather bag hung from his shoulder and his hand crept inside, taking hold of the brass and wood implement contained within.

The vestry door opened and a small, bespectacled man bustled out. His cassock strained at the seams against his ample stomach and, despite the cool evening air, his face shone with perspiration.

"Ah, Mr Tempest, Mr Chen, I am so relieved to see you, you've no idea how unsettled I have been this evening," he said, shaking their hands and mopping his brow.

"I am sorry you are so disturbed, Father Michael," Tempest replied. "Your message communicated a certain urgency, so we set off immediately."

"Yes, yes, I am very grateful for your response." Father Michael mopped his forehead some more, casting anxious glances around the dark shadows of the church. "Please, let's go into the vestry where we can talk a little more freely."

Tempest arched an eyebrow. Apart from the three men, the church was deserted and he could not imagine being able to talk any more freely than right here, but he said nothing. They followed the priest into the vestry. Vestments hung from one wall of the tiny room and the articles for providing communion sat on a simple wooden table in an opposite corner. Another table, slightly larger and surrounded by five plain chairs, dominated the room. Upon this table sat a large, leather-bound bible, open at the book of Revelation. Candles had been placed on every available spot, their yellow flames fighting the gathering darkness.

"Please, sit down," Father Michael said, indicating the chairs.

"Your church seems to have fallen into a state of neglect," Tempest said.

"Yes, yes, St James's has been earmarked for demolition for some time now. A new railway line is being built, connecting the inner city with some of the outer lying suburbs, and the church stands in its path." Father Michael sighed. "Even the good Lord himself must bow before the march of progress and technology it seems."

"Indeed, we live in an age of science and reason, a new dawn of enlightenment in which much of the old ways are disappearing. But we are in danger, are we not Father Michael, of forgetting the God of the Old Testament, and his jealous, vengeful nature?"

"He gave up his son as an offering for us all, Mr Tempest," Father Michael said. "Let us not forget that God the Father is compassionate too."

"What can we do for you, Father? Your message suggested a certain urgency was needed."

Father Michael leaned across the table, his cassock brushing the open pages of the large Bible. "This church has been closed and scheduled for demolition for over a year now, but still I have continued to come and pray and worship into the still hours of the early morning. In the last few months, Mr Tempest, I have become very unsettled. There have been certain . . . incidents which suggest to me that a demonic presence may be manifesting itself here."

"What incidents would these be, Father Michael?"

"I spend most of my time here in the vestry, studying the Word of God and praying. I find a peace here, a stillness of atmosphere I find little of elsewhere in the city, but after darkness has fallen that changes. There are noises from the main church hall, shuffling and whispering, the occasional sound of something heavy being shifted, sometimes a squeal of delight or terror, I am not sure which."

"Perhaps your imagination gets the better of you on such nights. It is not unlikely that your demonic presence may simply be a gang of children using the empty church for their own amusements, perhaps even purposely tormenting you?"

"These thoughts crossed my own mind, and I took to walking up and down the church when I heard these disturbances. Every night I would walk up and down, and every night I found no evidence of trespassers, children or otherwise, until a week ago, when I found this . . ."

Father Michael produced a loosely tied bundle of cloth from beneath the table and placed it before Tempest and Johnny Chen. His hands shaking a little he untied the string and unfolded the squares of dark material.

Five razor-sharp, bloodstained teeth lay in the cloth. They looked as though they had been torn from the gums, scraps of flesh still hanging from the roots. But it was their pointed edges that fascinated the most, like cannibal teeth that had been filed down to points.

Johnny Chen glanced at his companion. Tempest said and did nothing to indicate the teeth meant anything to him, but Johnny Chen saw the muscles in his jaw flexing.

"I found these by the altar, in a small pool of blood. The blood had begun congealing and I had some difficulty in pulling the teeth from the floor. After that night the sounds grew louder and more intense. I began to be afraid to step outside the vestry, and then the things began knocking at the door and whispering my name, inviting me to come outside and take communion with them. I have stood here Mr Tempest and spoken aloud the Word of God to the unholy things on the opposite side of that door, and they have laughed at me."

"And yet you still come here, night after night?"

"This is the house of my Father. Where else should I go?"

Tempest looked at the teeth, picking one up and examining it closely in the yellow candlelight. The needle-sharp point pricked his thumb and drew a perfectly round drop of blood.

Johnny Chen sprang from his chair at the sudden scratching on the other side of the vestry door, like cat's claws repeatedly dragging down the wood. Tempest dropped the tooth and looked at Father Michael. His face was pale, his eyes round with fear. He nodded almost imperceptibly, but said nothing as the frenzied scratching continued and then suddenly stopped.

"Father," whispered a voice in the awful silence, "Father forgive me, for I have sinned." The thing behind the door, for the owner of that voice could not be human, started giggling.

Tempest stood up and grasped the door handle, moving to one side so that he would not be in the doorway when he opened it. He nodded to Johnny Chen who reached into the leather bag and pulled a crossbow from inside. The bow was primed and he levelled it at the door and smiled. Tempest wrenched the door open.

The doorway was empty, the subdued, flickering candlelight of the church outside the vestry seeming to mock them in the silence. Johnny Chen crept into the church hall, gripping the crossbow. Tempest followed him, waving at Father Michael to stay where he was. As the two men walked through the church, down between the rows of wooden pews, a sudden urgent whispering grew in the shadows and the recesses of the old building.

. . . *tempesttempesttempesttempest* . . .

The low, evil murmuring slowly grew in intensity, gathering in the shadows like an approaching storm. The shadows cast by the sputtering candles began to take on human form, figures huddled in the darkness uncoiling, drawing up and ready to pounce. A dark shape fell from the rafters in the vaulted ceiling, dropping like a huge, malignant spider. Johnny Chen wheeled on the spot, pointing the crossbow upright and shooting the vampire through the chest. Before the gaunt, hollow-eyed thing had finished thrashing in its death throes on the stone flagged floor the Chinaman had primed his crossbow, ready for the next attacker.

. . . *tempesttempesttempesttempest* . . .

Another vampire leapt from the shadows, an unholy squeal ripping from its mouth as it bared its bloody fangs. Tempest pulled a pistol from his jacket and shot the monster in the chest. It recoiled, screeching in agony, and collapsed to the floor where it squirmed pathetically for a few moments before lying still.

. . . *tempesttempesttempesttempest* . . .

Two more vampires appeared on either side of Johnny Chen, almost materialising out of nothingness. He shot one in the chest and, only a fraction of a second later, spun round to punch the second in the mouth. The cadaverous creature let out a howl, staggering as blood spewed from its lips and some of its teeth fell to the floor. Before it had a chance to recover Johnny Chen drew a long, thin knife and stabbed it through the heart.

The whispering stopped. In the dreadful silence that followed both Tempest and Johnny Chen cast anxious glances around the flickering shadows of the church. The silence was broken by a single cry.

"No! Dear God in Heaven, protect me against this evil!"

Father Michael was pulled from the vestry, the vampire's arm encircling his neck in a stranglehold as the priest tried vainly to struggle free.

Tattered, dirty clothing hung from the vampire's emaciated frame, it's grey flesh stretched tight over bones and sinews. Dark, empty eyes stared at the two men, eyes empty of reason or compassion. Bloody fangs protruded from its open mouth, as it hissed in anger.

Tempest pointed his gun at the thing.

"Shoot me," it hissed, "and see how useless your toys are against me, as I feast on this fresh blood."

"Your companions felt the sharp end of our toys," said Tempest.

"They were weak, but I am strong."

The priest struggled in his arms, praying in hushed, urgent tones. The vampire opened its mouth, baring its vicious fangs.

Blood and bone erupted from the vampire's forehead as the bullet sank deep into its skull. Another bullet ripped at its shoulder, and the vampire let go of the priest, who collapsed in a faint.

Incredibly the thing stood its ground, bringing up its hands to its head, feeling at the wound.

"What devilry is this?" it hissed.

"Garlic-tipped bullets," Tempest said, as the thing fell to the floor, thrashing in its death throes.

Chapter Twenty
'Razor' Bob

Inspector Arthur C. Behrends of the Metropolitan Police Force looked around uneasily at the vile, wretched regulars of Paddy's Goose. The thick cloud of filthy tobacco smoke stung at his nostrils, and the glass of cheap gin he had bought burnt the back of his throat. But he swallowed it anyway, and tried to not look too conspicuous. Even out of uniform, though, he knew that he still stood out like a sore thumb, here among the thieves, prostitutes, murderers and beggars of the East End. Hopefully he would be taken to be nothing more than a gentleman slummer, looking for cheap drink and sex. Certainly both could be found here without any difficulty.

The last thing Behrends wanted was to be found out as a policeman. He was not entirely sure he would leave the premises alive.

Maybe that was what 'Razor' Bob wanted, why he had suggested they meet here tonight. He had made it pretty clear at their last couple of meetings that he wanted nothing more to do with Behrends. Oh yes, Behrends paid his informant well, reimbursed him for the risks he took, the dangerous double life he led to supply him with information, the kind of information only a copper's nark could get you. And he could see why Bob would want out of the life, to stop taking all those risks. It was not only Behrends who risked his life associating with 'Razor' Bob in Paddy's Goose. A copper's nark would probably fare a lot worse than a copper if found out among this kind of villainous crowd.

But then that was the hold that Behrends had over Bob; get the word out on the streets of the East End that Bob was a squealer, a snitch, and his life would not be worth the three ha'pence of gin he always liked to drink at their meetings. And so Behrends kept his informant on a short leash, tempting him on with more money for yet more information, but holding the threat of exposure over him to keep him in the game.

Still, it worked both ways, didn't it? 'Razor' Bob was a valuable informant because he was so well known among the London underworld. But, because he had so many contacts, surely it would not be that difficult for him to arrange a hit on Behrends? He could make up a reason as to why this particular peeler needed to be snuffed out, nobody would argue the point too much; after all, what was the loss of one more copper to the villains of London? A cause for celebration at the very least.

So Behrends had played his dangerous game with 'Razor' Bob over the years, had squeezed him for every last bit of information he could give, squeezed him so hard sometimes he thought he might not see him again. But Bob always came back when summoned. Never let him down once, had 'Razor' Bob. He had been a valuable resource, helped Behrends in solving many of his cases, and consequently helped his rapid promotion through the police force. Behrends owed Bob a great deal, more than the money and the drink he gave him.

Maybe then, now was the time to cut him free. One last job, one last valuable piece of information to help Behrends crack this final case of his long and distinguished career, and then 'Razor' could finally go his own way, free of Behrends and his demands for information.

The Inspector took another swig of his foul drink, grimacing as it burnt its way down his throat.

Hidden away in a darkened corner of the library, Jim watched as Oscar Slavin and the young man called Alex Crosely prepared for the summoning. While Crosely talked, Oscar glanced around briefly and, for a single moment, his gaze rested on Jim, who flinched involuntarily; but then he turned back to face Crosely, and Jim relaxed again. He had chosen his hiding place well, behind the ostentatious furniture, which had been pushed to the outer edges of the room, making clear a large space in the middle. Despite the shafts of late afternoon winter sunlight radiating weakly through the French windows, much of the library was in shadow and Jim felt sure he could not be seen in his hiding place.

Jim was determined to see Crosely perform his magical invocation, and summon a spirit. No one was going to order Jim back to his room, or anywhere else for that matter. Jim had never taken orders from anyone before in his life, not even old Mulready, who had left him to his own devices for most of the time. As long as he brought in the loot, Mulready had never cared much about ordering Jim around at all.

With the furniture cleared to the outer edges of the room, and the rug rolled up, a large, empty space had been made on the hardwood floor, upon which had been drawn a magical circle. Four pentagrams had been drawn at points around the circle, and in the middle of each of these sat a burning candle.

"How very fascinating," Oscar said, regarding the magic circle, and the words written around its perimeter, with much interest. "Anaphaxeton, Tsahtsehiyah, Hadraniel. Three of the many names of Metatron, am I correct?"

"Yes, that is correct," Crosely replied. "Now, you may wish to take a seat, this will take a few minutes." Oscar sat down on a nearby chair

144

watching, with some amusement it seemed to Jim, the young occultist close his eyes and raise his hands in an attitude of supplication.

Crosely began pacing up and down inside the circle, softly chanting the names of Metatron and carving elaborate symbols in the air with a ceremonial dagger. He continued in this fashion for a few minutes, and Jim struggled against a wave of tiredness sweeping through his body, tempting him to sleep.

"We're ready to begin," Crosely said suddenly, stepping cautiously over the lines drawn on the floor, careful not disturb them, and out of the circle.

Standing with his back to Jim, facing the ever weaker sunlight, he began his prayer.

"I do invoke, conjure and command thee, O thou spirit Matsmetsiyah, to appear and to show thyself visibly unto me before this circle in fair and comely shape, without any deformity or tortuosity, by the name and—"

"Hey guys, am I too late for the sideshow?"

Denver McCade stood in the open doorway of the library, hands on hips, a cigarette hanging loosely from her mouth.

She smiled lopsidedly at Crosely, and said, "Sorry, did I put you off?"

Denver sauntered across the floor, scuffing an edge of the carefully marked out circle as she went, and sat in a sofa near to Jim's hiding place.

"Really, I must protest," Crosely spluttered, hurrying to repair the damage done to his magical symbol. "The magical circle of Anaphaxeton must remain unbroken during and for a short time after the ceremony. I can't be held responsible for any malicious spirits that might escape due to others' carelessness. And I would ask that all of you show respect for the magical invocation that is to be executed here tonight, which is the result of many years' worth of—"

"Crosely," Oscar said, leaning out of the shadows in which he was becoming enveloped, "get on with it will you? Time is short and Mr Tempest will be back soon."

"Yes, yes, of course," the magician muttered, turning back to face the last, dying rays of sunlight entering the library.

He started his conjuration once more from the beginning.

"I do invoke, conjure and command thee, O thou spirit Matsmetsiyah, to appear and to show thyself . . ."

"This guy's a real blowhard," Denver whispered. "I swear, Jim, all this chanting's gonna give me a headache."

Jim started at the mention of his name and stared at Denver. She sat with her back to him and made no physical indication that she knew of his presence.

"Don't worry," she whispered, "I won't give you up. But if this all goes pear shaped, stick with me, okay? I'm not convinced this pea-brained trickster really knows what he's doing."

" . . . and by the name Ioth, which Jacob heard from the angel wrestling him, and was delivered from the hand of Esau his brother; and by the name Anaphaxeton which . . ."

Wisps of white smoke drifted around the room, picked out by the pale winter sunlight still seeping through the French windows. Jim thought of Murmur, and the sigil burning into his host's flesh, burning so deep it scorched at the bone beneath. Murmur had shown him the skull and talked of the fool who had summoned him, too weak to control him.

" . . . I do exorcise and command thee, by the four beasts before the throne, having eyes before and behind . . ."

The sun was disappearing now, casting the library into shadow, rendering the figure of Crosely little more than a dark, indistinct blur. And yet, it seemed to Jim that the wisps of smoke within the pentagram still retained elements of the winter sun, burning with their own pale, hazy light.

" . . . I do potently exorcise thee that thou appearest here to fulfil my will in all things which seem good unto me . . ."

"Can you feel it Jim?" whispered Denver. "Can you feel it?"

Suddenly the freezing cold hit Jim, enveloped his body, overwhelmed his spirit to the point of utter despair. The air shimmered before him, and he felt that he could see movement; the indefinable, subtle movement of ghosts flitting across his field of view, so indistinct he could have been persuaded that he imagined them.

" . . . I conjure thee, beautiful and majestic servant of God, Matsmetsiyah, to appear at my will and pleasure, in this place, in this circle, without noise, deformity . . ."

The wisps and curls of smoke in the magical circle radiated their own unearthly light now and swirled around and around as though caught in a whirlwind of their own making. Jim watched fascinated as the ghastly light began to take on a definite form.

"Come then, Matsmetsiyah, to do my will," Crosely declared, finishing his conjuration.

An unearthly silence filled the room, as the last echo of Crosely's voice disappeared into the ether. Jim trembled, the cold seeping deep into his marrow. His heart pounded so loud he was sure it would give away his presence at any moment.

The grandfather clock in the hall began chiming the hour, bludgeoning a hole through the silence of the library.

And then . . . nothing.

"What's happening, Crosely?" Oscar said, invisible now within the shadows.

"I don't understand," the magician muttered. "I don't understand."

Jim could feel the warmth flooding back through his body, felt his heartbeat slowing down. He looked at the wisps of smoke within the magical circle, drifting away in a light breeze, no longer emitting their supernatural light.

Had he imagined it all? The cold, the indefinable movement of the spectres flitting across his vision?

"Really, Crosely," Oscar said, sounding uncharacteristically angry, "against my better judgement I gave you a chance to prove yourself here, but I begin to feel that you are simply wasting my time. I wish I had never set eyes on you, that your family had never entrusted your education into my care."

Oscar strode out of the library, back to his papers and documents.

"Like I said," Denver whispered, "nothing but a pea-brained trickster."

Denver stood up and left the library, not even casting as much as a glance in Crosely's direction.

Jim watched silently as Crosely remained standing alone in front of his magical circle, the four candles casting a soft glow across his face. Finally, with a shake of his head, he too turned and left the room.

Jim pulled himself awkwardly out of his hiding place, stretching his limbs stiffened up from his enforced inactivity. He walked over to the magical circle. The four white candles, in the pentagrams, were still burning. Jim looked at the symbols and words scrawled around the circle, and the ceremonial dagger lying on the floor in the middle.

Had he imagined it all?

Had he?

Better go, thought Jim. He did not want Tempest to find him here when he returned from wherever he had gone.

As he turned to leave, Jim's heel scuffed the chalk outline of the magical circle, creating a tiny gap.

He walked to the door and opened it a sliver, peering out into the hall. Seeing that the hall was deserted, he quickly left the room, shutting the door behind him.

If he had stayed a moment longer, he would have seen the gap he unknowingly created in the magical circle widen of its own accord, and he would have felt the temperature dropping once more.

And then he would have seen the candles snuffed out one by one, plunging the library into darkness.

Chapter Twenty-One
The Gibborium

'Razor' Bob twitched and jerked his head whenever he spoke. When he was completely sober the twitch was so slight as to be almost unnoticeable. But 'Razor' Bob was rarely sober, and the more he drank, the more pronounced the twitch became. He stammered, too; and, like the twitch, the more he drank the worse became the stammer.

It was a wonder to his various contacts that he came by the information that he did. Perhaps it was his pathetic appearance: the purple scar running diagonally across his face and half closing his eye; the dirty, smelly clothes that he always wore; the filthy, trembling hands; and the fingers dark brown from all the cigarettes he smoked. Surely the last thought that would cross anybody's mind upon coming across this pathetic specimen of humanity was that he could be of any use, or importance, to anyone. And so perhaps people talked a little too freely when around him, not realising that he was actually paying attention; that his mind, as sharp as the razor that he carried with him and from which he earned his nickname, was assimilating and storing the information he was hearing for use at a later date.

After all, knowledge is power, as his old man had been fond of saying.

Knowledge is power.

Right at this moment, the knowledge that Inspector Arthur C. Behrends of the Metropolitan Police Force was sweating in terror at the possibility of being found out as a policeman, gave Bob a profound feeling of power.

He watched as Behrends mopped his brow and cast a swift, nervous glance around him.

"Yer alright," said Bob, his head twitching spasmodically. "There ain't n . . . n . . . no one's gonna recognise yer 'ere. When w . . . w . . . were the last time yer were on the beat? Life's b . . . b . . . brutal and short round these parts."

"I still think you could have chosen a more appropriate place for us to meet," said Behrends, casting another anxious glance around him. "After all, surely you're in as much danger of being found out as I am?"

'Razor' Bob laughed, and threw back the last of his gin.

"Nah, this ain't m . . . m . . . my stompin' grounds, this ain't," he said. "Now, why don't yer b . . . b . . . buy me another drink, and then we'll get down to business, alright?"

Behrends leaned forward in his chair, and said, "Another drink, always another drink, right Bob? Well, I'll buy you another drink after we've discussed business, and not before. I want you clear headed on this one, no slip-ups. This is too important."

"W . . . w . . . when were the last time I let yer d . . . d . . . down, eh?" Bob said, his head twitching violently to one side, as though he was winking at the Inspector.

"Never, you've been an excellent informant over the years, I have to admit. But this is more important than anything else you've done for me. This case could be the making of me, and believe me, if it is, I'll see you right, Bob, I'll see you right."

"In'restin'," said 'Razor' Bob, also leaning forward on the table, drawing in close to Behrends, their noses almost touching. "Then let's talk b . . . b . . . business, shall we?"

Jim struggled with the bedroom window, the rusty hinges protesting as it finally swung shut with a dull thump. What on earth had possessed Mary to air his room at this time of the evening?

He looked out across the rooftops and at the purple, darkening night sky. His reflection gazed back at him, distorted slightly by the ripples and imperfections in the rolled glass.

Tomorrow he would go to the Salvation Army headquarters on Queen Victoria Street, and find George and Emma.

What they would do next, though, he did not know.

Emma might try to persuade them to join the Salvation Army; they would have shelter and food at least. Not much chance of Jim falling for that, though.

Maybe he could find work in one of the factories, one of the match factories, possibly. He had heard they paid good money there, on account of the sulphur fumes supposedly being so dangerous. Or perhaps he would look for work down at the docks. They were always looking for hard workers at the docks. Or maybe he could sell matches, like the match seller he met the other day. That would be easy money.

And him and George would save up their money and buy that barrow. Maybe Emma had kept Jim's money she had found, and then they would have something to start off with, something to help them through until Jim found some work.

At least he did not have to worry about Mulready anymore.

Jim swallowed at the sudden memory of Mulready burning and burning before him, his scorched flesh dropping from his bony frame in fiery chunks. Then he thought of Marlow Crimps, chasing Jim through the tunnels, beneath the padding-kens and rookeries of the Dials, in a murderous rage, his shirt splashed crimson with the blood of the people who had helped Jim escape.

And then he thought of Murmur, and his shoulders tingled, as if he needed reminding of the Devil's Imp slashing at his back with its venomous claws.

No, Jim did not need reminding of any of it; he would remember yesterday's events for a long time to come.

Gazing idly out of the window, and daydreaming about his future, about how things would be different for him and George from now on, Jim suddenly became aware of movement in the ripples of the windowpane. He watched, entranced, as the amorphous mass, shifting and changing shape as it undulated through the flaws and blemishes of the glass pane, drew closer to him.

It was only when he heard the soft grunt, the exhalation of breath, that the spell broke, and he turned to face the thing behind him.

"Hunh," grunted Marlow Crimps, his creased, weather-beaten face still bearing splatters of blood. In one filthy hand he clutched his serrated, blood-encrusted knife.

Jim backed up against the window he had been looking through just a moment before, pressing himself flat against the glass.

"See this?" Crimps said, pointing at his black eye patch with his knife, resting its sharpened tip against the rough leather. "There ain't nothin' can get past ol' Crimps' all-seein' eye, an' ain't that the truth. Yer can run all yer like, lad, but ol' Crimps' all-seein' eye'll find yer in the end."

Slowly Jim searched out the handle of the window, his fingers closing around it, ready to pull the window open and leap from it.

"Aaahh, no lad, it were a devil of a job to get that window open, and yer had a devil of a job yersel' tryin' to shut it, an' don't deny it. I'm gonna kill yer, boy, and there ain't no point tryin' to put it off. But if yer stay still, then mebbe I'll kill yer quick like, an' not make too much fuss about it. But if yer thinkin' o' strugglin', an' tryin' to escape, then I'll take my time, 'ave a bit o' pride an' enjoyment in my work, mebbe even let you have a good look at yer guts an' stuff before I finish yer off. Now, 'ow 'bout that, there's not many as can say they've seen their insides, is there?"

"It weren't my fault," Jim said. "Old Mulready, he'd been drinking, and he were mad, and he were gonna kill Slum Lassie Sal, and George too."

"Yeah, that's right," Crimps said, his one, bloodshot eye blinking slowly at him. "An' now I'm gonna kill you."

Crimps took another step forward, reaching out with his free hand. Jim pressed back against the window, looking from side to side, but it was no good, he was hemmed in by the dresser and the wardrobe.

151

As Crimps closed his large, dirty hand around Jim's throat, raising his knife above his head, he began grunting with demented anticipation. Jim's stomach turned over as the foul, sickly sweet stink of Crimps' breath washed over him.

Suddenly a woman's scream ripped apart the quiet of the house, followed by the crack of a gunshot. Distracted, Crimps momentarily relaxed his grip on Jim's throat, and turned his head towards the source of the scream.

But a moment was all Jim needed. He knocked Crimps' hand away from his throat and dove for the floor, scrabbling between the big man's legs. Crimps grunted, and grabbed at Jim's ankle, but Jim kicked and squirmed, twisting free from his grip once more.

He pulled himself to his feet and dashed for the bedroom door. Crimps' knife slammed into the heavy oak panelling of the door beside Jim's head. He looked at the blood-caked knife shivering from the impact less than an inch from his face, and felt the vibration coursing through the wood beneath his fingertips.

Without looking back, Jim pulled open the door and ran into the hallway. Relief flooded through his body as he saw Johnny Chen standing at the head of the stairs.

"Master Kerrigan," the Chinaman said, as Jim ran to him. "You must go back to your room now, Denver . . ."

Jim ran behind Johnny Chen, and turned, pointing back to his open bedroom door.

Marlow Crimps walked out of the bedroom, clutching his knife once more.

"Hunh," he grunted, when he saw the Chinaman shielding his intended victim.

"Go downstairs," Johnny Chen said, "down to the kitchen. Don't stop to talk to anyone, just go straight down to the kitchen and wait for me."

Jim turned and ran, taking the steps three at a time.

Johnny Chen regarded Crimps implacably for a moment as he strutted towards him, tightening his grip on his knife.

"Well, well, what we got 'ere, eh?" Crimps said. "I do believe it's a Chinaman. 'Ow'd the Chinaman like to 'ave a little dance with ol' Marlow Crimps, then?"

Johnny Chen cracked his knuckles and smiled.

Crimps paused, a look of uncertainty passing over his creased face.

Jim ran into the kitchen and skidded to a halt on the stone flagged floor. Mary stood at the worktop, her back to Jim, chopping a joint of meat.

"Mary!" Jim gasped. "Crimps has broken into the house, an' he's trying to kill me."

The cook said nothing, but continued chopping the joint of meat. Jim watched silently as she raised the meat cleaver above her head, the red juices of the joint running down the silver blade, and then brought it down with a dull *thunk!*

"Mary?"

Thunk!

Jim stepped softly around the kitchen table as Mary continued working.

Thunk!

He could see her profile now, the veins on her forearms standing proud as she manhandled the joint of meat, her hands bathed in its red juices, and more red spotted across her face.

Thunk!

Pulling the cleaver free, Mary turned and looked at Jim. Her eyes rolled back in their sockets until all he could see were the whites. The flesh on her face looked slack, as though all the muscle had been removed, and a thick string of drool hung from her open mouth. She raised the meat cleaver above her head once more, and then hurled it with all her force at the young boy.

The cleaver spun through the air, nicking Jim on the arm as he dodged out of the way, and clattered to the floor behind him. Sitting on the kitchen floor, shocked and confused, he glanced down at his arm and saw a dark red patch growing ever larger on his torn shirtsleeve. He looked up at the cook, who had picked up a long, fat steak knife, and was running her finger lovingly down its sharpened edge. She turned to look at Jim once more. Jim pulled himself up off the cold floor and ran for the door, his heart pounding in his chest.

An instant later the cook flung the steak knife at him.

Jim threw himself under the expanse of the kitchen table, scrabbling over the chilly flag stoned floor, the knife skidding across the tabletop. Behind him he could hear Mary screaming, and pulling more vicious kitchen utensils from the wall to throw at him.

And then he heard the other scream again.

The scream that had distracted Crimps.

Only, it was not a scream, more of a . . . shout?

There it was again, clearer this time.

"Yeeeehaaah!"

It was Denver!

A sudden onslaught of kitchen utensils rained around Jim on the stone floor, and over him on the tabletop, a deafening clatter of knives and skewers and pans. Jim cowered under the table, looking for an escape route. He could see the kitchen door, half open; all he had to do was make a dash for it, dodging the deranged cook's impressive marksmanship with knives and skewers on the way.

But he had to escape from the kitchen.

"Yeeeeeeeehhaaaahhhh!!"

Listening to Denver shouting, Jim thought that it might be a good idea to leave the house altogether.

"YEEEEEEHHAAAAAAAAHHHH!!!!"

Denver leapt into the kitchen, her face flushed, and her eyes darting excitedly around her. She had strapped a holster to her trousers, and now she pulled the Colt .45 from it, and spun it around her finger several times.

Mary had stopped hurling kitchen equipment at Jim, and stood entranced at the sight of Denver.

"Well I'll be a doggone, mangy old cur! Look at the little boy hiding under the table," she said, spying Jim on all fours, and looking up at her.

She stopped spinning the gun, levelled it at Jim, and pulled back the hammer.

Jim clapped his hands over his head, and waited for Denver to pull the trigger. He wondered if he would hear the explosion of the gun barrel before he died.

Tempest stepped into the kitchen behind Denver, both hands gripping the handle of a large brass bedpan. He swung the bedpan at Denver, cracking it across her skull, and she collapsed, unconscious at Tempest's feet.

The Colt .45 slid across the kitchen floor, coming to a halt by Jim.

Before he had a chance to react he felt the cook's calloused hands gripping his ankles. Suddenly resuming her deranged, high-pitched screaming, she began dragging Jim from underneath the table. As he slid backwards on his stomach, kicking and struggling, he reached for the gun.

Jim rolled onto his back, still lashing out with his feet, as Mary pulled him clear of the table. Gobbets of spit flecked his face as Mary shrieked at him, picking up the meat cleaver once more. She stood astride him, one hand on his chest pinning him to the floor, the other brandishing the cleaver above her head.

Jim held the gun awkwardly in both hands, trying to point it at Mary's head, but unused to its weight and shape.

Above the sound of the cook's endless screams, Jim could hear Tempest shouting, "For God's sake, boy, shoot her!"

Jim looked at Mary, into her unfocused eyes rolling back once more in her eye sockets, her fleshy jowls spotted with red.

Tempest slammed the bedpan into her face, hitting her with such force he bent the brass handle.

Her heavy body trembled with the shock of the impact, and she dropped the cleaver to the floor beside Jim.

Still standing, the deranged cook turned to face Tempest, a slow smile spreading across her thick lips as blood began pouring from her broken nose.

Tempest hit her again.

Oscar Slavin opened the drawing room door a sliver and peered out into the hallway.

"Is she still there?" said Crosely.

"No, I think she has gone downstairs to the kitchen," said Oscar.

"Thank God for that."

Oscar closed the door, and turned to look at his young companion.

"God? I thought you worshipped deities other than God."

"I worship no one. When I call spirits forth they do my bidding, not I theirs."

"Except today."

"I can't be blamed for this, someone must have damaged the integrity of the magic circle of Anaphaxeton that I created in the library. You saw what that cocky American cowgirl did to the circle. I warned everyone about the dangers."

"What exactly is happening out there Crosely?"

Crosely said nothing for a moment, and glanced at the floor uncomfortably. Then he said, "During the summoning of a specific spirit or deity, other spirits are sometimes released too. That is why it is important that the circle of protection remain unbroken, so that the spirits cannot go free, and cause havoc."

"You mean to say that Denver is possessed by something that you unknowingly summoned?"

He paused again, as though weighing his words carefully, and said, "Yes. To be specific, I think she has been possessed by a Gibborium."

"A what?"

"Gibborium. Demonic, mischievous little spirits, also known as Terrors, and Derangers. I think there's probably more than one out there."

"More than one?"

"Yes, yes, I would think there are probably two of them at least. They possess a person for a while, causing mayhem, but they are only minor demons, and struggle to inhabit anybody for long."

"And what happens then?"

"Oh they tend to jump from person to person, until they find someone who is particularly dull of wit and intelligence. Then they have been known to possess someone for a long, long time."

* * * *

Keeping Johnny Chen in his sights all the time, Crimps slowly knelt down and began patting the floor around him until he found his knife. As he stood up, he wiped the blood from his lips with the back of his hand, and spat a fragment of tooth across the hall.

Getting past the Chinaman was proving to be more difficult than he had anticipated.

"Hunh," he grunted. "That's some fancy moves yer've got there, Chinaman."

Johnny Chen stretched his arms above his head, and then slowly lowered them, calmly regarding his adversary at all times.

Crimps slashed at the air before him with his knife, and chuckled.

"But ain't I got a couple o' fancy moves meself?" he said.

Johnny Chen tensed, ready for the next attack. He needed to finish this quickly, go downstairs and help the others. It worried him that Denver had suddenly stopped her shouting.

He watched as Crimps worked his jaw, his single eye narrowing down to a tight little slit as he tensed, ready to pounce.

But then the villainous old man's body suddenly relaxed, and the knife fell from his hand. Crimps shook his head, as though trying to clear it of an incessant buzzing. He tried walking toward the Chinaman, and staggered slightly, his shoulders slumped and rounded.

Johnny Chen took a step back, wondering if this was some strange kind of act to trap him unawares.

It was no act. Crimps' entire body began to tremble and pulsate. As Johnny Chen watched, fascinated, he noticed the skin on Crimps' face coming alive, quivering and undulating as though hundreds of maggots crawled just beneath the surface.

Crimps closed his one good eye, and when he opened it again it glowed with a demonic, unearthly light that had not been there before.

"Hunh," he grunted.

Swifter than he had ever moved before, Crimps retrieved his knife and leapt at Johnny Chen, making frenzied slashing motions in the air.

The Chinaman stepped aside just in time, the knife slicing a button from his waistcoat. Crimps snarled in frustration, spinning round on the spot, the knife again slicing though the air Johnny Chen had occupied only moments before.

The Chinaman saw his opportunity and seized Crimps by the wrist, trying to use his own momentum against him, and overbalance him. But Crimps, suddenly possessed of a demonic energy, was too quick for him.

He fell against Johnny Chen, pinning him to the wall with his bulk, and head-butted him.

Colourful fireworks exploded across the Chinaman's vision and, stunned, he felt himself pulled to the floor.

"Hunh," Crimps grunted again, sitting on his chest and holding his knife against his throat.

A gunshot exploded in the confines of the hall, and Crimps yelped like a wounded dog. He leapt off Johnny Chen and backed away from the three figures standing at the top of the stairs, blood flowing from his shoulder.

Denver, standing between Jim and Tempest, pointed her gun at Crimps' hunched, retreating figure.

"Hold it right there mister," she said.

Crimps ignored Denver and stared at Jim, a flicker of recognition showing in his contorted features. Growling his anger, he turned and ran for Jim's bedroom.

The Colt .45 kicked in Denver's hand as she fired at the empty space left by Crimps. As one, Tempest, Jim and Denver ran after him, but they were too late.

By the time they got to the bedroom, Marlow Crimps was gone.

Chapter Twenty-Two
Tom's Last Chance

How many chances did a man deserve in his life? How many chances to make good his life, to be able to look after himself and the ones he loved? To get a job and provide a roof over his family, to feed them, and clothe them, and maybe, just once in a while, to take them somewhere special away from the daily drudgery of simply existing?

Some people were born into wealth, and some were born beneath a lucky star and it didn't matter what their station in life as a babe in arms, because they could do no wrong, and made their fortunes without even trying.

Some men made their fortune through sheer hard work, and by grasping every opportunity that came their way, and some made their fortune in adventurous travels in undiscovered parts of the world.

Some men stole, and cheated and murdered.

And then there were men like Tom, sitting on the muddy cobblestones of Ratcliffe Highway in the darkest hours before the dawn, waking from an alcohol-induced coma, and looking at his bruised, bleeding knuckles.

Pulling his worn, tattered jacket closer about him in a vain attempt to fend off the cold and the damp, Tom began struggling to his feet. Suddenly his vision doubled and blurred, and he felt the blood rushing through his veins, making him feel giddy and nauseous. He sat down again, reaching out his battered, bloodied hands to steady himself.

No good, he thought, not ready to stand up yet. But he needed to get up, to get moving, to start walking. It didn't matter where, the important thing was to move; it was the only way he could think of to escape the memories of what he had done, of what he had become.

But now, sitting on the wet, cold ground, in the dreadful silence of the night, he had no choice but to remember, and to confront those memories.

How many chances did a man deserve in his life?

It seemed to Tom that he had run out of chances, and that a miracle was what he needed for his wife and children to escape the life of misery and torture he had created for them.

It had not always been that way, when he and Martha were first married, eight years ago.

They had both had high hopes for the future. Neither of them had any money, and they had a child on the way, but Tom was young and strong, and willing to work every hour he could to support his family. He had ambitions to lift his family out of the slums of the East End, to make a better life for them.

They found a room above a tailor's sweatshop for eight shillings a week, and Martha worked in the tailor's by day, while Tom went out looking for work on the docks. But competition for work was fierce among the men of the East End; so fierce that fights often broke out among the crowds of 'casuals' and 'irregulars'. Tom often came home with his clothes torn, and stories of fights so brutal that he saw men's ears ripped from their heads. But he kept at it; he had to, as Martha's work in the sweatshop barely covered their rent, let alone provided them with food and clothing and heat for their shabby little room.

The work came, but it was irregular and infrequent. Sometimes Tom earned thirty shillings in a week, and then sometimes nothing for a fortnight or more.

As the years passed, and the work became less frequent, Tom began to spend more time away from home, in the local pubs, wasting his wages on drink and petty gambling with the other dockers. Often he returned home drunk, in terrible black moods, and would argue with Martha.

Last year he started hitting her.

That first morning, when he awoke from his drunken stupor, thick-headed and wondering why his hands were stiff and sore, he cried as he realised what he had done. He begged Martha's forgiveness and bathed her bruises with warm soapy water, promising he would never hit her again.

But his promise was a hollow one, and soon the beatings became a regular part of their married life together. And every morning Tom would wake up and see Martha's bruised face, and he would cry.

They had a second child now, a little baby boy, sickly with the damp and the cold. His children were the only reason he kept his sanity and he held fast to a promise that he would never hit them, at least.

Earlier tonight, that had all changed. Tom had come home in a drunken rage, and assaulted Martha and Kate. Martha had tried to protect their daughter, fending off the worst of the blows, sobbing and begging him to stop, and praying that he would leave the baby alone. Finally his fury had passed, and he had stood in the open doorway of their dirty little room, looking blank eyed at his family, and breathing deep, ragged lungfuls of stagnant air, his fists clenching and unclenching by his sides.

As he came to, looking at Martha and Kate huddled together on the floor, sobbing and clutching at each other, their thin arms and faces mottled with bruises, and the baby bawling in the corner of the squalid room, Tom was overwhelmed with an utter sense of self-loathing and disgust so deep he could not bring himself to look at his family any longer.

And so he turned and fled into the welcome embrace of the freezing night, ran to the nearest pub and drowned his self-disgust in more of the alcohol which had already torn his life apart.

Now, several hours later, the effects of the booze wearing off, Tom was once more consumed by a hatred of everything he had become, and a sense of helplessness that that was all he could hope to be from now on.

Tom had had his chance at a decent life; Martha was a good woman who deserved better than him, and his children deserved a father, not a drunken bully.

Tom pulled himself to his feet once more and began staggering down the road, unaware of where he was going or what he might do when he got there. As he walked he was overcome with emotion, and he started to cry, the pain spilling from the depths of his being in great, powerful sobs. He walked like this for ten minutes or more, weaving his way down the street, howling his grief, his arms sometimes outstretched to the darkened sky above him, his head sometimes bowed to the ground below him. But moving, always moving, in a futile attempt to escape the monster he had become.

Finally, as the last of his strength left his body, bringing him close to the point of collapse once more, something compelled him to look up, to see the place he had been destined to arrive at when he had begun his apparent aimless wandering.

Yes! This was it; his last chance. His last chance at turning his life around, and providing a decent living for his family, and showing them the love they so deserved.

Tom staggered into the grounds of the churchyard, weaving unsteadily between the dilapidated, moss-covered gravestones, towards the gloomy, imposing church.

They said that the church would be demolished soon, and all the graves dug up, to make way for the new railway they were building. Tom paused, leaning against one of the gravestones. No rest for the wicked, or the good either then; not even in death.

But the church was still here, and would serve his purpose for tonight.

One last chance to make things right.

One last chance . . . for redemption.

Tom staggered up the worn stone steps to the great, dark doors, the woodwork decorated with black iron studs. He pushed at the doors and they swung open easily and silently, not even the creaking of hinges to disturb the silence of the night.

Staggering down the length of the church between pews dimly perceived in the darkness, Tom began sobbing again, his hands held out before him in an attitude of supplication, grasping desperately for one last chance of hope; hope for a better future, a life worth living.

"Oh God," he cried. "Oh dear God, Jesus, please help me."

He fell on his knees on the stone flagged floor and his body sank forward until his forehead touched the chill ground. He remained like this for several minutes, alternately crying and whispering his prayers to the God above.

Finally, his outpouring of emotion having drained him of what little strength he had had left, Tom dragged himself to a pew and sat down on the hard wooden seat.

Maybe God had heard him; maybe everything would be different from now on.

Maybe . . .

Tom looked up at the sound of movement, and voices. Two shadowed figures were talking as they walked into the church, and behind them scurried countless more bodies, flitting this way and that, leaping and scuttling between the pews.

Tom shrank back into the shadows, hoping and praying that he would not be discovered; something evil and malignant emanated from these people.

The two men stopped walking, and the things around them stopped also.

"Tomorrow night, Talos, and the fragments of the sigil will be complete once more."

"And then begins the eternal night," Talos said.

"Yes, the eternal night, and you and your vampires will have a river of blood upon which to slake your thirst forever."

One of the vampires struggled towards Talos, dragging a large canvas bag behind it.

"We want to drink its blood," it hissed.

Talos glanced at the bag and then back at the man, ignoring the vampire's request.

"Tempest is close on your heels once more, Kralik," he said.

"Ah, Tempest, Tempest," spat Kralik. "Once I have completed the summoning, you won't ever have to worry about Tempest again. Perhaps I was a day late in tracking down the fragment to Antrobus's shop, but the fat old fool soon told me who he had sold it to. And now there is just one piece left, and Tempest has no chance of catching me now."

"We want to drink its blood," hissed the vampire again.

Tom risked raising his head a little above the pew to see the bag better. A feeling of horror overwhelmed him as he saw that something inside the bag was struggling to get out.

"Open the bag," Talos said.

The vampire pulled at the rough twine, and the bag fell open. Tom bit his fist to prevent the cry spilling from his mouth as he watched the little girl crawl out, her hair all messed up, her face and arms covered in scratches.

The vampire pulled her to her feet, and she began crying quietly.

She looked to be about the same age as Tom's daughter Kate.

Talos held out a hand and said, "Bring her to me."

The vampire roughly pulled at her, half walking, half dragging her to his master.

The little girl's sobs grew in intensity, shuddering through her frail body. She wore a pale blue dress, ripped in places and smudged with dirt. Tom noticed now that there was a small gash on the side of her neck.

Talos knelt down and took the girl gently in his arms, wiping away the tears from her face.

"You have suffered much," he said softly. "Too much for such a short life as yours. I should have killed you hours ago, but instead, like the cat with the mouse, we have played a cruel game with you, needlessly increasing your torment."

The child said nothing, more tears flowing freely down her face.

"And yet," he whispered, "I cannot deprive them. They must feed."

"No!" Tom shouted, unable to contain himself any longer. "Leave her alone!"

He leapt over the pews, dodging the vampires as they reached out for him. More of the ghastly things surrounded him, reaching out and dragging him down as he fought and punched. There were too many of them, and within a few seconds he was overcome.

"Bring him here," commanded Talos.

Squirming and struggling he was pulled towards their leader, getting his first good look at him. His dark eyes pierced Tom to the depths of his soul, and he felt an icy chill surge through his body.

"Would you sacrifice yourself for this girl? A life for a life, blood for blood?"

Tom nodded, his body seized by a sudden, uncontrollable trembling.

"Go," said Talos, turning to the child and pushing her away from him. "Run, run with all your might, for tonight you live."

As Tom watched, the little girl, sobbing now, turned and ran down the length of the church, stopping at the open door to look back.

"Go on!" Tom shouted. "Run!"

The girl disappeared from view, and Tom turned back to the horror that surrounded him.

"I cannot deprive them," Talos said. "They must feed."

Tom looked up at the crucifix on the wall above the altar.

How many chances did a man deserve in his life?

One last chance to make things right.

One last chance . . . for redemption.

Chapter Twenty-Three
London Wakes Up

The black cat with the green eyes padded through the bustling crowds of people, weaving between their legs, his black tail swishing behind him. Sometimes a young child might bend down to pet him or yank at his tail, but the cat simply scampered away, leaving the child to be scolded by his mother.

Lucifer ran on, over the cobblestones slick with water and oil, his nose tingling with the smell of freshly caught fish. The Billingsgate Market stallholders knew him well by now. So regular were his early morning visits that they ignored him and carried on with their business. Standing on their tables, in their greasy, fish-smelling trousers, the fishmongers competed for customers, advertising their goods by shouting at the tops of their voices.

"Had-had-had-haddick!"

"Fine cock crabs! All alive O!"

"Now or never! Mussels a penny a quart! What do yer think to that then?!"

"Oy! Oy! Oy! Fine grazzling sprats! All large and no small!"

Lucifer ran around the huge black oyster bags, glistening bright in the early morning sun, and between the legs of the porters, carrying sacks of fish on their shoulders, and cursing and laughing at each other. He stopped to inspect a large crab slowly crawling sideways underneath a table, until the crab was picked up and thrown back into its heap.

Someone threw a fish head at Lucifer, and he heard the coarse laughter behind him as he began running again, past the fishmongers' carts and the costermongers' barrows.

He ran and ran, until he found what he wanted; the fat, middle-aged lady in her apron, unloading the piles of slimy wet haddock and cod onto her table. From her apron pockets hung cod tails, and this is what the cat was after. As quick as a lightning strike, Lucifer stood on his hind legs, his front paws against the woman's legs, and pulled a cod tail from her apron. The woman shouted at Lucifer, but she was too late, he was already dashing through the market once more, his prize between his teeth.

Finding a quiet corner, he hunched down over his plunder, licking at the scaly flesh and purring loudly. After eating the fish and crunching its bones, Lucifer left the market, dashing between legs and under tables, and on through early morning London.

He ran down the side streets and dirty alleyways, into the poorer areas of the city. The rag-gatherers were out now, poking their sticks into the piles of rubbish in the back streets, looking for anything they could sell or eat. Sometimes he would be chased by one of these pitiful beggars, hoping to feast on some cat's meat for breakfast, maybe. But Lucifer was always too quick for these decrepit old men and easily escaped them.

Finally he came to his next destination, the tailor's sweatshop, where he leapt on the windowsill, and peered inside the dark, overcrowded room.

A man and woman, with their three young children, shared this single room, where they slept, ate and worked. The children were picking at their breakfast, their faces blank with hunger and misery.

"Blackie!" the youngest child suddenly cried, a smile splitting his grimy face in two, and ran to the window, leaving his meagre breakfast of bread and tea forgotten behind him.

Lucifer purred contentedly as the boy stroked him, and tickled him behind his ears. After a while the child began tugging at the cat's collar, examining its strange symbols. Lucifer rubbed his head against the boy's hand, purring even louder, their regular early morning ritual almost complete now.

"Shoo! Shoo!" shouted the thin, tired-looking woman, bustling towards him and waving a dirty rag before her. He jumped from the sill back into the street, and looked up at the boy and his mother from relative safety.

The mother put her arm around the boy's shoulder and hugged him close.

"Ain't I told you before, don't play with the cat. There's summat not right about that cat. You stay away from it."

Lucifer turned and ran.

"Bye, Blackie!" the boy shouted.

On he scampered, back towards the West End, past the running patterers and chaunters selling their pamphlets and ballads; the old men with their trays of cough drops and hot elder wine; the Highland bagpipe players, the Ethiopian serenaders and the gruff, gaunt sword swallower shouting out his next trick.

"You have seen me swallow coal, you have seen me swallow fire. Now you will see me swallow sawdust!"

On he ran, through the West End, dodging the hansom cabs and the kicks of the horses, and then down the quieter side streets, jumping over walls and squeezing through tiny gaps just wide enough for his thin, supple body. Finally he jumped through the broken, first-floor window of a sombre, dilapidated building, fronted by a rundown shop with a wooden sign upon which was scrawled a single word: 'Magick'.

The inside was dark and cool, and Lucifer's ears twitched at the faint sound of rats and spiders scuttling beneath the floorboards.

The cat padded silently along the bloodstained landing, and down the stairs. The broken shop window had been boarded up with rotten planks of wood hammered crudely into the frame. The cat ran into the back of the shop, threading his way between upturned boxes and crates, their evil contents spilling onto the dirty floor. His master was gone, Lucifer could sense that, but he would not have gone far. Murmur needed Lucifer, depended upon him too much, to be far from his side for long.

Denver McCade sat on the front steps of Tempest's house, watching the fine ladies and gentlemen go by, and smoked a cigarette. She was quite a sight, in her hard-wearing trousers and shirt, looking like a casual labourer taking a tea break. She stared right back at anyone she caught staring at her, and they soon looked away, flustered by her brash attitude.

Denver felt twitchy and unsettled. Since waking up this morning, she found that she could not sit still for more than a couple of minutes; she felt trapped and hemmed in by the house.

She also knew that if she listened to any more of Crosely's whingeing about the integrity of his magic circle having been violated, she would have to shoot him.

So she came outside and sat on the front steps of Caxton Tempest's house, and smoked her cigarette.

The cigarette helped calm her down, but not as much as she would have liked.

What she really needed right now was an opium cigarette.

Carefully she felt the back of her head, running her fingers over the painful lump on her scalp. Tempest sure had hit her hard, but then it had done the trick, and when she had woken up a few seconds later she was no longer possessed.

That had been weird, weirder than any other experience in her life; the feeling of another entity, another being of such evil and malice inhabiting her body, sharing her space with her own spirit. She wondered if Kralik had felt that too, if he still felt it now. After all these years, though, could there be anything left of the man she had once loved, except a shell of flesh and bone in which lived an evil, demonic presence?

Denver took another drag on her cigarette. Thankfully she could not remember too much of her own experience. All that really remained was a feeling of utter horror and self-loathing; enough to understand why Murmur might want to obliterate his existence occasionally with a trip to Moon Lee's.

So here she was, living in Caxton Tempest's world less than forty-eight hours, and already she had been possessed by a demon and hit over the head with a bedpan.

"Well, girl," she said, "that's what you gotta expect when you hang around with the great and mighty Caxton Tempest."

She should never have come here. It had seemed like a good idea that night, after Johnny Chen found her, and she rescued Jim from Murmur; just drop by Tempest's place, say hi, and ask what in hell was going on? But no, so far it had not worked out like that. She had hoped for some answers, but had received nothing more than a sore head and a bad case of demonic possession. And she still hadn't told him everything, still hadn't told him about the Order of Ahriman's questions, their incessant, relentless questions.

Who is Caxton Tempest?
Where is Caxton Tempest?
Why does he hunt vampires?
Where did he disappear to for all those years?
Why are the Council of Seven so afraid of him?

How the hell was she supposed to know? She had never even met him before. But she soon came to realise they asked everyone the same question, every poor sucker they caught in their trap and kept locked up in their dungeons beneath their mansion on East Fifty-sixth Street. And there were plenty of them, including her old friend Murmur.

And so she had come to Tempest's house, hoping for answers.

But what she had found, that foggy night at Caxton Tempest's house, had totally confounded her; Jim, lying in Tempest's arms, half dead from the Devil's Imp poison. Denver had watched in silence as Tempest laid him gently on the bed and began tenderly ministering to him as though he were his own flesh and blood.

Denver sucked hard on the cigarette, drawing the smoke deep into her lungs, imagining it was the opium, helping her to forget.

There was too much to forget now, though, too many memories, gnawing away at her, plaguing her nights with unseen terrors, indefinable horrors. The longer she lived, the more she saw, the worse it became. Five years spent wandering aimlessly from place to place had not exactly been easy, but it had the advantage of not allowing her the time to form any close relationships. If you had no one you loved, then there was no chance of ever losing them.

Denver flicked the cigarette away from her, and it landed on the street in a shower of sparks.

This was doing her no good, no good at all. Maybe she could just stop by Moon Lee's, just one more time.

It wouldn't do any harm.

"Denver?"

"Hey, kid, how ya doin'?" Denver said, twisting around to look up at Jim standing behind her.

"Okay," said Jim, sitting down beside Denver. "D'you think he'll come back?"

"Who, Crimps? Yeah, maybe, but we'll be ready for him. Besides, Crosely seems to think that those Gibboriums, or whatever they're called, will have sent him bananas by now, and he'll have forgotten all about you."

"I hope so."

Denver reached out and placed her hand on Jim's head, gently ruffling his hair.

"Hey, you've had a pretty alarming couple of days, but it's over now."

"But I still need to find George. You said you'd help me."

"Yeah, I did," said Denver, taking her hand from Jim's head, and pulling a battered cigarette from her shirt pocket. "Well, if you know where to start looking, why the hell don't we go now?"

She lit her cigarette, banishing all thoughts of Moon Lee's Opium Den from her mind.

'Razor' Bob sat on the edge of the damp, dirty bed, picking at his blackened fingernails with his cut-throat razor. As he worked at maintaining his own warped sense of personal hygiene, he sucked noisily on a boiled sweet, rolling it about in his mouth and knocking it against the few teeth he had left.

The morning sunlight filtered through the room's single, grimy window, casting a pale glow across the tangle of filthy sheets, from beneath which emanated loud, wet snores. After a while, when it became obvious to Bob that the sleeper was not going to wake up soon, he prodded impatiently at an exposed mound of fleshy thigh.

The sleeper grunted and pulled the sheets tighter around himself.

Bob prodded him again, a little harder this time.

"Unghh, geruunff!" came the muffled response.

Bob chuckled throatily. This was going to be fun.

He pulled back the sheets to expose more of the white, hairless skin and gave the man's leg a powerful slap.

The man yelped and pulled back the sheet, sitting up in the bed, ready to protest at his rude awakening. But, upon seeing his tormentor, he said nothing, and his fat, jowly face turned bright red with a mixture of embarrassment and indignation.

"What . . . what in God's name are you doing here?" he said, finally.

'Razor' Bob sucked on his sweet some more, before answering, "Just stopped by for a f . . . f . . . f . . . friendly little chat, that's all."

The man dragged the soiled bed sheet up to his shoulders, trying to mask his embarrassment and hide his nakedness.

Then he noticed the sunlight filtering through the window.

"Oh, dear Lord," he whispered. "What time is it? How long have I been asleep?"

Bob chuckled and said, "Yer too late for breakfast, I can tell yer that. I had Elsa slip a little somethin' into yer drink last night, before she brought yer to b . . . b . . . bed, jus' to make sure yer weren't goin' nowhere before we'd had chance for a little chat."

"Good God, man, don't you understand? I have a political reputation to think of, and my career in the city! And my family, what about my family?"

"Yer'll think o' somethin', yer always do. Yer m . . . m . . . more in danger of bein' found out if'n yer catch a dose of the clap, but then yer'd probably talk yer way out of that too," 'Razor' Bob replied, as he attempted to control a sudden onset of head twitching.

The Right Honourable Richard Brownrigg scowled at 'Razor' Bob, and said, "I wish I'd never met you, I curse the day that our paths ever crossed."

"Ah, that's not what yer said at our first meeting, now is it?" Bob said. "Yer were more than grateful for the services I provided for yer back then. Some men 'ave appetites that can't be m . . . m . . . met through the normal channels of polite society, ain't that right? I just helped yer along the way, introduced yer to a few people, gave yer an outlet for yer . . . desires. An' now I've come for me payment like, a return f . . . f . . . favour, yer might say."

"It seems to me that I have repaid your 'favour', as you call it, many times over. It seems to me that you are nothing more than a petty little thief and blackmailer."

'Razor' Bob inspected his black fingernails carefully, and said, "Well, you m . . . m . . . might be right there, and no mistake. M . . . m . . . maybe I would've liked to 'ave pursued a more noble career, a career in p . . . p . . . politics, p'raps, like yer good self. But there's none of us 'ave much say about the cards we're dealt when we're born, an' ain't that the truth, an' it s . . . s . . . seems to me that the good Lord always 'ad it in his mind that I'd be a thief and blackmailer, so who am I to argue?"

Brownrigg rubbed at the stubble on his chin, and licked his lips. For a moment or two Bob thought he might throw up.

Instead, the fat man said, "What the devil do you want from me this time? Come on, get on with it, man, and then I can get out of this cesspit, and go home to my family. Oh God! What am I going to say to them?"

Bob inspected his fingernails for a few seconds more, and then said, "Caxton Tempest. What do yer know of him?"

"Tempest? That's what this is all about? Caxton bloody Tempest?"

'Razor' Bob continued cleaning his filth-encrusted fingernails, industriously digging away at them with his razor, and dropping the bits of dirt onto the bed.

"I don't know. He's some kind of adventurer, isn't he?" Brownrigg said, rubbing his chin once more, the fat, soft flesh of his hand scraping against the stubble on his face.

"Yer can do better than that," Bob said, his head twitching spasmodically.

"Oh God, I don't know. I've never met the man. I've seen him in the city a couple of times, saw him at the opera once I think, and he has plenty of friends in high places so I've heard. Why, who wants to know?"

"Never you mind," Bob said.

"Been a naughty boy, has he?" Brownrigg said, and giggled.

Bob stood up, folded the cut-throat razor up and slipped it into his pocket.

"I'd appreciate it if yer could ask around a b . . . b . . . bit for me, know what I mean?" he said. "Find me some nice, juicy gossip on this Tempest geezer and, well, yer dirty little secret's safe with me."

He walked to the door, opened it, and then turned back to the fat man, and said, "For a little while longer, anyway."

Chapter Twenty-Four
George

The morning sunlight fell through high, narrow windows, highlighting the whitewashed walls of the long, empty corridors, which echoed with hard footsteps and hushed voices. The walls were mostly bare, apart from the occasional handwritten sign, exhorting the reader with a parable or a psalm.

Every one that is proud in heart is an abomination to the Lord.

Denver's boots echoed in the long corridor.

He that despiseth his neighbour sinneth; but he that hath mercy on the poor, happy is he.

The smell of disinfectant dried out the back of her throat and made her eyes water slightly. Beside Denver walked Jim, and they walked in silence. They could hear the faint cries of children playing in some distant corner of the building. Denver kept her eyes fixed firmly on Salvation Army Captain John Billingham who walked ahead of them.

Finally he stopped at a door and pulled a set of keys from his pocket.

He paused for a moment and turned to look at Jim and Denver.

"Are you sure you want to do this?" he said.

Denver looked at Jim, who simply nodded.

The Captain inserted the key into the lock and struggled with it for a few moments until finally, with a protesting squeak, it turned. He opened the door and stepped inside, holding the door open for Denver and Jim, and then closing it behind them.

"We won't be disturbed here," he said.

The room was bare, apart from two hard, wooden chairs and a bed. On the bed lay a body, with a white sheet draped over it from head to toe.

Jim walked over to the bed. He stood and looked at the sheet, at its contours and folds, at the shape of the body hidden beneath it.

"The young lady brought him to us the day before yesterday, in the evening I think," Captain Billingham said. "He should have gone to hospital really, but then I'm not sure what they could have done for him that we didn't."

"And you said she didn't stick around long after she got here?" Denver said.

"She stayed long enough to cradle the poor boy in her arms until he had passed away. We tried to persuade her to stay, she was exhausted, must have half carried the boy to us he was so weak, but she refused to stay any longer. Wouldn't even tell us her name, or where she lived."

"Her name's Emma Harris," Jim said, unable to take his eyes off the body under the sheet.

"And what's your brother's name?" Captain Billingham said.

"George Kerrigan." Jim said.

The Salvation Army Captain walked over to the bed, standing beside Jim, and took hold of a corner of the sheet. He turned to look at Jim once more.

"You okay, kid?" Denver said.

Captain Billingham pulled back the sheet.

George lay on the bed, his face white and drawn. A tiny splash of red on his forehead, just beneath his hairline, brought back memories of his brother screaming as the Devil's Imp clawed at his scalp. He seemed thinner than Jim remembered, smaller even.

"Is this him? Is this your brother?" said Captain Billingham.

"Yeah," said Jim. And then, as if explaining something, he said, "We were gonna be costermongers."

As Denver watched silently, Jim slowly leant over his brother and kissed him on the forehead. Denver dropped her gaze and studied the floor for a moment, unable to look anymore at Jim's slight, vulnerable frame, his back towards her, his shoulders bowed.

Here was another memory to haunt her sleep, another piece of misery that she would rather forget in a fog of oblivion.

Denver looked up at the sound of sudden movement to see Jim bolting for the door. Before she could react, he had run out of the room, and his footsteps echoed as he ran down the corridor.

With one last look at the body of the boy on the bed, Denver followed Jim outside, running down the corridor, past the proverbs and psalms.

"Jim!" she shouted, her voice echoing back at her uselessly.

She followed him outside, where the streets had filled with pedestrians and hansom cabs. Denver looked around her, pushing people out of the way as she ran, trying to locate Jim in the crowds.

Suddenly she saw him, in the distance, running as though his life depended upon it. She set off after him, drawing many curious glances as she dodged through the crowds of people and between the horse-drawn carriages. Her breath came in short, sharp gasps as she tried to keep up with the young boy, tried to keep her eyes fixed on him as he appeared and disappeared between the pedestrians and the horse-drawn cabs. Soon the inevitable happened, and she lost sight of Jim in the hustle and bustle of city-centre London, lost him in the city that he knew so well but was still a mystery to her. She slowed down to a walk, and eventually came to a stop, trying to catch her breath.

"Damn!" she said, looking around her in one last futile gesture.

It would be okay. Maybe he would go back to Tempest's. After all, where else could he go? As far as Denver knew, George had been Jim's only family.

Denver began walking back the way she had come, but with no firm idea of where she was. If she could get back to Tempest's house, and wait for Jim there . . .

Denver stopped when she saw a street she recognised.

She was only a couple of streets away from Moon Lee's Opium Den.

Maybe she could stop by, just one more time.

One last chance to forget.

After all, it wouldn't do any harm.

Johnny Chen daubed Mary's purple, swollen nose with a yellow, sticky ointment. The cook winced at every touch of his fingers.

"I'm sorry," he said, "I'm trying to be as gentle as possible. This will help reduce the swelling, although, I'm afraid, Mrs Mulligan, that your nose will never look the same again."

"Why he had to hit me in the face, I don't know," Mary said, wincing again as the Chinaman applied more ointment.

"I do not think Mr Tempest had much choice in the matter. From what he tells me, you were about to attack Master Kerrigan with a meat cleaver, and time was of the essence."

"I can't believe that I would do such a thing. I just don't what happened to me, Johnny."

"You weren't yourself. You were possessed by an evil spirit. The same thing happened to Denver, and she tried to shoot Jim. There, that's all the ointment applied for now."

Johnny Chen smiled at Mary as he replaced the lid on the tiny jar of ointment.

"Well," said the cook, struggling to her feet, "I suppose I'd better put the kettle on. Young Mr Crosely will be down soon wanting hot water for some more of his infusions, and goodness knows what they are, but he drinks them all the time, and they smell worse than this ointment, even."

"Please rest, Mrs Mulligan," Johnny Chen said, standing up. "Mr Crosely can boil his own water today. The ordeal you went through yesterday will have taken more from you than you think."

"Well, if truth be known, I don't feel myself still," said Mary. "I just wish I could remember more about what happened. It's all such a haze, and I just get so confused when I try to remember."

Johnny Chen took Mary gently by the shoulders and guided her to the stairs.

"It's probably better that way," he said. "Please, take the rest of the day off, and sleep. Sleep is the best thing for you, right now."

"Oh, Johnny," said Mary, taking him by the hand, "you've always been so kind to me. I know I'm just a foolish old woman, but this house has been a little lighter ever since you arrived. I don't like to speak ill of Mr Tempest, he's always been so good to me, so loyal, but sometimes he can be . . . well, a little cruel, if I'm honest."

"Mr Tempest has been through much darkness and walks a path that few others would dare tread. You must forgive him when he is less thoughtful of others than he should be."

"Oh, I know, I know, and I feel terrible for saying anything at all. Please, take no notice of me."

They reached Mary's bedroom door.

"I do hope Jim and Denver are alright," said Mary. "They've been gone a long time, haven't they?"

"Do not worry, Mrs Mulligan, and try to get some sleep."

"Oh, go away laddie," said Mary, waving a hand at the Chinaman. "How many times do I have to tell you, call me Mary, for goodness' sake?"

Johnny Chen opened Mary's door and stood back to let her pass. He inclined his head slightly to the cook, and, smiling his warm, gentle smile, said, "Please rest . . . Mary."

Back in the kitchen, Johnny Chen prepared two cups of China tea. He prepared them in traditional Chinese cups, looking more like wide, shallow soup bowls. He did not boil the kettle for young Mr Crosely's infusions, as he knew that Tempest had already ordered Crosely to leave the house, angry at his meddling with supernatural powers beyond his control. Tempest had been on the verge of ejecting Oscar Slavin from the house also, but Johnny Chen had pointed out that they still needed his expertise, especially now as he seemed to be on Kralik's trail.

Tempest, huddled over his desk in his study, looked up as Johnny Chen entered with the steaming cups of tea. On the desk lay the teeth he had recovered from Father Michael.

"The church, Johnny," he said, his eyes looking at his friend but not truly seeing him. "That church is the key, I am sure of that now. Perhaps we need to keep up a watch there. Perhaps tonight one of us could go and investigate further."

"I am sure you are right," Johnny Chen said. "Perhaps we could ask Inspector Behrends . . ."

"No, that man's a fool, refuses to believe the evidence when it spits him in the eye. Let us wait until nightfall and then one of us can go and observe the comings and goings of the vampires."

"They will know of our visit last night."

Tempest opened a drawer in his desk and swept the vampire teeth into it. "There is nothing we can do about that."

"Has Oscar spoken with you about his recent findings?"

"Indeed he has. Sit down Johnny, sit down."

Johnny Chen took the seat opposite Tempest. The two men had a respect for each other born out of shared adversity and tragedy. Neither was superior to the other, and both knew that they would one day go their separate ways. Until that time, they walked the same path of danger and mystery, one goal common to both.

"It seems that Kralik, or the demon that possesses Kralik if Denver's story is true, has been scouring the Western hemisphere for the scattered fragments of the Sigil of Semjaza. Once pieced together it is assumed he intends to summon the demon Semjaza, who is bound at the gates of Hell. Once summoned the gates will be open and all the demons of Hell will follow him into the world."

"How many fragments are there left to find?"

"Oscar is waiting for a telegram from a contact in Paris, but he believes this will only confirm what he already knows; that Kralik needs just one more fragment."

Johnny reclined in his chair, sipping at the hot tea, his brow furrowed in thought. "Ought we also to pay the demon Murmur a visit? Why did he direct Inspector Behrends to Denver McCade? He must have his own motives for giving up this information."

"That's a good idea," Tempest replied. "Murmur has his own part yet to play in this drama, I am sure."

Chapter Twenty-Five
"A surer candidate for the fires of Hell . . ."

Denver struggled fitfully from a nightmarish dream, clawing her way back from restless sleep to an uneasy wakefulness. She felt feverish and sick.

The opium did that sometimes.

She lay on her back on a wooden pallet, and when she moved her shirt felt warm and moist with sweat. Denver's body ached, and her breath came in gasps, as though she had been running hard. She lifted her hands in front of her face, and saw they were trembling.

How long had she been in Moon Lee's? The light looked different now, somehow, even in the smoky, darkened atmosphere of the opium den. Must be later in the day; maybe it was evening.

She struggled up into a sitting position, her head swimming with the effort. Her mouth and throat felt dry, her tongue like a swollen chunk of stale bread.

How long had she been here? How much of the opium had she smoked?

She took a deep ragged breath in and then exhaled. Her throat felt sore.

She had to get back to Tempest's, tell them about Jim.

Tell them about George . . .

The very thought of the demon Murmur sucking the life force from the young boy turned Denver's stomach. She should have killed him at their last meeting, emptied the Colt .45 into his chest as she had so often thought of doing.

She felt for her gun, tucked away in a secret holster inside her shirt. The textured grip on the handle felt comforting, secure.

If Murmur came here tonight, she would kill him.

Denver ran a shaky hand through her blond, tousled hair, pushing it back from her face damp with sweat.

Strange, though, about the light. There was something wrong with it, some subtle difference that registered in an unconscious part of Denver's mind and troubled her.

No time to worry about that now, though. Had to get back to Tempest's.

Tell them about Jim.

She tried licking her dried lips, tried working up some saliva to moisten the inside of her parched mouth, but it was useless.

And where the hell was everyone? No matter the time of day or night, there was always somebody gracing Moon Lee's den of iniquity with their custom.

Apart from today.

The attic room was empty, completely deserted.

Except . . . no, that was wrong, too. Because there was somebody else here.

Denver screwed her eyes shut and shook her head, trying to clear the mist that seemed to have fallen across her vision.

She could see a man now, walking across the attic room towards her. His face was cast in deep shadow, and all she could see of his face was the occasional flash of his eyes as he approached her. But she felt that she knew him, that he was very familiar to her.

"Who are you?" Denver said. "What do you want?"

But the man said nothing, drawing ever closer, the only sound that of his weathered boots hitting the wooden floor with a hollow thump.

Suddenly overwhelmed by a wave of nausea, Denver looked down, dragging her eyes from the approaching stranger. The sight that met her eyes stabbed her through the heart.

Her pallet was surrounded by dead bodies lying on the floor, twisted and tangled around each other, but all with their faces turned towards her, staring at her accusingly. There was Tempest, his collar open to reveal the scar on his neck, which was bleeding now. And there was Jim, and next to him Johnny Chen, and Mary.

All of them looking at her, their eyes round and wide, and fixed on her in a death stare.

Denver suddenly realised that the sound of the man's boots hitting the floorboards had stopped, that there was now complete silence in the opium den. She could sense the man standing just in front of her, looming over her and waiting for her to make the first move.

She reached for her gun, but her fist closed around empty space where the gun should have been. She looked up at the man, unable to shake the feeling that she knew him. But still his face was obscured by a dark shadow, only his green eyes blazing out at her like gas lamps in the night.

"You killed my friends," she said.

"They weren't your friends, Denver," the man said. "They were your enemies. The Council of Seven's influence extends everywhere, Denver. Everywhere."

"No, no," whispered Denver, as darkness engulfed her, and she allowed the faint to swallow her up in its welcome embrace.

But the darkness only lasted a second and then she was struggling fitfully back into a waking reality, back from her restless sleep.

"A nightmare," she muttered, shakily pulling herself upright, and glancing around her at the bodies lying on the long, low benches in the smoky gloom of Moon Lee's opium den. "It was just another freakin' nightmare."

She rubbed vigorously at her face with both her hands, trying to dispel the last shadows of the dream.

"You've gotta get a grip, girl," she said. Just as in her dream, her tongue felt dry and swollen, and her hands trembled when she held them up in front of her.

Across the darkened, smoky attic, one of the figures sat up from his pallet.

For some reason she could not fathom, the sight of the man sitting up sent a thrill of fear through her. She reached behind her and felt for the Colt .45, its familiar fit inside her hand instantly reassuring.

Denver pulled herself to her feet and took a moment to steady herself, waiting for the room to stop spinning and swaying, and making her feel sick. Feeling a little steadier, she walked carefully through the huddle of bodies, silently puffing on an opium pipe being passed around the cramped, darkened attic room.

She felt a hand take hold of her shoulder, clawed fingers digging into her flesh and pulling her, twisting her round. She reached behind her, fingers closing around the Colt .45, but Murmur had knocked it from her grip before she had raised it above waist height.

"Aaahhh, Denver my lovely," the demon whispered, his foul breath flowing over her in a suffocating stink, "I believe we have unfinished business."

The gun had skidded across the rough wooden floorboards and lay beside a pallet on which reclined an old man, passed out in a haze of obliteration. Denver glanced at the gun, out of reach. Murmur closed a hand around her jaw and turned her face back so that she looked into his dead eyes. Denver grabbed Murmur's wrist, her other hand bunching into a fist as she swung it at the demon's jaw. Before it could connect Murmur had wrapped his arm around her and dragged her to him in a lover's embrace, pushing her off balance and arching her back into a painful angle.

"No, no, my sweet, precious Denver," he murmured, "that's no way to greet an old friend, after all we have been through together."

"Let me go!" Denver hissed.

Murmur pushed her on her back onto an empty pallet and straddled her, sitting on her stomach. His clawed hands pinned her arms by her sides and he leaned over her, hot saliva dripping onto her upturned face. "You didn't really think I would let you get away did you? Not after your interference the other night when you stole those two precious little boys from me."

"If you hadn't sent Tempest after me then I never would have showed up that night, and you could have fed to your heart's content."

"And such are the unintended consequences of many a man's actions. I try to do what is right, what is best for all of us, and yet my actions come back to haunt me, come back to *kill* me."

Denver struggled fitfully for a moment, but Murmur held her fast. His clawed fingers dug into the flesh of her arms, but she knew it would be useless appealing to his better nature; he simply didn't have one. Still, something he had just said . . .

"What do you mean, you tried to do what's right? Why *did* you send Tempest after me?"

"I have betrayed the angels in Hell, and their fury shall know no earthly bounds when they find me. Time is short, my comely little cowgirl. Let us consummate our relationship now, while we still have time."

"I should have blown a hole through your chest the first time I saw you here," Denver hissed, gagging at the demon's foul breath washing over her.

"Ah yes, perhaps you should have. But then the road to Hell is paved with good intentions, is it not Denver McCade? Let us kiss, and I shall show you what Hell is really like."

Murmur leaned closer to Denver, writhing impotently on the hard wooden bed. It was useless, the demon had her pinned down, his frail body far stronger than it appeared. She snapped her head forward, her forehead smashing into the demon's nose, and flinched as cold blood splattered her cheek and stung her eyes. Murmur simply shook his head and then pressed his cold, dry lips against hers, the stink of his mouth invading her mouth, making her retch and cry out in revulsion.

With a bone-crunching thud Murmur was catapulted from the bed, slamming into the floor with a hollow thump. Denver rolled off the pallet and leapt to her feet. Her Chinese friend, the knuckle cracker, stood by the bed, lowering the booted foot he had kicked Murmur in the head with.

The demon struggled to his feet, a rivulet of blood dripping from his nose and splashing on the floorboards. Scarface joined knuckle cracker, both staring at the demon, relishing the prospect of a fight.

"You go now!" Moon Lee shouted at Murmur, gesticulating wildly, an opium cigarette dangling from her lips. "You no welcome here anymore. I see you here again my two boys sort you out!"

Scarface and Knuckle cracker smiled.

Murmur spat a bloody tooth onto the floor and shuffled from the opium den.

"See you in Hell, Murmur," Denver said, and smiled.

* * *

The man, sodden with drink and aged beyond his years, reached out a trembling hand to pick up the bone lying on the cold, hard kitchen floor. As his fingers touched it, a young boy kicked the bone out of his reach, and the gang of children around him laughed. The man rested his forehead on the dirty floor for a moment, before shuffling forward on his hands and knees, and reaching for the bone once more.

Another child kicked the bone, sending it scudding across the floor.

The man lay down on his side, lacking the strength to carry on.

The communal kitchen of the cheap doss house bustled with men and women cooking up their next meal. Scraps of meat, bones with nothing more than gristle left on them, vegetable peelings and cold potatoes, all begged, borrowed, stolen or foraged for that morning, were all thrown into old pots and rusty tins and boiled up into a thin gruel.

The children who were not involved in the taunting of the old drunk stood by their parents, holding out their empty plates in impatient expectancy.

One of the boys picked up the bone and squatted before the tramp, waving it in front of him, but just out of reach.

"What'ser matter, mate? What'ser matter? Come an' get yer bone, like a good little doggy!" he said.

Jim, sitting apart from the others, watched as the scrawny, filthy man lifted his head from the floor and looked at the boy, his bloodshot eyes imploring the child for a release from his misery.

The boy held the bone tantalisingly close, and then snatched it out of the way as the man reached for it.

The small crowd of children squealed with delight.

"Leave 'im alone," Jim said.

The boy looked at Jim, a sneer creeping across his grimy face.

"What's it ter you?" he said.

"All he wants is summat to eat. Let 'im 'ave the bone."

The boy turned away from Jim, and began waving the bone in front of the drunken man again.

A sudden, unexpected surge of anger welled up in Jim's chest, and he rushed at the boy and barrelled into him, sending them both skidding across the floor. They began punching each other furiously, and the other children now gathered around the two of them, grateful for another diversion to help them forget their gnawing hunger.

A stout woman with florid cheeks pushed her way through the circle of boys and girls, and pulled the two lads apart by the scruff of the neck.

"You!" she shouted at the boy, shaking him violently. "'Ow many times do I have ter tell yer, leave the old man alone!"

She pushed him from her, and the boy turned and shot one last vicious glance at Jim before skulking away.

"And as fer you," she said to Jim, not unkindly, "I ain't seen yer round here afore, so I'll lets yer off this time, but from now on yers best ter mind yer own business."

Jim struggled free of the woman's grasp and picked up the bone. He handed it to the old man who began sucking and chewing at it with what little strength he had left in his frail body. Seeing that the bone had already been picked clean of all its flesh, Jim took a scrap of unidentifiable meat from the table and tossed it to the man. He scrabbled at the scrap of meat like a voracious dog, chewing at it with his toothless mouth and grunting unintelligibly.

The woman's face turned even redder with anger, and she cuffed Jim around the head, sending him sprawling across the floor.

"Why, you mangy little toe-rag . . ." she muttered, advancing on the boy.

Jim leapt to his feet, ready to fight her, ready to fight all of them.

"Hold it, 'Mother', not too hasty now, eh? Don't you know who that is?"

'Mother' turned round to look at the rangy man pushing his way through the crowd of children. He cast an amused look over Jim and said, "This here's Jim Kerrigan, who were solely responsible for old Marchek Mulready's baptism of fire the other night."

The woman took a step back.

"That were you?" she said.

"Yeah. What about it?" Jim said. For a moment the events of the last few days threatened to overwhelm him. He struggled to hold back the tears, his eyes blazing with defiance.

"If'n yer want to come an' eat with us, Jim Kerrigan, then yer welcome," said 'Mother'. "An' most other folk round 'ere'll say the same."

"Aye," said the man. "There were much rejoicing when news got out about the old man's demise. There were plenty of people would have liked to have done the same, but none had the bottle for it."

The man looked at Jim thoughtfully for a few seconds and said, "You know Crimps is after you, don't you?"

"Yeah. I know."

"An' this lot," he looked around him and sighed, "well, they'll pat you on the back and shake your hand, and some of them will buy you a drink, and some of them will let you share their food. But when it comes to Marlow Crimps, you're on your own, lad. They'll turn their backs on you, and they'll disown you quicker than Judas Iscariot disowned his master, and for a lot less silver, too. What's your business here, Jim?"

"I've come to see you," Jim said. "I've been waiting all afternoon."

"Is that so? Then you'd best step up to my office, where we can talk in private."

Jim followed the man out of the kitchen, past the men, women and children looking at him with a horrified respect, and up a flight of gloomy, rickety stairs.

In his damp, dingy room the man sat on the edge of his bed. There being nowhere else to sit, apart from the floor, Jim remained standing.

"Them's some fancy clothes you're wearing there, Jim lad."

Jim looked down at his shirt and trousers, remembering with some surprise that he was still wearing the clothes provided by Johnny Chen. They were muddied now, and the shirt was ripped a little.

Tempest and Johnny Chen and Denver, they all seemed a lifetime away now, even though it had only been this morning he had last seen them. Jim had spent the rest of the day wandering the city streets. He had got into a fight with some mudlarks on the banks of the Thames and narrowly escaped arrest. He had wandered and wandered, until he had finally come to a decision, and then he had come here.

"Come on, lad," the man said. "What is it you want from me?"

"I want a gun," Jim said.

"Ah, do you now? Got some more killing to do, have you? Got a taste for it now, is that the case?"

"Mulready always said, if you needed a gun, you were the man to ask."

"He did that, now, didn't he? He had many faults did the old man, and being burnt to death seemed a most appropriate way to send him on his way, as a surer candidate for the fires of Hell you couldn't imagine, apart from his mate Crimps, that is; but I'll tell you one thing, Jim, he were never slow about recommending me to people when the need arose, and I'll always be grateful to him for that."

"What about it, then?"

"Aye, what about it. Well, you're in luck, Jim. It just so happens I've been waiting to do a deal on a nice little pistol I've got tucked away here, but the buyer never turned up. I'm expecting him to turn up sometime soon, but most likely by now floating face down in the Thames with a shiv stuck in his back."

The man got off the bed and knelt down to rummage beneath it. He pulled out a dark oak box with a brass carrying ring. He placed the box on the bed and opened it up.

In the case lay an ornate pistol. Beside the pistol were a small screwdriver, an oil bottle and a cleaning rod.

The man lifted the pistol out of its case and held it delicately in both hands for Jim's inspection.

"This, my young friend," he said, "is a French, silver-plated, six-shot, eleven-millimetre single-action revolver."

Jim looked at the gun and said nothing.

"Try not to be too impressed, young man. If you show too much enthusiasm, I might be forced to put the price up. Here, take it."

Jim took the gun from the man. It felt lighter than Denver's gun, and it fit more snugly into his hand. The wooden grip felt warm to the touch.

"Have you ever fired a gun before?"

Jim shook his head.

"Well, it ain't difficult, and that's the pity of it. You just point it and squeeze on the trigger. Squeeze, mind, nice and gentle like, and if you're up close it should do enough damage for what you want."

Jim held the gun out at arm's length, pointing it at the wall behind the man.

"Careful," said the man, "it's loaded."

Jim lowered the gun, looked at the man and said, "I ain't got no money."

"No, I didn't think you would have," he said. "It's yours, Jim. Just be careful what you do with it. And the next time you come round here, make sure Crimps has already joined Mulready in Hell, okay? That'll be payment enough."

Jim turned and walked to the door, slipping the gun inside his shirt.

"Don't you want the carry case?" the man said.

Jim paused for a moment at the open door and turned to look back at him.

"I ain't got no use for it," he said.

And then he was gone.

Chapter Twenty-Six
To Kill Murmur

"There's got to be a way out, there's got to be," muttered Billy Rackitt as he followed Maria through the labyrinth of dark tunnels, just visible by the glow of the oil lamp she carried with her. She took him a different route to the one she had brought him by; this time they followed the course of a small, gurgling underground stream. The sound of the water was pleasant to Billy, reminding him of normality, of the outside world. Maria said that there were many more streams and brooks bubbling their way beneath London.

Above ground late afternoon was slowly turning to evening, but Billy knew none of this. Isolated from any sense of passing time, he had no idea if it was day or night. He had slept some more after they had finished eating and then Maria had woken him up, saying that it was time to do some vampire hunting. Billy felt a little uneasy at this, already having had more than enough to do with the vampires than he ever wished. But, not wanting to show his fear to this tiny slip of a twelve-year-old girl, he said okay, and watched silently as she picked out her weapons.

"Here," she said, handing him a couple of the sharpened stakes.

He looked suspiciously at them and then stuffed them into the waistband of his prison trousers.

"Why are we going after the vampires?" Billy said. "Do we need more food, is that it? Are we stealing stuff?"

"No," the girl said. "This is just for fun."

Fun, thought Billy. Great.

Maria was a strange girl, unlike any he had ever come across before. But then how long had she been down here? How old had she been when the vampires killed her parents and carried her underground with the intention of sucking her blood at their leisure?

This place was enough to send anybody mad with fear and grief, let alone a little girl, with nothing but a pet rat named Jesus for company. And yet she had shown incredible resilience and fortitude, turning from victim to attacker. But she couldn't live this life forever; she needed the companionship of normal people, of children her own age. And besides, they would catch her one day; she couldn't hide from them forever. And what then? Would the outraged vampires settle simply for sucking her blood, or would they want her to suffer some, for all the killing and stealing she had done over the years, all the inconvenience she had caused them?

No, Billy was going to find a way out of this dungeon, and when he did he was taking Maria with him.

"Maria!" he hissed. "Maria!"

The girl stopped walking and turned to face Billy, the light of the oil lamp giving her face a yellow, ghostly glow. Jesus peered out from her tangle of red hair, his nose twitching.

"There's a way out of here, there's probably more than one way out of here," he said. "How hard did you look, how hard did you try to escape?"

"I wandered up and down these here tunnels fer ages," said Maria. "But there's too many of them, you could spend months wandering around down here, and never find yer way out."

"No, it's got to be easier than that," said Billy. "The vampires who caught me and brought me down here, they knew where they were going, even in the pitch black. And Talos, the boss man, he were wearing a suit that weren't even creased. Did you try all the passages and tunnels down here?"

"Yeah, all of them," Maria said.

Billy sat down on the dirt floor, his back against the wall, and closed his eyes.

"Except one," she said.

Billy opened his eyes.

Jim had never even thought of killing Crimps; not until the man had suggested it, anyway. But now that the thought was in his head, it seemed like a good one.

Later, maybe.

If he had enough bullets left.

Murmur was first.

Jim wiped the sweat from his forehead with his shirtsleeve and glanced around him. The dimly lit, dank hallway was just as he remembered it. The bookcases stuffed full of ageing, rotting books; the heavy, grey, dust-encrusted cobwebs swaying in the damp breeze; the mildewed wallpaper curling from the walls; and, over all of that, the heavy, coppery smell of blood.

Jim pulled the pistol from inside his shirt, where he had tucked it into his trousers. Get in close, the man had said.

He would make sure of that.

According to Denver, there was no way he could kill Murmur, only the body that he possessed. But if that was all he could do, if he could only send him back to Hell, then at least he would have accomplished something; a vengeance of sorts, for George.

Jim slipped the gun back inside his shirt, taking care to make sure it was well hidden.

Get in close, the man had said.

Jim walked the length of the landing, his shoes squelching on the blood-drenched carpet. No light emanated from underneath any of the doors, so Jim reasoned that Murmur was downstairs. He had no desire to investigate the bedrooms if he had no reason to.

Jim paused at the top of the flight of stairs, looking down into the inky darkness below. For the first time since the idea had come to him of killing Murmur, he felt a pang of fear.

He gripped the handrail beside him, his palm damp with sweat. Doubts began to crowd his mind, prodding at him with uncertainties and questions.

What about the Devil's Imp? He would have to be careful; the thing almost killed him last time. If it got free again, or if Murmur set it free to kill him, what chance would he have?

And what else did the demon have at his disposal? Murmur had spent his time on earth collecting the paraphernalia of occultism, devising means of murder, possession, enslavement to the demonic. He had to be on his guard at all times.

Jim wiped his dirty sleeve across his forehead again, as beads of sweat began to drip into his eyes.

"This is stupid," he said. "Just got to pull yourself together. Remember, there ain't no one can hurt a Kerrigan."

But that was what he used to tell George, and George was dead now.

Jim shivered in the damp air, the cold sweat on his back chilling him to the bone.

"If you're gonna do it, then do it now," he said.

Taking a deep breath, he began his descent of the stairs.

He reached the bottom of the steps without falling down, despite his legs suddenly turning to jelly and almost buckling beneath him. He was in the long, dark corridor now, and he found that he could not stop trembling. Was it the cold that made him tremble, or the icy lump of fear in the pit of his stomach?

One hand touching the gun through his shirt, the other feeling along the damp, mildewed wall, he began slowly walking the length of the corridor. The door to the main living room was slightly ajar, and a cold yellow light spilled out of the gap. Jim could hear movement inside now, the sounds of something heavy being shifted.

Jim crept up to the edge of the doorway, pressing himself flat against the damp wall, and peered around the edge of the doorframe. The destruction of the once grand living room was just as Jim remembered it; the open crates, their contents spilling onto the filthy carpet, the mounds of

189

rotting, ancient books scattered throughout, the layer of filth covering everything.

But the room was empty as far as Jim could see, and the sounds of movement had stopped. The young boy took hold of the gun, clamping his trembling fingers around its grip, and stepped across the threshold of the door.

He had taken just a couple of steps into the room when the pistol was knocked from Jim's hand and sent scudding across the floor, kicking up a plume of dust as it went.

"Master Kerrigan," said a familiar voice, "you should not be carrying a gun. You are young, too young to understand that these tools of death do more than kill your enemies; they murder your heart and soul while you avenge your loved ones."

Johnny Chen stepped from the shadows and placed a gentle hand upon Jim's shoulder. Jim began to tremble, the strength leaving his body like water flowing down a drainage ditch. Suddenly he felt weak and drained, and Johnny Chen caught him as his legs collapsed beneath him. He felt the Chinaman pull him close and hug him tight.

"I wanted to kill him," Jim said, his voice catching and tears rolling down his cheeks. "I wanted him to pay for what he did to George."

"I know, Master Kerrigan, I know," Johnny Chen whispered. "In time Murmur will pay for what he has done, for all his victims, but right now we need him. He may be the only one who has the answers we seek, and time is running out."

"I don't care," Jim said, pushing free of Johnny Chen's embrace. "I don't care about that. He should die, that's all I care about."

Jim walked deeper into the room, weaving between the boxes and open packing crates. He struggled to control the tears, but it felt like trying to stem the flow of a river with a sheet of newspaper; the tears came anyway, unwanted, unbidden.

"Master Kerrigan, we should return to Mr Tempest's house. He is very worried about you."

Jim halted by the trunk containing the Devil's Imp. An insane desire to open the lid, to set the Hellspawn free, almost overcame him. He struggled with it, fought the suggestion some dark corner of his mind had made; he needed to get out of here, away from this place, all these memories.

He turned to face Johnny Chen, and as he did so his foot touched the gun. The light was dim in here and he felt sure Johnny Chen would not have seen it, hidden among the dirt and detritus covering the floor. As Jim wondered how he could possibly pick up the gun without being noticed, a sudden rapping at the front door of the shop distracted them. Johnny Chen waved at Jim to keep quiet. Dissolving into the shadows of the hall, he looked into the shop. The glow of a gas lamp filtered through the window caked with grime and illuminated the shelves laden down with occult items.

Again somebody knocked on the door and then tried turning the handle, rattling the door in its frame. Johnny Chen stared intently at the dark, hunched figure, silhouetted by the yellow glow of the street lights.

Jim slowly knelt and picked up the gun, slipping it inside his shirt. The man at the door finally gave up and moved away, disappearing from view.

Johnny Chen turned and looked at Jim.

"Let us go," he said, "Mr Tempest will be waiting for us."

Chapter Twenty-Seven
A Message for 'Razor'

Marlow Crimps clutched his glass of 'blue ruin' as though it were a lifeline, the only thing that kept him from drowning in a stormy, darkened sea of utter insanity.

Around him, life in The White Swan continued as normal. The rogues, the thieves and the bag men, all sat around their rickety tables, in their tight little groups, conducting 'business', a thick cloud of cigarette smoke almost obscuring them from view. The sailors on shore leave brawled, and the desperate women of the night sold themselves for a pittance.

But the shouts and the fights barely disturbed Crimps.

The casual observer, sitting alone at a nearby table, with nothing better to do than observe his fellow drinkers, would have seen little to indicate the inner turmoil that Crimps was currently experiencing. Perhaps he would have noticed the fierce grip with which he held on to his glass, so fierce that the glass was in danger of shattering. Or perhaps he would have noticed the occasional twitch in Crimps' battered features and heard the occasional grunt escape his tightly clenched mouth.

But, apart from these tiny telltale signs that all was not as it appeared, the casual observer would have noticed nothing more than a fellow drinker, alone for the evening like himself.

Inside the tortured mind of Marlow Crimps it was a different story. The Gibboriums' high-pitched voices filled his head with their gibberings and screechings, sometimes commanding him to do things for them, sometimes not making any sense at all. Crimps had tried blotting them out with alcohol, tried to lose them in a fog of drunkenness, but to no avail.

The voices were wearing Crimps down, eating away at his mind, at his senses, at his very ability to think, and feel, and act. But they were also fusing with him, becoming one with him. The Gibboriums had found a deep vein of hatred within Marlow Crimps, a rich seam of unadulterated hostility, which they could feed on, thus helping to keep them alive.

Crimps lifted the glass of cheap gin to his lips and downed the drink in one. Slowly, carefully, he lowered the glass to the table, but found he was unable to let it go. His knuckles turned white as his hold increased on the glass, and his arm began to tremble under the force of his grip.

Suddenly the glass shattered, tiny shards of glass exploding from his clenched fist and scattering across the table. And then the blood began leaking from between his fingers.

"Hunh," Crimps grunted, the pain barely registering in his brain.

The voices screamed and yowled and jabbered, becoming spikes of terror and confusion prodding at his alcohol-addled brain.

Crimps put his head in his hands, oblivious to the shards of bloodied glass now sticking into his face.

"This is it, it's got to be," muttered Billy Rackitt, as he gazed at the padlocked, black iron gate, and the steps on the other side, cut out of the rock and which led upwards.

He closed his hands around the wrought iron and pressed his face against the bars, looking up to try and detect even the faintest glimmerings of daylight. He felt so close to freedom now, so close it hurt.

"There ain't no use," Maria said from behind him, keeping guard. "There ain't none of the vampires even allowed to use it, just Talos and Mina. They're the only ones who have a key for the padlock."

"That woman, Mina, she's human," Billy muttered. "She needs fresh air and daylight; she needs proper food, not blood. This must be for her, so that she can get above ground sometimes, and easily too, not having to crawl through dirty tunnels on her hands and knees. This is it, it's got to be."

Billy leant his forehead against the cool of the iron bars and closed his eyes. He felt close to desperation now. How would they ever get the keys off Talos or Mina?

"Someone's coming!" hissed Maria.

Billy turned, ready to run and hide, but it was too late; they had already been discovered.

The two vampires' bloodshot eyes grew wide in astonishment as they looked at Billy and Maria standing before them. Swift as lightning, Maria had plunged a stake into the first vampire's chest, sending it crashing to the floor, dying as it went.

She was too slow for the second vampire, though, which jumped on top of the young girl, baring its fangs and screaming a high-pitched squeal. Billy leapt at the two figures, entwined in a deadly embrace as the young girl did her best to keep the vampire's teeth from closing around her exposed neck. Pulling a stake from the waistband of his trousers, Billy watched the girl and the vampire fight, unable to stab at the vampire for fear of hurting Maria. But he wanted to kill this bloodsucking fiend as quickly as possible, before the others were drawn to investigate the commotion.

Suddenly the vampire fell from Maria, and was silent, clutching at the stake that protruded from its chest. Maria climbed unsteadily to her feet, wiping the vampire's blood from the rags that she used as clothes.

194

"Yer've gotta be quicker than that," she said, giving Billy an accusing look.

"Yeah," he said, shaken by the young girl's ferocity.

"I told you there ain't any way out of here," said Maria, and turning to walk to back down the tunnel they had just come up.

"But there is," came a voice from behind Billy.

Maria and Billy both turned round to see Mina standing behind them. Billy instinctively lifted the stake in his hand, ready to defend himself.

Ignoring him, Mina said, "Come, follow me," and turned and walked away from them into the darkness of the tunnel.

Billy looked at Maria, who shook her head, her red, tousled hair whipping across her grimy face, her chin jutting out defiantly.

"It's a trap," she said.

"It might be our only chance of getting out of here," Billy whispered. "She's got the key, and we ain't, so why don't we follow her and see if we can find it?"

Maria looked at Billy uncertainly but, his mind made up, the escaped convict began walking after Mina down the dark tunnel, ready to execute his second escape from certain death.

Maria followed him.

Within moments they were in Mina's living quarters, the fire burning just as fierce as the last time Billy had seen it. He looked anxiously around the room, half expecting Talos to leap at him from some darkened corner.

"Do not worry," Mina said, as if reading his mind. "My husband is not here, he is outside, in the freedom of the night. He keeps me locked up in this dungeon. Palatial though it might be, that is all it is, am I right? A dungeon."

"What do you want?" Billy said, trying not to stare too hard at the beautiful Mina. Once again she wore a figure-hugging dress, which showed off her sybaritic body to full effect. "We ain't got time to chat about the niceties of vampire etiquette."

"Then let me get straight to the point. You're looking for a way out."

She paused and looked at Billy for a long time. He felt as though she could read his mind, that she knew of his keen awareness of her body's shape.

And then she held out a key, swinging it slowly from a short, silver chain.

"This is the key to the padlock," she said. "It is yours if you wish. Tonight you can both be back above ground, free to live your lives once more."

Billy looked at Maria and then back at Mina.

"What's the catch?" he said.

The insistent rapping on the door dragged 'Razor' Bob from his disturbed sleep and back into reality. He sat up in the bed and automatically reached for the razor underneath his pillow.

"What is it?" he said. "What's all the r . . . r . . . racket fer?"

"I got a message fer yer, 'Razor'," a boy's voice said.

Grunting his displeasure at being disturbed, Bob swung his legs over the side of the bed and fumbled for his clothes, which lay in a jumbled heap on the floor. There had still been some light left in the room when he had gone to sleep, but now it was much darker. The cold night air goose pimpled his flabby flesh, and he shivered as he struggled to unravel his clothes. He pulled on a shirt and a pair of trousers, and they felt damp against his skin.

Ever cautious, Bob unfolded the razor and concealed it in his right hand.

The female form lying beside him in the tangle of sheets sighed softly, and buried herself deeper beneath the covers.

"Don't worry love," Bob said, running a finger down a bare arm, which had slipped out from under the sheets, "I'll be right back."

The young scruffy street urchin stared expectantly up at Bob when he opened the door, one hand out before him, palm up, waiting for payment, the other hand scratching industriously at his flea-infested body.

"W . . . w . . . what do yer want, boy?" said Bob. "I ain't gonna p . . . p . . . pay yer fer somethin' somebody else has asked yer to do."

"I got a message fer yer 'Razor'," the boy said again.

"Yeah," Bob said, his head twitching to one side. "Yer already told m . . . m . . . me that. Ain't the feller who gave yer the m . . . m . . . message already paid yer for yer trouble?"

"Nah, he said *you'd* give me summat."

Bob sighed and pulled a couple of pennies from his pocket, dropping them into the boy's hand.

The young boy stuffed the pennies into his trouser pocket, and then screwed his filthy face up as he tried to recall the message.

"C'mon, lad," said Bob, feeling the cold and wishing he was back in bed. "I ain't got all night."

"It were a gen'lman, wot asked me," said the boy. "He told me to tell yer to meet 'im in 'Jack's Hole'. Said yer should go there right now."

"And what were this gentleman's name?"

The boy screwed his face up again and thought for a long time.

"Dunno," he said eventually, and began running down the corridor, his job finished.

196

"Oi!" Bob shouted after the boy, bringing him to a sudden halt. "What's so bleedin' important, that I have to g . . . g . . . go now?"

"Dunno," said the boy again. "The man said it were about Mr Tempest, and that yer should go now."

Brownrigg, thought Bob, as he closed the bedroom door behind him, the boy's footsteps still clattering down the stairs. It made sense that the message came from Brownrigg now that he thought about it; only he would have sent a young ragamuffin like that running halfway across town with nothing more than promise of payment at the other end. The man was inherited rich, but tighter than a crab's arse.

Still, if he had come up with the goods on Tempest, then none of that mattered. All 'Razor' Bob wanted right now was to get Behrends off his back, for good. And if the information that he received tonight did that particular trick, well, maybe Bob would be generous enough to leave the Right Honourable Richard Brownrigg alone from now on; alone to pursue his deviant desires in peace.

Bob pulled on his shoes and ran a comb through his greasy black hair. Pulling down a tiny, blemished mirror from a shelf, he held it close and examined his reflection in the dingy light.

Bob ran his finger down the scar that crossed his face, pulling down the one eyelid and giving him a slightly lopsided look. He massaged the stubbly skin on his cheeks and opened his mouth to inspect his few remaining teeth. Stuffing a finger in his mouth he poked at one of the loose molars in the back.

"Yer getting' old, 'Razor'," he said softly. "P'rhaps it's time yer moved on, got out o' the life once an' fer all."

If the information he received tonight was what Behrends was after, then maybe this was the opportunity he was waiting for. Behrends would reward him handsomely for his trouble, and 'Razor' would get his chance to move on and find himself a new life away from the slums of the East End.

Replacing the mirror on the shelf, 'Razor' Bob slapped the sleeping girl on the rump and laughed.

"Don't you go nowhere, Slum Lassie Sal," he said. "I'll be back before yer know it."

Chapter Twenty-Eight
'Jack's Hole'

Denver took the steaming mug of black coffee from Tempest and sipped at it carefully. Tempest sat down opposite her at the kitchen table.

"How's Mary?" Denver said.

"She'll be alright with a bit of rest," Tempest said. "She's asleep right now."

"You hit her pretty damn hard with that bedpan, and in the face too."

"She was about to chop Jim up into tiny little pieces," said Tempest, glancing sharply at Denver. "What should I have done?"

Denver took another sip of her coffee and shuddered.

"I get the feeling thing's ain't looking too good right now," she said.

"No, they're not. Oscar is waiting for a telegram from one of his contacts who might be able to tell us where the last piece of the sigil is. If Kralik has already found it . . ."

"Yeah, I know," whispered Denver, and then said, "He invites all the demons of Hell to come and stay on earth for a while. Like forever. Yeah, you said."

"You didn't tell us the whole story the other night, did you? I got the feeling you left out a lot more."

"Maybe."

"What happened, Denver? What happened after you passed out in Central Park?"

"One of the Order of Ahriman found me and took me back to their brownstone," Denver said, staring at the top of the table, unable to look up at Tempest. "They'd caught Murmur by that point, caged him up in the basement. They put me down there too."

"Then what happened?" Tempest said, quietly.

Denver said nothing, looking at the thin tendrils of steam rising from her coffee.

"You really want to hear this?" she said finally, looking up at Tempest once more. "It's not a pretty story."

"I think I can handle it," Tempest replied.

Consciousness, and with it physical feeling, rushed back at Denver McCade like a torrent of cold water. One second oblivion, the next wakefulness, pain, confusion. She lay on her back on a cold stone floor, staring up at an arched ceiling of rough brick. Her head ached terribly, as though her skull had been clamped in an oversized vice and squashed. She attempted to reach up a hand to rub at her eyes but her muscles set up an instant protest at being asked to move, screaming in such agony that she gave up and lay still.

She remembered nothing of what had happened to her since waiting for Kralik in the drifting snow. They had been due to attend a meeting of the Order of Ahriman, she remembered that much. Denver tried moving her hand again, and this time her muscles protested a little less, enough that she carried her manoeuvre through and rubbed at her eyes.

An arched ceiling of rough brick. A cold stone floor. Seemed like she was in a cellar maybe, and with that thought a flood of memories smashed into her mind, almost suffocating her in their intensity. The orgiastic party, the summoning in the basement going horribly wrong, fleeing from Kralik through the New York streets.

But where was she now? She remembered Kralik finding her in Central Park and attacking her. She even remembered defending herself with his own knife and Kralik fleeing as he clutched at his stomach.

But then what? Had she fainted?

Have to sit up, have a look around, she thought. No good lying here.

She placed her palms flat against the cold floor and pushed, bracing every muscle in her back and thighs, struggling upright. Her body screamed at her to stop, her mind shouted at her to stay lying down, she would feel much better that way. But her spirit, the unstoppable McCade spirit, compelled her to fight, to get up on her feet and fight.

Sitting upright she froze when she heard the low, dry giggle. Heart pounding, she slowly turned in the direction of the voice.

The man with the shaven head, with the symbol carved into his forehead, squatted only a few feet from her, legs bunched beneath him like a monkey. He looked at her through lifeless eyes and giggled again. His arms hung down before him and his fingers twitched spasmodically.

Instinctively Denver knew he was about to pounce.

She slid her legs beneath her, trying to find purchase with her feet. Too late the man leapt, a snarl ripping from his mouth. Denver braced herself for the impact, throwing her hands up over her head in a protective gesture.

But the man snapped back in midair, as though an invisible wall had been placed between them. He scrabbled at the floor, snarling and spitting, but could get no nearer her. Then Denver noticed the chains across his chest and around his waist, linking up with the bars behind him.

The bars of the cell that imprisoned them both.

Denver backed away from the snarling thing and rested her back against the iron bars. She could hear footsteps now, echoing down a

200

corridor, approaching them; somebody coming to investigate all the noise perhaps.

Denver's hands fluttered across her waist, trying to find the Colt .45. But, of course, she had given it to the fat butler, handed it over like the naive fool she was.

The footsteps sounded louder now. She looked up as they drew close and saw the man with the silver hair approach the cell out of the shadows beyond the single gas lamp on the stone wall.

"Good, you're awake," he said, as though he were a doctor attending his favourite patient.

"Where in God's name am I?" Denver whispered. Her throat hurt to speak. She tried swallowing, but her muscles locked up and she almost gagged.

"Please, don't try to speak," the man said. "You've been through a great deal these last few hours and you must be weakened. Oh, and don't worry about Murmur, he's quite harmless as long as he is chained up."

Murmur spat at the man, his dead eyes suddenly alive with utter hatred.

"Set me free and I will crack open your skull and suck at your brains!" he hissed.

The man did not reply. He pulled a handkerchief from his waistcoat and wiped the gobbet of spit from his shoe. Denver remembered the last time she had seen him he had been wearing a long, black robe. Now he was attired in an evening suit.

With a shock she suddenly realised she too was no longer dressed in the robe; somebody had undressed her and put her back in her own clothes.

"Now," said the man, ignoring Murmur, "please try to rest. I have a function to attend to at the moment, but I shall be back later. I have much I would like to ask you, Denver McCade."

"Why are you doing this to me?" Denver croaked, but the man did not answer, simply turning and walking away.

Endless hours passed, a meaningless amount of time to Denver who had no way of marking the passing minutes. She sat hunched against the cell bars as far away from Murmur as she could in the confines of their prison. The demon stared at her for a long time, but finally grew bored with her and curled up on the cold floor. Only when she was sure he slept did Denver dare to stand and examine her surroundings a little more closely.

That she was in a basement was in no doubt, and she felt certain that she was in the basement of the brownstone belonging to the Order of Ahriman. She held her breath, straining to catch the slightest sound of the party still happening upstairs, or maybe something else that might help her in some way.

But there was nothing, just an endless, deep silence.

She fell asleep too, for a while. Unconsciousness crept up on her, and she only realised she had been asleep when she awoke, slumped in a corner her head resting against a cell bar. The first thing she saw was Murmur gazing at her, his lips wet with drool.

Denver screamed.

Finally the questions started. Sometimes the man with the silver hair asked them. Sometimes other men visited Denver and asked them. Even the fat butler came to the cell one day and interrogated her. But always, no matter who asked them, always the same questions.

"Who is Caxton Tempest?"

"Have you heard of him?"

"What do you know of the Council of Seven?"

"Why did you infiltrate the Order of Ahriman?"

"Did your friend know Caxton Tempest?"

"What do you know of Caxton Tempest?"

"Do you believe the Council of Seven are all powerful?"

"Do you believe they could ever be defeated?"

"Why are the Council of Seven so scared of Caxton Tempest?"

And on, and on, and on, the endless questioning, the same questions over and over until Denver wanted to scream and to throw the thin, hot soup they gave her every day into their faces.

One day the questioning stopped. That same afternoon Denver realised that Murmur was dying. During their time together in the cell Denver had seen Murmur turn from a powerful, healthy looking man into a walking cadaver. Grey flesh hung from his bones in leathery folds. His hair had fallen out in patches revealing skin stretched parchment thin over his skull and threaded with veins. His teeth had rotted away and regularly fell out, hitting the stone floor like a dropped penny, and tumours had grown on his face and bare arms. Denver felt sick just looking at him.

The Order of Ahriman seemed panicked by this turn of events. They desperately wanted to keep Murmur alive, but did not have the faintest idea of how to accomplish this. When asked, the demon said nothing, regarding his interrogators with hate-filled, watery eyes.

One morning, at least she assumed it was morning, Denver awoke to see Murmur sprawled across the floor like the victim of a vicious mugging, empty eyes staring glassily at the ceiling.

"Hey!" she called. "Hey, someone get down here now!"

A moment later the obese butler appeared from the shadows, as though he had been waiting for her call. He looked at the dead demon for a few seconds, his face as impassive as a block of stone. Then he pulled out a set of keys and unlocked the cell door.

It was while Denver watched the butler lean over the prostrate demon checking for any signs of life that she suddenly realised Murmur's eyes always looked empty, that they had never once had the appearance of life within them. Before she could cry out, Murmur had overpowered the butler, thin fingers scratching and pulling at his hair, dragging him to the floor where he nestled over him like some black, malignant spider. Horrified but impotent, Denver watched as the demon kissed the obese man, watched as his struggles grew weaker and weaker, until finally something so unexpected happened the young girl rubbed her eyes in disbelief.

Murmur fell from his victim, collapsing in a tangle of limbs on the floor. The butler clambered a little unsteadily to his feet and brushed flecks of dirt from his clothes. He turned his dead, empty eyes on Denver, and she suddenly realised this was no longer the same man who had greeted her and Kralik at the door the other night, or the one who had entered the cell just a few moments ago.

Somehow the demon had transferred himself from one body to another. From a diseased, listless, walking corpse to this healthy, powerful man.

Murmur smiled at her, the folds of fat on his face bunching up so that his eyes almost disappeared, and then he left the cell.

A moment later Denver followed him.

The silence stretched out between them, the only sound that of the grandfather clock ticking away the seconds at the top of the stairs. Somewhere a corner of the house creaked slightly.

"And that's it," Denver said finally. "I managed to escape the Order of Ahriman, and Murmur and I went our separate ways. When he turned up in Moon Lee's opium den a few months back I hardly recognised him, but for the flicker of recognition in his dead eyes of course. We kind of both left each other alone after that."

"Until Murmur told Inspector Behrends about you. Why did he do that? What could he have possibly benefited from by sending me to you?" Tempest said.

"I think he's scared. He knows all about Semjaza's sigil and the consequences of opening the gates of Hell. My guess is he should have been searching for some way to set all his demon pals free, too. But he hasn't, he's been too busy enjoying what earth has to offer him."

"The lives of prostitutes and street children."

"I should have killed him years ago," Denver said, her hands curling up into fists, the knuckles turning white under the pressure. "If I had, then Jim and his kid brother never would have encountered him, and George would still be alive right now."

"You can't blame yourself for that, Denver," said Tempest. "You've suffered enough, you can't take on everybody else's suffering too."

"Yeah? Why not? It seems I don't have much choice. I spent the last five years hiding out, trying my damndest to not get mixed up in this whole business again, but look what happened. Here I am talking about demons and dead children and the end of the world."

Tempest looked away, but not before Denver had seen the look of vulnerability pass across his face. Something she had said, the comment about dead children . . .

Denver reached out a hand to touch his, her fingers finding their way around his. She opened her mouth to say something, but before the words had even begun to form, Johnny Chen entered the kitchen. Denver snatched her hand from Tempest's and picked up her coffee mug.

"There is a prowler outside," the Chinaman said. "He keeps to the shadows where I cannot see him."

"Then let's go and have a look," Tempest said, rising to his feet.

The three of them ran upstairs to the ground floor. Johnny Chen ran to the back of the house, and Tempest approached the front door.

"Stay here," he said, waving at Denver to keep her distance.

"Hey, don't worry about me, I ain't no feeble little girl you have to protect," Denver hissed, her eyes blazing with indignation.

Ignoring her, Tempest opened the front door and stepped outside. The air was cold, and occasional heavy droplets of rain hit the ground with a loud splash, threatening a deluge to come.

Denver moved closer to the front door as Tempest disappeared from view. A damp, chill gust of wind blew through the reception hall, ruffling Denver's shirt and hair. She pushed her hair back off her face and saw a lithe, dark shape darting towards her. For a moment she watched transfixed as the thing hurtled at her and into the house, bolting past her feet. Once inside, the black cat stopped running and looked around, its tail swishing silently from side to side.

"Damn!" Denver hissed as she looked at Murmur's cat, and automatically reached for the Colt .45 by her side.

Wherever Lucifer was, Murmur was never far behind, that was for sure. She ran to the door, the Peacemaker in her hand, and outside, large drops of water hitting her and spreading out in wide, dark patches of damp on her shirt. She looked around, trying to locate Tempest and Murmur.

The darkness cloaked itself around Denver, obscuring her vision. Looking up at the sky she could see nothing but a heavy blackness pressing down on her, and felt the oppression of the broiling clouds full of rain. She shrank back as the heavens suddenly opened up, and disgorged their contents onto the street. Holding an arm over her face to protect herself from the furious onslaught of the rain, Denver ran back to the house, through vast puddles already formed on the ground.

Once inside she turned to look back out of the door and saw Tempest sprinting for the shelter of the house.

"There's nobody out there as far as I can see, but ..." he stopped talking, noticing the gun in Denver's hand, and then looked to where she indicated at Lucifer prowling up and down the reception hall, flashing his large green eyes at them.

Johnny Chen appeared at the back of the house, closing a door behind him, rivulets of water running down his face and into his soaking wet clothes.

"There is nobody outside now," he said. "Whoever the intruder was has gone."

Tempest pointed at the cat and put his index finger to his lips, indicating silence.

Slowly, quietly, he walked over to the drawing room door, which stood slightly ajar, and pushed at it. The cat ran between his legs and into the room, purring contentedly.

Johnny Chen and Denver followed Tempest as he stepped inside. The room was darkened, a fire in the hearth giving out the only light and casting crazy, flickering shadows across the walls. One of the high-backed chairs had been pulled up close to the fire, and sat with its back to them. The dull, heavy throb of the downpour outside was the only sound to be heard.

The cat stopped running in front of the fire, and began rubbing its head against one of the chair legs, its purring growing louder. A wizened, skeletal hand appeared from the depths of the high-backed chair and stroked the cat between the ears.

"Please, put the gun away, Denver McCade," Murmur whispered. "It would be unfortunate if you used it right now, as I am in sole possession of the answer to all your problems."

In recent months the trade at 'Jack's Hole' had suffered somewhat from the attentions of Frederick Charrington, self-appointed crusader against the East End's dens of iniquity. Rather than speaking out to advocate the values of Christianity and wholesome living, as many of the other moral campaigners did, Charrington crept through the streets of the

East End in the dead of night, reporting to the police on any public houses illegally running a brothel.

After having applied successfully for a warrant for the arrest of several brothel keepers, the nocturnal trade of these desperate houses of pleasure began to suffer drastically, especially at 'Jack's Hole', the most notorious of them all.

Threats of violence against Frederick Charrington were taken very seriously, and he was given police protection to continue his crusade.

But tonight, as 'Razor' Bob scuttled his way through the dingy, narrow streets of the East End, his collar turned up against the torrential downpour, he noticed trade was on the up again. It was said that several local bully boys had recognised Charrington on one of his night time visits, and that he had been alone. This had been an opportunity too good to miss. Later, they had boasted of having given Charrington a 'good seeing to'.

No one expected to see the self-appointed moral crusader in these parts for a long while to come, if indeed ever again.

'Razor' Bob loitered at the doorway of 'Jack's Hole' for a moment, as a large, buxom woman, her face heavily painted with make-up and wearing bright, garish clothing, pushed past him on her way outside, a gaudy, tatty umbrella her only defence against the elements. Bob paid her no attention. His earlier good humour had suddenly evaporated, the heavy rain extinguishing it like a freshly lit campfire. And why had Brownrigg wanted to meet here, in this God-forsaken place? Even for a dedicated slummer such as him 'Jack's Hole' was a dive; a place where, if you were lucky, you would leave in the morning with nothing more than a terrible hangover and the clothes on your back. If you were unlucky, you never left at all. Not alive, anyway.

Still, when was the last time that Bob had let something like that get in the way of acquiring some juicy titbit of information? That was his job, after all.

'Razor' Bob pushed open the door and stepped inside.

Brownrigg grabbed hold of him immediately.

"For God's sake, man, where have you been?" he hissed.

"What's yer 'urry?" Bob said, shaking himself free of the big man's grasp.

"I've had to call in a few favours for this information, and I hope tonight to see the last of you," the fat man whispered.

"Just calm yerself down and buy me a drink why don't yer?" Bob chuckled. "Then we'll talk."

Chapter Twenty-Nine
Charlotte and the Vampire

Billy Rackitt and Maria hugged the rocky wall, flattening their bodies against its cold, damp surface, trying their hardest to become invisible. Billy's breath floated from his mouth in a white vapour, and his heart pounded within his chest.

They stood near the top of the stone steps, closer to freedom than they had ever been before. Billy could see movement above them and the yellow light of several oil lamps being carried around. A gust of chilly air told him they were very close to the outside world, and the darkness told him that it was night, although what time of night he had no idea. He could hear two voices talking together, but could not make out what they were saying over the thunderous pounding of the rain. Little streams of water had begun to snake their way down the stone steps, and the occasional drip of filthy water splashed on his scalp.

"What's happenin'?" Maria whispered from behind him.

"Someone's up there," Billy whispered back. "If we try and get out now we'll be spotted."

Only an hour before, Mina had unlocked the padlocked iron gate for them and led them up the dank, dark stairway. After dangling the key to the padlock in front of them she had said very little, and Billy thought that she seemed rather sad. The climb up the stairway took a long time, and it was only after an endless trudge up the gritty, slimy steps that Billy began to realise how deep underground they had been.

As they neared the top Mina came to a halt and turned back to Billy and Maria.

"You must stay here," she said. "I can hear my husband's voice; if he finds you here then you die, and I most likely will join you."

"Why are you doing this?" Billy said. "Why risk your life to set us free?"

"Why indeed?" Mina said. She reached out a hand and stroked Billy's cheek, wiping away some of the dirt and grime. "You really think you will be free, Billy Rackitt? You are an optimist, one for whom life is full of opportunities to be grasped, chances to be taken. I envy you your naiveté. But let me tell you Billy, you will never be free. Your life was mapped out for you before you were born, before you were even conceived. You have no choices, you have no freedom, you are a puppet, little more than a pawn in a cosmic game of chess between the forces of evil."

"I don't understand," Billy said.

"Hide, Billy. Hide here in the shadows and listen, and then perhaps you will understand," Mina said and turned away to climb the remaining steps.

She quickly disappeared from view, and then Billy and Maria heard a door opening above them.

Billy listened intently to the voices above him, which now echoed down the stairs.

"Mina, my darling, this is a surprise."

Billy recognised the voice immediately, although he had heard it spoken only once before, and then but briefly.

It was Talos.

"I need some fresh air," said Mina. "I feel like a rat cooped up down there. I need to walk, to stretch, to breath."

"Don't go far, my darling," Talos said. "After all, tonight is the night, come at last."

"Tonight?" said Mina, a sudden note of uncertainty in her voice. "So soon? Have all the fragments been found then?"

"I collect the last one tonight," another voice said, one that Billy did not recognise. "And then the summoning can begin. Already the heavens tremble at the power of Semjaza's Sigil, even though only three of the pieces are joined together. Once I have the final fragment nothing can stop me."

"And then we begin the eternal night," said Mina.

"And you will be queen of that night, Mina, queen to my king," Talos said. "We will rule over the night, and we will rule over the vampires."

Suddenly there was a tremendous roar, a cacophony of noise, causing Billy and Maria to shrink back in fear. Then Billy realised what was happening; it was raining.

But it was raining harder than he had ever known before.

Mina said something else then, but Billy could not catch it above the noise of the storm. He strained to listen, but could not decipher what was being said. He wanted to creep closer, to find out more about this summoning, but dare not for fear of being found.

After a while, he realised the note of the voices had changed; that he was no longer listening to Mina and Talos, and the mysterious stranger, but that others had taken their place.

And so Maria and Billy waited for their chance, waited for the exit to the stairway to be left unattended, so that they could finally escape.

Jim sat in the kitchen with Denver. He ate ravenously, having had nothing since breakfast. He found it hard to believe that it had been only this morning that he sat on the front steps of the house with Denver, talking about finding George.

Outside, the rain still pounded on the cobblestones, rivers of water flowing down the streets. The charcoal black sky gave no hope of the rain ceasing soon.

Above them, in the living room, Tempest and Johnny Chen were in consultation with Murmur. Tempest had said they needed to find out from him what he meant when he had said he was in possession of the answer to their problems.

Denver had said they should just let her shoot him.

"I just don't like it," she said. "Murmur's got his own reasons for coning here, but I bet it ain't for our benefit."

Jim felt at the pistol, still tucked into the waistband of his trousers beneath his shirt. He had not told the others about the gun, preferring to keep it his secret.

Denver glanced over at him and, noticing something in his look, said, "You okay, kid?"

"Yeah," said Jim.

"Tempest's only dealing with that parasitic scum because he has to, you know that don't you? As soon as this is all over with, well . . . we'll deal with Murmur once and for all."

"Yeah, I know," Jim said, because he knew that if nobody else was prepared to do it, then he would deal with Murmur for sure.

Charlotte MacKinnon drew back the curtains in her living room and looked out of the rain-streaked window. The thundering, torrential downpour obscured her view of the street almost completely. Not fit for man nor beast to be outside, and yet that was where her husband was right now, unless he had left the Royal Geographical Society later than anticipated and seen the torrential downpour. But then Charles MacKinnon, famed explorer and adventurer, was unlikely to be put off by an 'inoffensive little English shower', as he would call it.

Charles had seen much more in the way of extreme weather than most people, his famed explorations taking him into the most hostile and inhospitable corners of the world imaginable. He had also encountered dangerous animals and exotic peoples, suffered from tropical diseases and severe malnutrition and narrowly escaped death when caught between warring tribes. He generally liked to regale anybody who would care to listen with his experiences, but of late Charlotte had become convinced that her husband was embellishing his stories somewhat, as they rang less true, and increasingly more fantastical, with each telling.

Even their eight-year-old boy, Edward, seemed to be harbouring suspicions that his explorer father was not telling him the complete truth.

"Did Daddy really wrestle an alligator to the ground and kill it with his bare hands, Mummy?" the little boy had asked her at teatime just this evening.

"If that's what your father said happened, then that's what happened," replied Charlotte, although she sounded less than convinced even to herself.

Still, if Charles wanted to embellish his stories, then that was up to him. If his ego still needed massaging after all the years of famed exploration and discoveries he had made, after the plaudits from the learned societies and journals, then that was his problem.

Of course Charlotte knew what the root of the problem really was; the great Richard 'Mjasiri' Speke, once again stealing Charles' thunder from underneath his nose. From the moment that Speke had returned from the first unsupported trek through the swamplands of the Ituru forest, home to many unknown species of insect life and fauna, and the fierce cannibal tribes that had stopped many other explorers in their tracks, he had become the most famous British adventurer of recent times. Now leading a scientific expedition into the Antarctic, every telegraphed report from the ship was awaited with bated breath by the British public.

It was unfortunate that Charles had chosen this time to return from his travels in Iraq with what he believed to be a fantastic archaeological find. He had been most excited on his return to England, but was met with a certain amount of indifference, and only a vague, polite interest in his find.

And now it lay around their house, on the sideboard, sometimes on the floor where it was licked occasionally by the dog. Charlotte, letting the curtains fall back into place, shielding her from the weather, picked up the rough piece of rock and looked at it for what seemed the thousandth time, wondering what on earth its importance could be.

What had Charles called it?

A sigil.

Only it wasn't a whole sigil, simply a fragment of one, the last fragment to be found, if Charles was to be believed.

Charlotte sighed.

Perhaps if it had been the first fragment to have been found, then there would have been more interest.

Charlotte started at a knock at the front door. It was unlikely to be Charles, unless he had lost his key; but she could not imagine that anybody else would be out on such a horrible night. Taking pity on the poor wretch currently standing on the front step, no doubt close to drowning under the weight of rainwater pouring from the sky, Charlotte hurried to the door.

As she passed the bottom of the staircase, a shadow caught the corner of her eye, and, without even bothering to turn her head, she said, "Edward, go back to bed. Now."

A sigh from near the top of the stairs told her that she had been heard and that Edward was returning to his bedroom.

Charlotte opened the front door. A tall, thin man, the collar of his raincoat turned up against the elements, stood on her step. He wore a wide-brimmed hat, from which poured a steady stream of water.

"Good evening," he said. "I am sorry to trouble you on such an evening, Mrs MacKinnon, but I believe your husband has recently come into possession of the last remaining fragment of the Sigil of Semjaza."

"Yes, that's right," Charlotte said. "I suppose you're a collector, Mr . . .?"

"Kralik. Zedekiah Kralik, and yes, you suppose right. Excuse me, but I am rather wet, and the rain does not look like stopping . . ."

"Oh!" Charlotte exclaimed. "Of course, do come in. Where are my manners?"

In the living room, Kralik removed his hat, and Charlotte got her first good look at his face. She quickly looked away.

She felt as though Kralik's eyes had burnt into her and sullied her soul, dirtied her beyond her comprehension.

Don't be silly, she thought to herself. But she could not bring herself to look him directly in the eyes again.

"Is Mr Mackinnon here?" Kralik said.

"No," Charlotte said, immediately regretting her answer. "But I'm expecting him back any time now."

But Kralik wasn't listening. Instead he was moving, almost gliding it seemed to Charlotte, across the carpeted floor, towards the fragment, where she had let it fall when she heard the door knocker. Kralik picked the fragment up, holding it reverentially before him, a small sigh of satisfaction escaping his lips.

On the verge of saying something, not wanting him to handle the fragment for some reason unknown to her, she snapped her mouth shut when she heard a sound behind her.

Edward, sneaking back downstairs again.

Charlotte did not want him in the same room as this cold, sinister stranger. She turned, ready to tell him off and send him back to his room, but instead emitted a tiny scream at what she saw.

A gaunt, semi-naked figure crouched before her, dripping rainwater onto their expensive carpet, its grey, vein threaded skin glistening slightly under the glow of the gas jets. Its bulging, bloodshot eyes narrowed in anticipation of its kill, and it hissed at Charlotte, revealing its long, pointed fangs dripping bloody saliva.

"Please don't move," Kralik said. "If you do then the vampire will kill you. It is a long time since he has fed on the blood of a human, and stray cats and dogs are no substitute."

"Have you got what you came for?" Charlotte said, her voice surprisingly calm and flat.

"Yes, I have," Kralik said.

"Then please leave, now."

"Mummy?"

Edward stood in the hall, wearing his pyjamas, and looking into the living room, his eyes round and wide as he looked at the crouching vampire already turning towards him.

"Edward, go back to bed now," Charlotte said.

Edward looked from the gaunt, hungry vampire to his mother, his jaw dropping in surprise. The vampire regarded Edward carefully, sizing him up perhaps, calculating how much resistance he was likely to put up as it pounced on him.

Edward took a step back, looking at the creature before him once more.

The vampire leapt at the child, its mouth open and ready to close around the soft flesh of the little boy's neck, ready to suck his blood from the veins that pulsed just beneath the surface of the skin. Charlotte screamed, a high-pitched, piercing shriek, and the vampire juddered to a halt on the floor in front of Edward, shaking its head in confusion and irritation.

Seeing the vampire's confusion, Charlotte took a deep breath and screamed again, holding the scream as long as she could. The vampire clapped its hands over its ears, shaking its head from side to side, trying to rid itself of the awful noise that pierced its mind and confused it so.

Edward turned and ran up the stairs, his tiny, slippered feet slapping furiously against each of the steps in turn.

Charlotte was suddenly hit in the small of her back and slammed face down onto the floor, her scream cut short as she gasped for air. She felt Kralik's heavy weight on top of her, pinning her down. She lifted her head and looked up to see the vampire gathering itself up and leaping for the stairs in pursuit of her son.

"Let the vampire have the boy's blood," Kralik whispered in her ear, "for in only a matter of hours none of this will matter any more."

Charlotte struggled for a second, and then sobbed and let her head fall to the floor. Kralik was too strong for her; she would never fight him off in time to run upstairs and rescue her boy.

But then suddenly he was gone. She looked up and saw his shadowy shape running for the door and out of her sight. Charlotte pulled herself up onto her knees, a scream of agony escaping her lips. The small of her back exploded with pain, shooting hundreds of red-hot needles through her torso and paralysing her where she knelt. Gritting her teeth until she thought her jaw might break, Charlotte reminded herself of the monstrous thing upstairs, possibly sucking the blood from her child right at this very moment.

Taking a deep breath and ignoring the pain, she staggered to her feet and walked unsteadily to the foot of the staircase. She halted as she heard Edward scream.

"No, you will not have his blood," she muttered, and ran stumbling up the stairs, her shaking hand gripping the banister with all her strength, the pain in her back spreading through her limbs and up into her head, until her whole body felt as though it was on fire.

She halted once more at the top of the staircase, frozen in shock at the gruesome tableau before her. Through the bedroom door she could see the vampire crouched over Edward who lay on his bed, his head buried beneath his arms in an attempt to block out the horror before him. Once again the thing opened its mouth, baring its fangs, and uttered an anticipatory whine of satisfaction.

Charlotte ran to the bedroom, shouting, "Edward! Edward!"

Her child sobbed and drew his knees up into his chest. The vampire ignored her and lunged for the boy's neck.

Charlotte took a deep breath and screamed at the top of her voice.

The vampire's head snapped around at the sound of the scream, its bloodshot eyes staring at Charlotte. Her body racked with pain, she took another breath and screamed again as the vampire clapped its hands over its ears, trying to shut out the sound it hated so.

Charlotte let the scream drag out until her lungs were empty and then drew another deep, ragged breath of air, clutching at the door-frame for support. In the time it took her to fill her lungs once more, the vampire climbed from the bed and began advancing on Charlotte, blinking its grey skinned eyelids at her.

Another scream, and the vampire halted in its advance again, covering up its ears and trying to block out the awful sound that the woman made.

But Charlotte could only make the scream last so long, before her lungs were empty again, and in the time it took her to draw another breath the vampire had advanced on her some more, drawing ever closer. An excess of oxygen began flooding through her body with each deep lungful, and her vision clouded over, the effects of hyperventilation making her feel faint. One more paralysing scream was all she could manage and then the thing would have won, and it could suck the lifeblood from her and her little boy.

She screamed her last, a feeble effort this time, which hardly bothered the vampire at all as it continued advancing upon her. Suddenly it was on top of her, pushing her to the floor, one clawed hand on her chest and holding her down, the other pulling at her hair, yanking her head back to expose the soft flesh of her neck.

Maybe Edward will have time to run, she thought, as she felt hot splashes of the foul thing's saliva dripping onto her throat. Maybe this is the only way I can save him.

Charlotte's whole body stiffened in shock as the vampire lunged at her, as she felt its fangs piercing her flesh, as she heard its disgusting sucking noises, and felt her life force dribbling away from her.

She clasped her arms around the vampire's gaunt, skeletal body, hoping to hold on to it as long as she had strength left within her, keep it from taking her boy.

"Oh please, dear God, let it not take my boy," she whispered. "Please Lord Jesus, not my boy, not Edward."

But it was useless, the thing was too strong, and it wrenched free of her grasp, suddenly emitting a high, mournful keening noise. Charlotte placed a trembling hand over the wound on her throat, stemming the flow of blood, and looked up at the vampire through a haze of tears. It thrashed violently from side to side, its hands scrabbling at something behind its back.

It was only when the vampire had fallen face down on the floor beside her that Charlotte noticed the long bladed knife protruding from between its shoulder blades, and the deep crimson blood that oozed from the wound.

She looked up at Edward, standing above them both, his face white with shock.

"Did . . . did you do this?" she whispered.

Edward nodded, unable to take his eyes from the bloodsucking monster lying lifeless beside his mother.

"Where did you get the knife from?" she said.

"Daddy gave it to me," her little boy said. "He said he used it to kill a lion in the Congo when it tried to eat him."

Charlotte pulled her son to her and hugged him fiercely. Downstairs she heard the front door open, and her husband's voice call her name.

"Don't worry," she whispered. "Daddy's home."

Chapter Thirty
An Uneasy Alliance

Jim kept to a shadowed corner of the room, out of sight of Murmur's gaze. The demon had already seen him when he entered the living room, but paid him scant attention. Once he had been a curiosity perhaps, an opportunity to feed on definitely, but now he was nothing in the demon's sight.

Still, Jim felt compelled to keep his distance.

Murmur still sat in the high-backed chair in front of the fire, holding court with Tempest and Johnny Chen. Denver sat a little away from them, but closer than Jim, close enough to make her presence known to the demon.

"I don't believe what I'm hearing here," she was saying right now, still staring at Murmur, but talking to the others. "You're seriously telling me that this piece of shit is our only hope of stopping Kralik?"

"It seems that way, yes," Tempest said.

Lucifer curled his lithe body around Jim's leg, making him jump. The cat looked up at Jim and blinked his green eyes at him, a contented purring now emanating from deep within his throat.

Jim pushed the cat away with his foot, wanting nothing to do with it, or anything else associated with Murmur. His skin crawled at the touch of its fur against his flesh.

Denver was up on her feet now, pacing up and down the living room.

"Explain it to me one more time," she said. "Just so's I can get it straight in my head."

"Murmur said that, once the invocation to summon Semjaza has been performed, nothing can reverse it," Tempest said. "There is only one recitation in existence that can reverse this particular invocation, and that is recorded in The Heptameron of Arcanity and Pacts, which we know is lost in central Africa."

"But you're saying you know another way," Denver said, wheeling on Murmur, who had followed Denver's every move with his black, soulless eyes.

"Yes, that's right," whispered the demon, his grey, thin tongue snaking out from between his lips for a brief moment, and then disappearing again. "If the invocation used in the summoning were to be recited backwards, then the summoning could be stopped and the demon returned to Hell, even a demon as powerful as Semjaza. But this will only work in the moments after the invocation has been completed. Leave it too long, and nothing can be done, and the forces of Hell will occupy the earth forever more."

Again the cat rubbed its body up against Jim's leg, its purring growing ever louder. Jim pushed it away again. Not to be deterred, Lucifer leapt onto Jim's lap and, resisting the boy's attempts to push him off, curled up to go to sleep.

"And you're the only one who can recite the incantation backwards?" Denver said.

"No, not the only one," Murmur whispered, the ghost of a smile passing across his gaunt features. "I'm the only one here who can recite it. To be effective, the incantation must be recited backwards by a demon."

"I don't get it," Denver said. "Why would a demon want to stop the summoning of another demon? It doesn't make sense."

"You know nothing, Denver McCade," Murmur hissed, his eyes suddenly alight with an unholy fire. "Why don't you go back to sucking on an opium pipe, obliterating your miserable life from your tiny little mind?"

"And what makes even less sense," Denver said, ignoring the demon and turning to face Tempest and Johnny Chen, "is why this particular demon wants to reverse a summoning which would open up the gates of Hell?"

Jim pushed at the cat, trying to get it off him, and his fingers slipped beneath its collar. He looked a little more closely at the collar now, at the strange symbols drawn on it. Magical symbols of some kind, perhaps.

And then a thought occurred to Jim; why would a demon feel the need to keep a pet cat?

"Once I am found by the spirits with which I shared Hell," Murmur said, "I will be caught and tormented for the rest of eternity. Upon my release onto earth I should have spent my time searching for a way to set them free, but I did not, choosing instead to take pleasure in what your pathetic little lives have to offer in the way of enjoyment."

Jim pushed at the cat again and this time sent it tumbling to the floor, where it landed with a thump.

Denver glanced briefly in the direction of the sound and then turned back to Tempest, and said, "And you believe him?"

"Yes," Tempest said. "I believe him."

"Time is running short," Murmur whispered. "Already the heavens signal that Kralik has the last fragment of the sigil; its power grows now that it is almost whole again. Kralik can begin the summoning at any moment. We must act."

"But where will he perform the summoning ritual?" Denver said. "We can't stop him unless we know where he is."

216

"I know where he is," Tempest said, his eyes suddenly alight. "Johnny, let's open up the armoury, we need to be defended against Talos and his horde of undead. Denver, are you coming with us?"

"Just you try and stop me," Denver said, her hand reaching for the Peacemaker, her fingers curling round its familiar grip.

"I'm coming too," Jim said, standing up.

"No you're not," Tempest replied, barely even glancing in his direction. "You're stopping here."

"No one tells a Kerrigan what to do," Jim said. "I told you, I'm coming with you."

Tempest stopped and turned slowly to face Jim. Jim swallowed, a tiny knot of fear suddenly tightening in the pit of his stomach. What had possessed him to challenge Tempest's authority like that?

"Let the kid come," Denver said. "Hell, it's not like he's any safer here than with us, right? Because if we don't stop Kralik tonight then we all lose, every single one of us."

"Alright then," Tempest replied. "You can come with us."

The knot of fear in Jim's stomach grew. It was too late to back down now.

Chapter Thirty-One
Caxton Tempest at the End of the World

They stood in silence in the thunderous rain and looked at the grey, dilapidated East End church. The building shivered and trembled as though it were alive, the brick walls and the slate roof undulating in the darkness, like some mighty mythical beast waking from its slumber. Jim blinked several times in an effort to dispel what he thought was an optical illusion, but the effect persisted. It seemed as though the ancient church building would uproot itself from the ground at any second and lumber towards them, intent on crushing them beneath its stonework. But as they moved closer, threading their way through the maze of tumbledown, moss-covered gravestones, he realised that it was not the church that undulated so, but what covered it.

A mass of black, grotesque insects crawled across the church, covering every little nook and cranny, scurrying over the roof and through the windows. Beneath the pounding of the rain hitting the ground, Jim could now hear another sound, the rapid, staccato click of thousands of tiny legs, scuttling across the worn stonework. Looking down at his feet he saw more of the evil looking things crawling from the mud. Black, bulbous spiders, bigger than his fist, thick, gnarly stick insects large enough to straddle a man's head, monstrous, hairy centipedes, swollen cockroaches and other indescribable creatures crawled up from the bowels of the earth, skittering over his shoes and making him shudder in revulsion.

Jim kicked out at the monstrosities under his feet and took a couple of steps back. He looked up at the others, standing beside him, blinking as heavy raindrops splashed in his eyes.

"Do not fear the insects," Johnny Chen said. "There is far worse yet to be let loose from the depths of Hell."

Jim swallowed and looked back to the grey, moving mass that covered the church building. A fiery, orange light seemed to be growing within and emanating from the windows, between the scurrying bodies of the insects.

He took a firm hold of the crossbow he had been given by Johnny Chen, its grip unfamiliar to his young hands. Beside him stood Tempest, also carrying a crossbow, but larger and sleeker than Jim's.

Next to Tempest stood Denver, her Colt .45 Peacemaker at the ready. Beside Denver stood Johnny Chen, a long, curved sword in his hands, which the Chinaman had told Jim was a Pudao, a weapon used many years ago in the Chinese infantry, with a blade so sharp it was capable of slicing a man's arm off in a single stroke.

Behind them all lurked Murmur, his gaunt frame stooped and clawed, his eyes flicking from side to side. He paid no heed to the grotesque insects, and they crawled freely over his crooked body, lending his already unsettling appearance an even more freakish, terrifying aspect.

"So, Kralik has been here all along, hidden from us and protected by Talos," Tempest said.

"It's not Talos we're after tonight," Denver said.

"We are after anyone who comes between us and Kralik," Tempest replied.

The five figures looked at the church in silence for a few seconds more.

"Let's go," Tempest said, arming the crossbow and striding through the rain and mud towards the church, his booted feet kicking the gruesome insects from his path as he walked.

Jim moved forward with the others, slightly behind them. He could sense Murmur at his back, a tingling sensation between his shoulder blades where he felt the demon might strike at him at any second, still unable to trust his motives. Suddenly hearing a hissing, squelching noise, Jim turned swiftly bringing the crossbow up in front of him, ready to fire at Murmur as he pounced upon him.

But he was wrong. Murmur had hissed, but it was not at Jim he looked, but at a dilapidated gravestone, and the bubbling, boiling mound of earth in front of it.

"The dead are being wrenched from their graves," hissed Murmur. "The summoning must be near completion."

As Jim watched transfixed, a dirty, skeletal hand clawed its way from the mound of soil, and then another, and these two lifeless, animated hands began pushing and pulling their way out from the blackness of the grave. The cadaverous arms were visible now, reaching up to the filthy sky, rainwater running down their pale, hairless length to mingle with the mud. And from that churning, boiling mass of mud Jim saw a head appearing, a grinning skull, scraps of hair and flesh still hanging from it, and its black, empty eye sockets staring straight at the boy.

For a moment Jim thought that it was Marchek Mulready, come to get his revenge on Jim for the horrible, fiery death he had suffered. He stepped back, only to feel cold hands grabbing at his ankles, frenziedly pulling and scratching at him.

Swallowing the urge to scream, Jim kicked at the hands that were scrabbling from the graves around him and then raised the crossbow and aimed at the corpse pulling itself from the mud and slime of its earthly tomb. Only its legs were hidden now, its grey, rotting torso streaked with mud and sections of its ribcage now visible between patches of decayed flesh. It struggled towards Jim, ignoring Murmur.

Jim fired the crossbow, the steel-tipped arrow piercing the thing's skull, and sending it crashing into the ground. Incredibly it struggled upwards once more, hands pulling at the arrow protruding from its skull.

A sudden flash of lightning lit up the night sky, illuminating the graveyard for a second as bright as the noonday sun. All around them, in the stark, harsh relief of the lightning strike, could be seen hundreds more animated cadavers, mud and rotting flesh dripping from their bones. Some still struggled from their graves, others stood beside their former resting places, dazed and confused, wondering at their new found freedom.

And some already approached the living, staggering towards them like the drunks that Jim had seen so often on his late night forays in the city. But none of the drunks he had ever seen had been possessed of such a single-mindedness of purpose as these living dead seemed to have.

"They crave our flesh," hissed Murmur. "Brought back to life they realise that their own flesh is dead, and so they crave the taste of living flesh, to try and regain what they have lost."

The corpse that Jim had shot was free now of its grave and advanced upon him, the arrow still protruding from its skull. Jim loaded the crossbow again and loosed another arrow at the living corpse, hitting it in the chest. The ghastly thing before him continued its advance, barely noticing the arrow protruding from its ribcage, its arms reaching out at full length towards Jim, its bony fingers twitching to grasp hold of him. Transfixed by the ghoulish sight of the undead thing's advance, Jim lost the ability to move, to act, and stared in frozen terror as the corpse took hold of him.

The thing opened its mouth to sink its teeth into his face when suddenly its head flew from its shoulders and landed on a tombstone only a few feet away, the teeth still snapping together as though chewing on its prize. But the headless corpse continued to grasp at Jim, until Johnny Chen hacked at it again with the Pudao, slashing first at its arms until it let go of Jim and fell to the muddy ground, and then chopping the rest of it up into little pieces where it lay. Incredibly the segments of gore and bone continued wriggling towards Jim with a life of their own.

Johnny Chen pulled at the boy, dragging him towards the church.

"Come Master Kerrigan," he shouted over the roar of the pounding rain. "If you stay here you will die!"

Followed by Murmur they ran to join Tempest and Denver, who stood facing an army of undead blocking their path to the church, their rotting flesh sloughing from their bodies in the powerful deluge, creating a bubbling pool of gore around their feet.

221

Jim turned to look behind them, but already they were hemmed in by another army of living dead, trudging a relentless path through the mud of the graveyard towards them.

"Take Murmur and follow Mr Tempest and Miss McCade into the church," Johnny Chen said, leaning down close to Jim. "The demon is our only hope now to reverse the summoning."

And then, letting out a blood-curdling howl, the Chinaman ran into the midst of the corpses, brandishing the deadly Pudao at anything in his path. The night air was suddenly filled with an unearthly high-pitched screaming as the dreadful corpses scattered before the Chinaman and created a clear path to the church doors.

"C'mon," Jim shouted at Murmur, sickened by the sight of the demon's haggard body still covered in shiny black bugs and other loathsome insects, some crawling over his face now, and in his mouth and nose.

As the Chinaman continued his single-handed assault on the mob of undead, Jim and Murmur ran to the church steps to join Tempest and Denver.

The massive wooden church doors lay wide open, the fiery orange light spilling out of the building and illuminating the four figures standing on the stone steps. Yet more corpses staggered from the shadows, one of them ahead of the others grabbing Murmur and sinking its teeth into his shoulder. Denver shot the thing in the head, its skull exploding in a shower of brains and bone, its headless body recoiling from the force of the bullet impact.

"Get inside!" she shouted, firing the Colt .45 frantically into the army of living dead that approached them. "I'll fend these jokers off, you guys stop Kralik before it's too late."

Tempest stepped inside the church, with Jim and Murmur close behind him. The church floor was flooded, hundreds of insects floating in the rainwater, their legs pistoning crazily as they tried to get a purchase on something solid. Jim watched in horrified silence as Tempest closed the church doors on Denver and then pushed the bolt into place. Denver had been hastily reloading the Colt .45 as the ghouls advanced upon her, close enough to reach out and grab her, as Tempest closed the doors, and then Jim saw her no more.

Tempest began walking down the centre aisle, between the hard wooden pews. The empty building echoed with the noise of the rain hitting the roof, and the scurrying and scratching of the thousands of tiny insect legs.

At the end of the church, standing over the altar on which lay the four fragments of the Sigil of Semjaza, was Zedekiah Kralik. His torso was bare, and on his chest was drawn the symbol that was represented on the stone sigil before him. Already the dark lines of the magical symbol were smoking and burning into his flesh.

"Caxton Tempest!" he shouted, a crazed smile stretching across his face, his flesh trembling and twitching as though it might rip apart at any second. "How good to see you. Talos told me you might drop by, and you couldn't really have chosen a finer moment."

Tempest raised the crossbow, aiming it at Kralik's chest.

"It's over, Kralik," he said. "Come with us, and we can find some way of exorcising the demon within you. If there's still a part of you left, you can make that choice."

"Choice? There are no choices, Tempest. Your life, my life, it was all mapped out for us, before we were even born. You might think you have a choice, you might think that you make your own, independent decisions, but none of that is true. The theologians argue over predestination and free will, but they might as well be dogs, trying to fathom the mind of their master, for all they know. There are only two powers that have ever operated in this world: God and the Council of Seven. The Council of Seven will soon be no more, and God, well, God has turned his back on his miserable creation and forsaken you forever. When Jesus cried on the cross 'It is over!' it wasn't a victory shout, it was a cry of defeat. It *is* over Tempest, the day is drawing to a close, and soon the night will come."

"You're wrong," Tempest said. "That's not you talking, it's the demon."

Kralik laughed. "I exorcised that demon years ago, Tempest, but not before he had told me many things, the power of Semjaza's Sigil being one of them. I wish I had time to enlighten you on a few more, but as you can see, events are a little out of my control now."

"If I have to kill you to stop this summoning, then I will, Kralik."

"Stop the summoning?" Kralik shouted, the skin stretched across his ribcage rippling like the sea. "Can't you see it's already far too late? The summoning is over. Semjaza is entering my body even as we speak, and the gates of Hell will open soon after, flooding the world with every kind of evil that has ever existed since the beginning of time. How does it feel, Caxton Tempest, at the end of the world? Does it feel good?"

Jim heard a raspy rustling from above, and he looked up to see a darkened shape dropping from the shadows of the rafters. Instinctively he raised his crossbow as the vampire crashed into him. It let out an agonised scream and dropped at Jim's feet, an arrow sticking from its chest.

Another vampire hurtled towards Tempest who turned and shot it in the chest with the crossbow. Jim looked up again to see many more of the grey-skinned figures dropping from the church rafters and leaping over the pews for them. Jim fired the crossbow at another leaping for him and hit it in the chest. It fell squealing to the ground, clutching at the arrow sticking from its ribcage, its blood pulsing over its hands.

The mass of vampires shrank back for a second, suddenly aware of the power before them. Tempest aimed the crossbow at Kralik once more, who was now trembling so badly that his body was barely distinguishable as human.

Before he had a chance to fire the crossbow, the vampires attacked once more, falling upon them as one. As Jim watched, horrified, Tempest was overwhelmed by a mass of scratching, biting creatures of the night. Jim loosed another arrow from the crossbow, before succumbing himself to the countless attacking vampires.

Darkness overpowered Jim, the rancid, coppery smell of blood and death filling his mouth and lungs, threatening to suffocate him. He kicked and punched at the bodies that smothered him, fending off the twisted, distorted faces, their mouths wide open to reveal their vicious fangs as they strained frantically for the soft flesh of his throat. As he beat and pushed at them, his arms grew red with crisscrossing rips in his skin.

"Leave them!" a voice shouted, cutting through the night air.

The vampires pulled themselves off Jim, leaving him gasping for air on the cold, hard floor. He clambered unsteadily to his hands and knees, looking around him for Tempest, who was struggling beneath the weight of a group of vampires pinning him to the ground.

He could not see Murmur anywhere.

"Let them watch their final moments on earth," said a powerful-looking vampire – Jim assumed it was Talos – standing at the altar beside Kralik, now nothing more than an indistinct blur and letting out a high-pitched moan, slowly building in intensity.

We failed, Jim thought. *We tried our best, but we failed.*

Chapter Thirty-Two
Billy and Maria

Rainwater flowed down the stone steps, a shallow waterfall filled with grotesque cockroaches and centipedes, which scurried around Billy's feet and tried to climb up Maria's legs. The little girl, so brave in the face of the underground hordes of vampires, screamed and kicked at the insects, and Jesus climbed onto her shoulder and hid beneath her hair.

Billy plucked a particularly large and loathsome cockroach from his trouser leg and threw it against the wall. Its shell made a loud popping sound as it exploded against the hard rock.

"I told you there weren't no way out," the girl said, all the while kicking at the water around her. "We should go back. We were safe down below."

"No," Billy said, looking up at the orange light emanating from the top of the stairs. "I don't know what's happening up there, but one thing's for sure; up ahead there's freedom, and back down below there's nothing but death."

"No, I ain't going up there," Maria said, shaking her head. "It were that woman, she tricked us."

Billy looked up the stairs again. He was sure that Mina was not tricking them, that she had had her own purpose for leaving tonight that did not involve them, but that she had not intended to trick them.

"Come on, Maria," he said, taking hold of her hand. She did not struggle or resist as he began ascending the stairs, his feet slipping in the water and on the bodies of cockroaches.

A few seconds later, they were at the top, behind an old wooden door pushed slightly ajar by the force of the running water. Billy peered through the gap and drew in his breath at the sight of all the vampires. They seemed to be inside a church.

"Your whistle," Billy said to Maria. "Have you got it with you?"

"Yeah," said the girl, pulling it from the tatters of her clothing.

"You're gonna need it," Billy said.

Black despair filled Jim's heart, and tears welled up in his eyes at the thought of all he had been through recently, only for it to finally end like this. Within the storm that only a few seconds before had still been recognisable as Kralik, Jim could now see a new form taking shape, a powerful, evil-looking, demonic shape. Semjaza was finally free, and behind him would come the hordes of Hell, suddenly set loose from their prison to roam the earth for eternity. Jim tried again to pull himself out from under the vampires that held him pinned to the floor, but it was useless; they were far too strong, and he was weak.

Jim closed his eyes, finally giving up all hope, when suddenly the piercing sound of a policeman's whistle filled the church, and the vampires let go of Jim's arms. He opened his eyes and saw the vampires had clapped their hands over their ears, the sound utter agony to them. A young girl was running through the church blowing the whistle for all she was worth, and following her was a man running from a door set back in the chancel.

The girl took a deep breath, and in that moment the vampires got ready to attack, but then she was blowing the whistle again, and again the vampires were paralysed by the piercing sound.

Taking his chance, Jim pulled out the pistol hidden in the waistband of his trousers. His hand shook as he held the gun, the girl's whistle piercing through his skull and the sound of the vampires groaning in agony. He tried to lift the gun but it felt too heavy, too cumbersome. Then Tempest closed his hand around the revolver and pried it from the young boy's grasp. He aimed it at Kralik and fired six times at the demonic form materialising before them.

The smouldering red horned figure threw back its arms, a demonic roar filling the building, and then it was gone, and Kralik was visible again, six bullet holes in his chest, surrounded by the Sigil of Semjaza. He stumbled, clutching at his wounds, and fell with a splash to the floor, lying face down in the water on the cold flagstones.

For a few moments nobody moved, even the vampires staring in fearful silence at Kralik's lifeless body lying on the floor. The only sounds were those of the rain still pounding on the church roof and the clicking of the insect legs scurrying over the building.

"It's over," Tempest said, climbing to his feet and pushing the vampires from him.

"No," Talos replied, climbing up on to the altar and looking out over his horde of vampires, crouching on the ground. "It has only just started. The summoning was completed."

Jim suddenly became aware of a low vibration humming through the ground, becoming slowly stronger and deeper. After only a few seconds, he began to feel the rumble passing through his body, and, lifting up a hand, he saw that he could not keep it from trembling. The walls of the church were shaking now, and the stained glass windows began to shatter and crash to the floor, letting in swathes of rain.

"The gates of Hell are opening!" shouted Talos, raising his arms above his head.

"Everybody outside now!" Tempest shouted, running over to Maria and picking her up beneath one arm. He ran for the doors, Billy Rackitt following him. Jim ran too, struggling to keep his feet as the ground bucked and swayed beneath them.

Then he was outside, the rain pouring down his body, and hundreds of living corpses blocking their path out of the graveyard. Johnny Chen and Denver stood back to back, their bodies dripping with blood and gore.

"Tell me it's over, Tempest," Denver said. "Tell me that noise I hear is a victory roll and not the death-knell for our funeral."

Behind them from within the church there was a sudden explosion, a wave of heat pushing everyone to the ground. Face down in the cold mud Jim covered his head with his hands.

The waves of heat and light seemed to go on forever, but when they finally ceased, and Jim was able to lift his head from the muddy ground, the first thing he noticed was that the rain had stopped.

The next thing he saw were the hundreds of dead bodies lying scattered around the graveyard, completely and utterly lifeless. The church itself was on fire, the flames licking at the insides of the windows.

Jim struggled to his feet, looking for the others. Tempest was up already, the young girl by his side, and helping Denver to her feet. Johnny Chen was pulling the man up from the mud.

The ragged group clung together and helped each other pick their way between the still corpses, and away from the church. As they walked Tempest looked around him at the devastation, the grim set to his face reminding Jim of the first time he had seen him.

"What the hell's happening now?" Denver said, wiping blood and mud from her eyes.

"It seems the summoning of Semjaza is over with, and that he remains where he belongs; in Hell," Tempest said.

"How can you be sure?" asked Denver.

"Look around you," said Tempest. "The dead are no longer alive, possessed by an evil force beyond our understanding. It's over."

"Indeed it is," said Murmur, his gaunt, crooked body silhouetted by the glow of the burning church as he approached them, clasping the fragments of the sigil to his chest. "The summoning incantation has been reversed, the gates of Hell remain closed and the vampires have gone, dissipated into the night."

He let the four fragments fall to the ground.

"And now, Caxton Tempest, I advise you to destroy these fragments beyond repair, so that the sigil's power will be lost forever," Murmur whispered.

227

Denver pulled the Colt .45 from her holster and fired five bullets into the fragments, pulverising them to dust.

And then she raised the gun and pointed it at the demon's chest, her mouth twisting into a grim shadow of a smile.

"Now it's your turn, Murmur," she said.

"Denver, no," Tempest said.

Murmur said nothing, his hands twitching by his sides, his eyes staring at Denver.

"Don't give me any crap about how he helped us here, Tempest," she said. "Murmur helped nobody but himself tonight, and you know as well as I do that once he leaves here he'll be out hunting down the innocent and sucking their lives from them. He tried to kill me once, and he killed Jim's brother George, and given a chance he'll kill any of us, too."

"Then go ahead, Denver McCade," Murmur whispered. "Shoot me."

"This here's a Colt .45 Peacemaker," Denver said, "once used by Bat Masterson when he was sheriff of Ford County. It can blow a hole right through your chest, or in your case, your host body's chest. So while it might not kill you, it'll send you back to Hell where you belong . . ."

Denver paused long enough to pull back the hammer on the gun.

" . . . and that's good enough for me."

Jim winced at the roar of the Colt .45 and closed his eyes against the glare of the muzzle flash. When he opened his eyes again, Murmur was lying on the muddy ground on his back, his clawed hands clutching at his chest, his black, lifeless eyes still staring at Denver.

Tempest walked over to the ancient body and felt for a pulse in its neck. When he pulled his hand away scraps of parchment-dry flesh flaked from the corpse and fluttered away in a light breeze.

"Is he dead?" Johnny Chen said.

"I think so," replied Tempest. "It's hard to tell. What constituted life for the demon Murmur? Did his host body have any of the normal signs of life, such as a pulse or normal body temperature? Did his lungs breathe air for the purpose of living or simply to facilitate speech?"

"How long did he possess this body, do you think?" said Johnny Chen.

"Only a couple of years at the most," Denver said.

"Murmur's demonic energy must have placed enormous demands upon it, sucking it dry at an incredible rate."

"Well, he's gone, now," Denver drawled.

Suddenly the black cat leapt from the darkness, screeching and yowling, and jumped onto a gravestone. It looked at the gathering, its fur standing on end and its green eyes flashing angrily at them.

"Dammit!" Denver hissed, aiming the gun at the cat and pulling the trigger. The hammer clicked hollowly on an empty chamber, and she watched impotently as Lucifer turned and ran, disappearing into the gloom of the graveyard.

Chapter Thirty-Three
Lucifer

The pale, watery sun struggled over London's horizon of dirty rooftops, casting its weak light across the city. As day chased night, the dark rain-clouds sped away, disgorging their contents out at sea. A cold wind blew through the streets, catching screwed up remnants of newspaper and pamphlets, and propelling them down deserted alleyways. Large pools of water, reminders of the night's torrential downpour, made navigating the early morning London thoroughfares a tricky business.

Inspector Behrends weaved his way through the bales and sacks that littered the London Docks and shivered as the cold morning air penetrated his clothing. He stepped carefully around the large puddles of seawater, his shoes slipping on cobblestones glistening in the early morning light. Rough-hewn porters and sailors in their gaudy clothes pushed past him, loading and unloading their cargoes of wines, tobacco, exotic spices, coffee and tea. The sailors made up a multicoloured pageant of nationalities: the Frenchman, the Lascar, the Portuguese, the African.

The cold, weak sun silhouetted the forest of masts and rigging pointing skywards like the spires of many churches, along with the big, black funnels of the steam ships, belching out their filthy smoke. The shouts and curses of the ships' crews filled the air, some in English and others in languages Behrends did not recognise. The skippers barked out their orders, standing on the prow of their ships in oilskin coats.

The Inspector breathed deep of the aromatic smells of tobacco and spices. This at least was some recompense for having to rise so early and meet his guests at the dock. A heavy-set, bronzed sailor set down a packing case amongst its mates, his thick arms rippling with muscle.

"I'm looking for the *Etruria*," Behrends said. "Where is she docking?"

"Over there, Sor," the sailor said, pointing further down the dock where a huge steamer sat disgorging its passengers. Behrends pushed his way past the porters and the sailors, anxious not to miss his American guests.

The Inspector stood at the foot of the gangplank waiting patiently as the ship's passengers walked past him and towards waiting carriages. Behrends wondered how he would recognise the men he was waiting for. It had been many years since he last had any dealings with them, and time had dulled his memory of those events. Even as these thoughts passed through the Inspector's mind, he saw a man walking towards him down the

231

gangplank, and a shudder ran through his body as he recognised him and knew that he could never really forget after all. The man had a shock of silver hair, giving him a highly distinctive and memorable look. Behrends had hoped he would never see him again.

"Good morning, Inspector Behrends," said the silver-haired man, offering his hand to the Inspector in greeting. He spoke with an American accent. His companion stood silently beside him, and his eyelids drooped heavily, giving him a disturbing reptilian appearance.

"Good morning," Behrends said, giving up his hand to the American, who took it in a tight grip and pumped it up and down three times.

"Shall we take a cab, Inspector?" the silver-haired man said. "We really have no time to waste."

The American led the way across the slick, cobble-stoned docks, his gold-topped cane tap-tapping on the stones as he walked. His silent companion fell into step beside him and, after a moment's hesitation, the Inspector followed, his limbs suddenly heavy and slow with dread.

Once inside a hansom cab, the American thumped his cane against the roof and shouted, "On your way, driver!"

"What is it you want with me now?" Behrends said, removing his hat and wiping a hand over his feverish brow. He felt ill, thought he might be coming down with something, perhaps he would need some time off work and in bed.

Looking at the Inspector, as the cab trundled into motion, the silver-haired man smiled and said, "Really, is that the way to greet an old friend?"

"I'm surprised to see you, that's all. It's been a long time."

"Indeed it has been a long time. The years pass swiftly, do they not?"

"What is it you want?"

"Ah, good, Inspector, I see you have lost none of your propensity for plain speaking and coming straight to the point. Let us then follow your admirable example; we have need of your services."

"Go on."

"Caxton Tempest. You have had a chance to do some investigating, I hope?"

"I have had dealings with him recently, yes," said Behrends.

"Ah yes, the mysterious murder of Archibald Antrobus. I wouldn't worry yourself about that, Behrends, that is of little importance now. But I did not ask you about your dealings with the man, did I? Have you found out anything remotely interesting about Tempest?"

"May I ask why you are so interested in him?"

"Really Behrends, has it been so long? As a member of the Order of Ahriman, you know not to question its leadership. The Order always repays its members for their loyal acts of service, you know that. As for why it does what it does, well . . . that's not for you to worry about, is it?"

"No, no, of course not," said Behrends.

"And did we not cable you from the United States asking for information about Tempest in preparation for our visit here? Well?"

Behrends harrumphed and then organised his thoughts, thinking over what 'Razor' Bob had told him last night.

"It seems that about seven years ago Tempest's wife and son were killed in mysterious circumstances. No one knows what happened, there is no record of any investigation or of where they are buried."

"Yes, yes Inspector, we know all of that. Please continue."

Behrends shifted in his seat slightly, uncomfortable beneath the American's gaze.

"After he lost his family, Tempest then disappeared for a couple of years. There is absolutely no record of his existence or activities anywhere until he reappeared at his house in Regent Street, which his housekeeper Mrs Mulligan had been looking after for him in the event of his return. Nobody knows where he went or how he spent those two missing years."

"Yes, Inspector, quite so," the silver-haired man said, a little impatiently now. "All of this is common knowledge. Now, do you have any information we don't already know, or should we dispense with your services once and for all?"

"Just one more thing," Behrends said, wondering a little anxiously what the man had meant by dispensing with his services 'once and for all'. "It is part of the official record that Tempest's parents were English missionaries, living for many years in central Africa, but that is not quite the truth. You see, they were only his adoptive parents, not his natural ones."

"Is that so?" murmured the man. "How interesting."

"It seems that Mr Caxton Tempest has done all he can to remove this fact from the public domain, and there is consequently no information about the adoption process or who his real parents are."

"You surprise me Inspector, and we are indebted to you for that interesting tidbit of information. However, time grows short and we must be off. We shall be in town for the foreseeable future, and I have no doubt that our paths shall cross again. The Order will always have need of such valuable members as yourself." The silver-haired man thumped the carriage roof with his cane and shouted, "Stop here, driver."

The hansom cab came to a halt and the American opened the door for his companion who climbed out first.

"And remember," he said, before he shut the door, "discretion at all times. As few people as possible must know of your investigation. A few more nuggets of information like that will be very useful. We'll be in touch soon, to see how you're getting on."

Behrends leaned back in his seat as the cab trundled into motion again. He felt sick and, not for the first time, wished fervently that he had never heard of the Order of Ahriman.

In the city most people slept still, unaware of last night's drama. Some of London's citizens would awake with a 'heavy head', a feeling perhaps that their sleep had been a troubled one, or a vague, uneasy memory of a nightmare, of cold hands dragging them below the surface of a freezing lake while they gasped for air.

But then they would shake the feeling off and go about their daily business, and the dream would soon be forgotten amidst the hustle and bustle of London life.

Early this morning though, as the city still struggled slowly awake, a lone figure shuffled down the deserted streets, his back bent as though he carried a heavy load, his feet barely leaving the cobbles as though he had been carrying this load for a long time and was now exhausted beyond measure. Marlow Crimps grunted incessantly as he walked, sometimes gibbering long, rambling monologues under his breath. His wet clothes hung from him and his hair was plastered to his forehead. His face had a pinched, tight look about it, and he had lost his eye patch, the vacant, bloody socket open to the elements. Occasionally a maggot crawled from Crimps' empty eye socket and out onto his cheek. Crimps would then swipe at the maggot as though it were a bothersome fly and it would drop from his face. A little later, another one would crawl out.

Very little remained of Marlow Crimps within his Gibborium possessed mind and soul, but what little brain space he had left was still occupied with one thought, one overwhelming purpose.

To hunt down and kill Jim Kerrigan.

Lucifer ran through the London streets as the city slowly woke up. He ran through the Billingsgate fish market, ignoring the shouts of the fishmongers and the curses of the porters, and missed his usual appointment with the cod tail lady. He ran through the dirty alleyways and tiny backstreets into the poorer areas of the city, dodging the feeble attempts by the rag-gatherers to catch themselves some cat meat.

The black cat ran and ran, until he found what he wanted.

"Blackie!" the boy cried in delight. His brother and sister sat at the table, picking at their breakfast. The boy's mother rose uneasily from her chair as her youngest child ran to the window to stroke the cat before she managed to shoo it away.

The boy had only halfway stretched out his arm to tickle the cat under the chin when it leapt at him, screeching. The cat landed on the boy's face, its claws digging into his flesh, and pushing him to the floor.

His mother ran screaming around the table, ready to pull the cat from her son, but something stopped her at the last second. Some primeval fear compelled her to step back, a nameless shiver coursing through her body preventing her from rescuing her son.

Finally the cat jumped from the boy's face, shaking itself vigorously and staggering slightly. It jumped on the windowsill and turned to look at the others, a look of confusion on its feline features.

The boy stood up, wiping the blood from his face. He looked at his mother and brother and sister, all of them staring in silence at him, and then he lifted his hands before him and regarded them afresh, as though they were new appendages to his body.

"Timmy?" the boy's mother said, her voice trembling with an unnamed fear.

The boy looked at her with eyes suddenly grown old and evil.

"My name is Murmur," he hissed.

As the other children screamed, he leapt at their mother and began sucking the life from her, her flesh shrivelling and falling from her bones like dust.

And the black cat stood on the windowsill screeching, its fur sticking up in angry little spikes.

For more information on the Caxton Tempest books, free stories, competitions and more, please visit

www.caxtontempest.com

Acknowledgements

I would like to thank the following people for their help and encouragement. Pete and Nick, for reading an early draft, (although I thought it was the finished manuscript!) and commenting on it. Thanks are also due to Pete for help with the front cover design. Your eyes will live forever now!

A big thank you to Simon Bruntnell of Northlight Photography for all his help and encouragement. Go and look at his website (there's a link from www.caxtontempest.com) for some gorgeous photographs of glasswork and his portraiture.

The following books and websites were very helpful for my research, and I recommend them as interesting reads or visits: A Dictionary of Slang, Jonathon Green; Inventing the Victorians, Matthew Sweet; The Victorian Underworld, Donald Thomas; A Dictionary of Angels, Gustav Davidson; Casebook: Jack the Ripper (www.casebook.org) and Dictionary of Victorian London (www.victorianlondon.org).

Most of all I want to say thank you to my long-suffering wife Jo, for her patience and understanding as I spent many an evening locked up in the cellar scribbling away in the semi-darkness. And thanks for reading up to Chapter 8 before you got too scared and couldn't carry on!

I love you.

Printed in the United Kingdom
by Lightning Source UK Ltd.
122368UK00001B/226-255/A